That Speci[al]
A Psychologi[cal Horror]
Howie McIntyre

Copyright © Howie McIntyre 2022

All rights reserved

Howie McIntyre has asserted his right under the Copyright, Designs and Patents Act 1988 to be identified as the author of this work.

This book is a work of fiction and any resemblance to actual persons – alive or dead – is purely coincidental.

One

HEAD SWIMMING, BREATH hitching, Vanessa stared at the cut glass tumbler. It was turned upside down in the middle of the Ouija board, waiting and not moving. She looked at it wide-eyed and hopeful that, after the previous aborted attempts, it would finally work. It wasn't as if she was asking too much. She wasn't asking for the impossible... a miracle. She wasn't asking for him back. She wasn't that stupid. In fact, she wasn't in the least bit stupid. Her name on the front cover of a dozen best-selling novels attested to that fact. You could ask anyone, and they would be quick to agree that stupid people didn't earn what she earned or achieve her level of success without having more than their fair share of brain cells.

The problem was – and this was something Vanessa tended to conveniently push to one side – her brain cells were well and truly pickled. A brain soaked in vodka was likely to be at least a little bit stupid, and it wasn't beyond all reasoning to think that a pickled brain might make someone like Vanessa believe that it was a piece of piss to communicate with the dead.

Hence the Ouija board, on a dark night, in her bedroom, alone, and for the umpteenth time.

All she wanted to do was to communicate with her boy, to have an opportunity to tell him that she loved and missed him, to have him tell her that he was okay. She would be happy with just once. One measly time was all she prayed for.

Having assumed that because spotty faced teenagers, huddled and giggling in corners of their bedrooms, made it work, then for someone like her it wouldn't be a problem. After all, it wasn't exactly rocket science. All anyone had to do was lay out the board, put their finger on the glass, and then ask their question. What was so difficult about any of that?

The person didn't have to be sober to stick their finger on a glass and ask a question.

Is anybody there?

A simple, straightforward question... one that even someone as pissed as a newt would be able to get their tongue around.

'Is anybody there?'

The glass refused to budge, not even an inch. Vanessa was getting pretty close to picking it up and hurling it against the wall.

Perhaps it was because she used a tumbler instead of the thing that came with the board – the wooden pointy thing, the planchette. Perhaps that's why it didn't work.

She didn't know where the bloody planchette was. She'd turned the house upside down looking for it. There was a picture of it on the lid of the box, so she knew what it looked like, but could she find it... could she fuck. Eventually, she'd given up and tried the glass tumbler.

To date, she'd tried about twenty times. The sensible side of her brain told her that was nineteen times too many, but the grief-stricken, desperate side had told her to try twenty more times... to try as many times as it took to get the bloody thing to move.

'Is anybody there?'

Her voice was a mere croak. She worried that Simon might not recognise it. He'd only been six when he died... perhaps too young to be able to hold the memory of her voice for so long. It had been three years. Half his lifetime gone already.

She took a slug of water and tried again. 'Simon... baby... are you there? It's mummy. Please... are you there?'

Her finger trembled. The glass seemed to shift.

Startled, she lifted her finger, convinced that she'd unwittingly moved it herself.

Her heart thumped. She placed her finger back on the glass.

'Are you there? Is anybody there?'

A tear formed in the corner of one eye. She swiped at it. She wasn't going to cry. Simon, when he was withering away and dying right in front of her, had seen enough of her tears. She would be damned if she would inflict another one on him ever again.

Tears were selfish, indulgent, useless. Where had tears ever got her. Nowhere, that's where. She scrubbed at the offending eye with a knuckle. No more fucking tears.

She pressed down hard on the glass. She wasn't ready to give up. It was late, she was tired, and there were other things that she ought to have been prioritising, but it was her boy... her child... and three years was a long time to suffer the grief-stricken weight of her dead child's silence.

She hadn't told Richard about her attempts to contact their son. He didn't like her bringing up Simon's name and if he'd known what she'd been up to, his derision would've been too much for her to bear – not on top of everything else he ridiculed her about. She always seemed to be on the receiving end of his sarcasm, and since he'd walked out on her, it had got much worse.

Sometimes, she almost hated him... *almost*.

The Ouija board was her secret. The constant disappointment and added heartbreak were hers alone to suffer and bearing both the failure and the despair was taking a heavy toll on her physical and mental state – not that she cared. All she cared about was getting through to Simon. Until she did, she knew that she would continue living a half-life. She would never be whole again.

Having made a final attempt, she stood and contemplated some other means that might prove more successful. She supposed that she could consult a medium, but that would mean leaving the house, and Vanessa *never* left the house. She wondered if mediums did home visits. She wondered what it would cost. Whatever that cost was, she was sure that it would be worth it.

Above her head and out of sight, a creeping, crawling shadow almost oozed across the ceiling. Amorphous, it collected directly above her and seemed to pulse with malevolent energy. Vanessa wasn't aware of it.

For at least the past three years, Vanessa hadn't been aware of very much. She'd looked at the world through a haze of alcohol, interested in very little and stumbling from one day to the next without much thought about what had been going on around her. The years before – the relatively happy, successful years – had shown the world a completely different Vanessa. *That* Vanessa wouldn't have been completely oblivious to the ominous shift in the atmosphere or the sudden dip in temperature. *That* Vanessa would have been curious. She would have paid attention. Perhaps, she would even have been a little frightened.

Fear *would* come, and perhaps if she'd had some early indication that her whole world, her whole life, was about to be upended and forever altered, it might have stood her in good stead. If she'd been aware that evil had entered her home, things might very well have turned out quite differently.

But, that night – oblivious to everything but her disappointment and her growing need for a strong drink – her fate was sealed. From that moment on, Vanessa was snared.

With one last glance at the board, she turned and walked from the bedroom. There was a bottle of vodka chilling in the freezer with her name on it, and the anticipation of the ice-cold liquid sliding down her parched throat and easing away some of her tension was very inviting.

By the time the bottle was empty, she'd placed Simon behind the locked compartment in her mind. That locked compartment was special. It held every memory of her son. She didn't often prise it open to peek inside. Life was too much of a bitch without inviting even more grief.

Totally sozzled, she finally slept.

In the morning, she didn't recall the essence of the nightmare that had rampaged so viciously through her sleeping hours, and, on waking, she was left with only a vague sense of unease. Thankfully, another glass of vodka for breakfast soon erased that unease and she greeted the morning no differently than she had greeted it every other day for the past three years – half pissed from the night before and caring about nothing.

Two

'You have to stop letting him rule you, Vanessa. He's a two-timing bastard, a leech, and a moron. You have to cut him off, and you have to do it now.'

Vanessa Parker eyed her agent – and sometime friend – took a sip of her cold coffee, and grimaced. She'd heard it all before. Actually, she was sick to the back teeth of hearing it. Everyone seemed to have an opinion about her life, her failed marriage, her work, and even about how much vodka she drank. Just because she had her name on a few bestselling novels didn't mean she wasn't entitled to a little privacy. Just because she was behind on the final draft of her next book, didn't give Anita the right to barge into her home and start spouting crap and laying down the law.

Her marriage was her business. How much vodka she consumed was *definitely* her business. If she decided to strip naked and run down the street with a red rose clamped between her teeth, and another one jutting out from the crack between her not so well-rounded buttocks, she still expected everyone to keep their sticky noses out of it.

Well, fuck the lot of them. They could all go and screw themselves – and that included her feckless shit of a husband. She'd had enough of every last one of them.

Well, maybe not her feckless husband. It would take a great deal of crap being slung from his direction before she would ever consider writing him off. It was quite astonishing just how much shit she was prepared to take from him – shit she wouldn't accept from anyone else – and, sometimes, she was ashamed of herself for being the proverbial doormat.

Throwing a glower across at Anita, she shrugged deeper into her dressing gown. Pulling the belt tight, she dragged herself to her feet and padded across the kitchen floor to the huge American fridge-freezer. She loved that fridge-freezer and not just because it had been a gift from Richard. She loved it because it had one of those fancy drink dispensers and joy of joys, it even made its own ice. The drink dispenser kept the vodka just cold enough to warrant a single ice cube. Lately, she hadn't taken the time to fill it, finding it quicker and easier to put the vodka in the ice compartment, but she still made sure that there was always ice.

A single ice cube was best because it diluted the spirit just enough to take the rough burn away from the back of the throat, but without weakening the drink so much that she failed to experience the desired effect on her senses. To her mind, there was nothing worse than watered-down vodka.

She shuddered at the thought and poured herself a large measure before tipping her head back and swallowing it in two long gulps. God, that tasted so good. She smacked her lips and wiped them with the back of one hand. Growing up, whenever her mother had a drink, she'd often witnessed that same wipe of the mouth, that same lip-smacking satisfaction. Not for the first time, she wondered if alcoholism actually was a genetic timebomb, or if being married to utter bastards was what drove both mother and daughter to the solace that only the bottle would bring.

Her mother gave up the ghost two months before her fortieth birthday. She never got to see her daughter get married, never got to meet her grandson, and never lived long enough to turn her life around. Vanessa had long since stopped thinking about her. It wasn't that the memories were painful. To feel pain, you had to care. Vanessa simply didn't, but she sometimes wondered about the alcoholism gene and when she did, an image of her mother's face would flash behind her eyes.

She poured another drink, forgoing the ice, swallowed it, and gave an involuntary shudder.

Anita sat at the table with her mouth hanging open. As was usual for Anita, she overspilled her clothes and most of her bulk hung over the edges of the chair. Vanessa glanced over at her and immediately knew what she was thinking. She always knew what her friend was thinking, because she was one of those women whose every thought was signposted on their faces. And there it was, that look that said – *It's only just gone breakfast time and the stupid bitch is already half sozzled.*

Vanessa smiled, but it was a cold smile and one that barely cracked her face. She knew that her agent was worried sick about the latest draft of her work in progress – the book that was supposed to make amends for her last two fuckups. Vanessa wasn't stupid. She knew that it wasn't concern for her health that made Anita worried. No, it was nothing more than her agent's own bottom line that had her sitting there with a face like something gone sour. If Vanessa failed again, then Anita's pocket would suffer, and it didn't take a genius to work out that was the only thing that mattered to her.

What if she confessed to not having made a start on the new draft? What if she told her that all there was on her laptop was around forty-thousand nonsensical and incomprehensible words? She could confess to having nothing but a stinking pile of crap to show for nearly a year of work. It might be fun to ruin her day with that little snippet of information, but Vanessa decided against enlightening her. She wasn't ready to admit to being a complete and utter failure.

Anita wrinkled her nose, and said, 'You could at least take a shower... make an effort. You look and smell like some alkie homeless person.'

'Charming.'

'Well, it's the truth, Vanessa. It's about time you got a grip on yourself. I've got nothing against Alkie homeless people. I'm sure they've all got their reasons for living the way they do, and I suppose it's difficult for them to have a wash, but what's your excuse, Vanessa? You've let yourself go, and it's not a pretty sight.'

Vanessa rolled her eyes, poured herself yet another drink and said, 'You worry too much.'

'Worry too much?' She looked Vanessa square in the face. What she saw was a woman with hollow cheeks, greasy hair pulled back behind her ears into a messy ponytail, and dead, fathomless eyes. 'Do you know how many times I've had to cover for you? Too many times to count... that's how many.'

'Jesus, Anita... I didn't ask you to cover for me or lie for me.' Her words were beginning to sound slurred. 'That was your decision.'

Anita grunted. Vanessa was such an ungrateful cow. 'If I hadn't, you would've been out on your arse a long time ago.'

'What a crock. They'd never ditch me. I'm one of their biggest earners.'

'*Was* one of their biggest earners, Vanessa – *was* being the operative word.'

Anita was right, but Vanessa's ego was a little on the large side, so she refused to wholly believe it.

She flapped a hand. 'Every author goes through a dry spell. You know that.'

'Your dry spell has lasted across two books and looks set to flow right into a third one. If it wasn't for me...'

'Oh, give it a rest, why don't you?' Irritated, Vanessa threw herself forward, almost spilling her drink. 'I'm sick of listening to your shit. I've made you rich, lady – as well as all those bloodsucking executive publishers – so, instead of riding my fucking arse, you should be thanking me.'

Anita lit a cigarette with visibly trembling hands. Until she felt that first hit of nicotine and had taken a minute or two to calm down, she didn't trust herself to say another word. If she did, her tongue would eviscerate the bitch.

And Vanessa *was* a bitch. There was certainly no denying that fact. She was so far up her own arsehole that she could probably see daylight from her bellybutton. The sad thing was, at one time Vanessa would have had every right to be so cock-sure of herself. When it had come to storytelling and creating bestsellers, there weren't many who could hold a candle to her talent. Now, all that talent was being drowned in the bottom of a vodka bottle. The absolute waste really disappointed Anita.

She dragged on her cigarette and shook her head sadly. As well as being a waste, it was also a disgrace. Anita had lost count of the number of female authors who would've given their right tit to have had Vanessa's talent and opportunities. She couldn't imagine any of them pissing it all away. Then again, none of them had been ground down to dust being married to a selfish leech.

She blamed Richard for all of it, especially Vanessa's drinking. Why he couldn't keep his cock in his trousers – or at least not be so blatant about his affairs – was beyond her. Even after losing their son, he kept at it. The stupid bastard must've known that his screwing around had all but slaughtered the goose that laid the golden egg. Or maybe he hadn't comprehended any of it? It wouldn't have surprised Anita to know that Vanessa hadn't told her arsehole of a husband the extent of the mess she was in. He probably didn't have a clue that her last two books had tanked and that she was on the verge of being let go by The Publishing House. Vanessa had written for The House for nearly twenty years, but – when it came right down to it – the number crunchers were ruthless and had no compunction about binning her. Vanessa had to know that she was on her last chance. If she didn't – and it wasn't simply her ego telling her that she was invincible –

then she was in real trouble. If she hadn't confided in Richard, then she was in even more trouble than Anita first thought.

She exhaled and gazed up at Vanessa through the smoke. She studied her, alert to the weight she'd lost and the grey pallor to her skin. Vanessa was only thirty-eight years old but looked at least twice that – an old woman before her time. She would benefit from a good feed, but Anita doubted that there was much to chow down on in the house. As well as a good feed, she needed a good scrub under a hot shower. She'd said as much, but it seemed to have fallen on deaf ears.

Despite her concerns, Anita didn't feel all that sorry for her. Over the years they might have enjoyed a friendship of sorts but primarily, she was Vanessa's literary agent and, as such, she couldn't afford to allow that friendship – such as it was – to influence what needed to be said.

In some ways she was glad that Vanessa had landed flat on her face. After all, you often had to reach rock bottom before you were able to climb your way out of the shit, and Vanessa was already pretty close to rock bottom. Anita had no doubt about that.

'Have you had anything to eat?' she asked. 'I could make you some toast, fry you an egg?'

Vanessa held up her glass. 'I have all the breakfast I need but thank you all the same.' She swayed a little on her feet. 'Don't you have to be somewhere? I don't want to keep you from your busy life.'

Anita heard a plaintive note floating beneath Vanessa's words. Despite her actions suggesting otherwise, she knew that Vanessa hated being on her own.

'I'm in no rush to get off anywhere. Why don't you sit down before you fall down? I'm getting dizzy just looking up at you.'

Vanessa appeared to think about it, then pulled out a chair and flopped down at the table. Some vodka splashed over the rim of the glass, and she mopped at it with a finger before sucking it dry.

Unable to repress a look of disgust, Anita looked away.

The two women, now seated opposite one another at the kitchen table, couldn't look more different. Whilst Vanessa was rail thin and dishevelled, Anita was stout – some would describe her as fat – and perfectly groomed. The one thing that both women had in common was their love of books, especially the classics, and it was that love affair with literary fiction that had created a bond all those years before. It was a bond that Anita felt was being stretched beyond endurance.

Too fidgety and much too wired to sit for long, Vanessa was soon back on her feet and weaving her way around the kitchen.

'You can go if you want,' she said, draining her glass. 'I know you don't really want to be here.'

'And then what?' Anita returned. 'You'll get back to finishing that final draft?' She snorted and shook her head. 'Somehow, I don't think so.'

As Anita watched Vanessa move clumsily around the room, a tiny crumb of guilt threatened her equilibrium. Vanessa had been right when she'd said that she, and others, had managed to get rich off of her efforts. Not rich enough for Anita to retire, but certainly rich enough to afford a nice apartment and a couple of holidays abroad every year. The lure of another potential best seller had kept her by Vanessa's side far longer than was reasonable and it was the possibility of making another shitload of money – rather than their tenuous personal relationship – that had prevented her from walking away and not looking back. That was where the guilt came in. Anita knew that, deep down, she didn't really have Vanessa's best interests at heart. If she'd been a true friend, she would've told her to forget the book, forget chasing after what was lost, and book herself into rehab.

But, in the end, money – or the potential for money – always won out. She would wait until after the book was finished before encouraging her to get the help she so desperately needed. Meantime, she would badger her until she handed over the finished product. She only hoped it was better than her last effort.

She tried to shrug off the guilt. She made an attempt to remind herself that it was Vanessa's talent that actually kept her at her side.

That it would be tantamount to a moral crime to allow it to fester and die.

Anyway, there was also the fear that, if she walked away and then Vanessa pulled herself together, and if her next half a dozen books raked in millions, someone else would get her percentage of the royalties. There was no way that Anita would ever risk that.

So, she wasn't going anywhere. She would stay by Vanessa's side until it was obvious that she was flogging a dead horse. Then, friendship wouldn't enter into the equation because, for the astute Anita, business was business and friendship was very rarely profitable.

One thing was for sure – she wouldn't keep her trap shut. If she had something to say, then she would say it. It was time for the gloves to come off.

Vanessa was back at the fridge, pouring yet another drink.

'I wish you wouldn't,' Anita said. 'Don't you know that you're killing yourself?'

'We all have to die sometime.' Vanessa's voice was definitely beginning to slur. 'What do I have to live for anyway?'

Anita gave an impatient sigh. Self-pity was abhorrent to her. She had no time for it.

'Get a fucking grip,' she said. 'Jesus, Vanessa, knock the drinking on the head for a while.'

'Easy for you to say.'

'I'm not saying it would be easy, but...'

''What else do I have? Huh? My boy is dead, my husband has fucked off, and I can't write for shit, so you tell me... what reason do I have to give up drinking?'

'What about self-respect?'

'What about it?'

'Don't you care?'

Vanessa closed her eyes, mulled over the question, then opened her eyes once more, shook her head, and said, 'Nope.'

'Then, what about the respect of your loyal readers? Don't you care about that...about them? You can't keep putting out rubbish, fuelled on nothing but vodka, and expect them to stick by you. They deserve better than that.'

'Fuck them.' She took a long swallow of vodka, smacked her lips, and weaved her way back over to the table. 'And fuck you, Anita. Fuck the lot of you.'

'Nice, Vanessa... real nice.' Anita pulled herself to her feet. 'Give me a call when you're ready to see some sense.' She made for the door. 'But don't leave it too long. It's not just my patience that's wearing thin.'

Vanessa waved her glass in the air. 'Sure thing, Anita. Keep your phone close by. I wouldn't want you to miss that call.'

Vanessa didn't finish her drink. Placing the glass on the table she listened for the slam of the front door and then decided to take herself back to bed.

Getting up the stairs was a feat she only just managed. In the end, to get to the top landing, she had to crawl up each step on her hands and knees.

Resting her forehead on the bedroom door, she took a moment to swallow back on the bile that nipped at the back of her throat. God, she felt rough. Anita was right – she *was* killing herself. The thing was, she wasn't sure that she cared.

Pressing down on the doorhandle and shouldering the door, she couldn't understand why it wouldn't open. Momentarily confused, she tried again.

Finally, she concluded that something had obviously jammed it from behind. Try as she might – and the trying wasn't that strenuous because she simply didn't have the energy – it wouldn't budge.

She gave up and eventually folded down onto her side, curled up into a tight ball, and dropped into a drunken sleep on the landing floor.

It was a deep and dreamless sleep. Her slumber wasn't disturbed by either the slow creak of the bedroom door opening of its own volition or by the icy blast that erupted from within. Neither was her deep, alcohol-induced slumber disturbed when thin wisps of ink-black smoky tendrils snaked from the interior of the room and then gathered, and swirled, and danced in a hypnotic sway above her head.

Oblivious to what engulfed her, she huffed in dry breaths through her mouth, the smouldering haze being inhaled and exhaled with every snuffle.

Insensible to what was happening, she slept on.

Three

Anita sat in her car on the driveway, reluctant to move off. She tipped her head back against headrest and ruminated on what she ought to do next. She knew that she should give an honest assessment of the current state of play to The Publishing House. It was only fair that they be kept in the loop regarding the progress – or lack of it – of Vanessa's final draft. She knew that the right thing to do would be to share the whole sorry mess with those who had already paid an advance that had been in the tens of thousands.

She mentally fought with herself. On the one hand, Vanessa might still pull it off, but on the other hand, she was well aware of the fact that it wasn't only Vanessa's reputation at stake. In fucking herself over, Vanessa was also screwing *her*. Anita had more than an inkling that, if she didn't come clean, The Publishing House – one of the *Big Five* – would be reluctant to accept any more authors from her. She'd recently signed up two new authors and currently had a promising couple of novels in development from the two young women who Anita knew were on the cusp of greatness. It meant that she couldn't afford to piss off either of the executive editors at The House by assisting Vanessa in giving them the run-around. If she did, she would, in turn, be screwing those two fledgling authors because The House wouldn't trust her enough as their literary agent to touch them with a bargepole.

The roar of the wind grew so loud and so strong that it rocked the car, startling Anita out of her reverie.

Where did that come from, she wondered? Only moments before, the chilly morning had been graced with only the lightest of breezes.

A thin tree branch exploded past her window, startling her, and making her jump. Leaves danced in a manic swirl, lifted from the small edge of grass by the bluster, and the tree-lined driveway groaned as boughs bent and did their own, more ungainly, ballet.

The sky opened and dropped a heavy blanket of rain. It pelted down, thundering on the roof of the car and Anita suddenly felt as if she was under attack.

The unpredictable mood swing of that morning's weather was surprising but not ominous. Anita gave herself a mental shake and settled back to sit out the deluge. She'd made up her mind to go back inside and try to reason with Vanessa, knowing that it served no positive purpose to storm off and leave her to her own devices. She didn't believe it was sensible to throw the baby out with the bathwater and – although it wouldn't be pretty – she was determined to force Vanessa to pull on her big girl's trousers and knuckle down to some real work.it was either that or she would walk away, money or no money.

After ten minutes, the rain showed no sign of lessening its thunderous downpour. If anything, the cascade of water grew even heavier. She sat out the time thinking but the incessant drumming on the roof and windows made concentration difficult and she found herself flitting from one thought to the next without focussing on any one in particular.

She thought about Vanessa's first, wonderfully exquisite novels and the impact they'd had on the literary community. She thought of Richard's womanising, the death of the boy, and Vanessa's descent into alcoholism. She thought of how perniciously Vanessa's star had begun to wane and wondered what she could do to put a stop to her downward spiral.

Those last two novels had been absolute shite. To Anita's mind, they should never have been published, but The Publishing House had thought – quite wrongly as it turned out – that Vanessa's name alone would carry them. No one was going to be daft enough to make that mistake again.

If only she could make Vanessa understand that she was playing fast and loose with her final chance. A third damp squib wouldn't be tolerated and, quite apart from having to pay back the advance – something, because of what she knew about Vanessa's precarious financial situation, Anita knew to be impossible – Vanessa would be unceremoniously dumped, and that would be catastrophic for both of them.

She was under no illusions. She knew perfectly well that, even if Vanessa got her finger out, the final draft of her work in progress would need a lot of development. The edit would probably require huge swathes of change and Anita shuddered to think what a basic proofread would throw up. Nevertheless, she needed to see a finished version... *any* finished version. Something was always better than nothing.

She lit a cigarette, inhaled deeply, and watched the rain as it lashed at the windscreen. She had a strange feeling that the weather had conspired to keep her in the car and out of the house. She smiled at the thought.

As if.

Behind her, seen through the rear-view mirror, the house stood tall and imposing. Its shape rippled and shifted, made mobile by the almost hallucinogenic effects of the rain. She'd never liked that house. It harboured too much sadness and too many bad memories. Try as she might, she could never persuade Vanessa to sell it and buy something that sat within a community – somewhere that didn't harbour the lasting sounds of Simon's cries, or somewhere that wasn't steeped in Richard's infidelities. Being so far away from civilisation, and bearing in mind Vanessa's agoraphobia, it was the worst place on earth for her to be. She needed neighbours, needed the noise of traffic, the footfall past her windows. Vanessa needed to be anywhere but stuck out in the sticks with nothing but foxes for company.

At last, the rain eased, and the wind dropped. Anita stretched out a sigh of relief. She'd been sitting in the parked car for over an hour and her arse was numb and her head ached from all the noise of the inclement weather.

Moments later, dripping from the last of the rain, Anita stood at Vanessa's front door and grew furiously impatient when her knocking went unanswered. She tried calling through the letterbox, contemplated using the key that Vanessa had given her for emergencies, and finally decided to walk away. Imagining her slumped in a drunken stupor, she realised that there was no point in confronting her. She'd already wasted most of the morning and wasn't keen on flogging that particular dead horse – not when it was so obvious that Vanessa wasn't cognisant enough to even answer her own front door.

UPSTAIRS, WHEN THE last echo of Anita's loud hammering on the door faded to nothing, Vanessa stirred and shivered. Where the noise hadn't woken her, the cold air did.

Forcing open her gummy eyes, blinking and then quickly closing them again against the sudden glare, she wrapped her arms around herself and curled up into a tight ball, trying to stave off the effect of the frigid air. Full sleep was slow to shift and, in that place between deep slumber and full consciousness, she floated in a state of disorientation. She had no clue where she was. Not in her bed – she knew that much – but somewhere hard and uncomfortable. She was confused by the cold, knowing that the central heating was firing on all cylinders, but she was too exhausted to worry about it.

It took a full ten minutes before she felt inclined to open her eyes once more. Prising her lids apart took some effort and made her head throb.

She came to realise that she was on the landing, lying outside her bedroom door.

What the hell was she doing there?

Then, she remembered. She hadn't been able to open the door. It had been jammed on the inside. That was why she was on the floor and not on her bed.

She groaned and rolled onto her back. There was a hollowness in her stomach and in her head. She felt sick. Bile bit at the back of her throat. If she wasn't careful, she would end up choking on her own vomit so she struggled up and onto her knees.

Everything moved at one hundred miles an hour. The whole house seemed to be spinning. She rocked forward, gagged, and right in front of her she expelled a vile mouthful of something quite awful. She backed away from the stench, continuing to dry heave.

God, she felt bad.

Beneath the odour of sour vomit, she smelled something else. It wasn't terribly distinct but it seemed to remind her of the smell of spent matches. It hurt too much to consider exactly what it was, so she put it from her frazzled mind and, on hands and knees, worked her way back until she was perched at the top of the stairs.

It looked such a long way down. One wrong move and she knew that she would break her neck. For a scary moment, she contemplated throwing herself forward. A broken neck, in that crazy moment, seemed the answer to everything.

The shivers increased and her whole body spasmed. *Why was it so fucking cold?* The house was a monster to heat, but it was never *that* cold.

Bumping down each step on her arse, and clutching at the banister, she made it to the bottom in one piece. She sat for a moment on the bottom step, her chin on her knees, and tried to work out what she should do next. Her stomach rumbled.

She needed food.

The kitchen seemed miles away. In fact, it was a mere couple of meters but, to her, the journey was something she didn't believe she could make, not without crawling.

She wasn't adverse to crawling. Drunks often found themselves on their hands and knees, but the tiled floor felt like ice beneath her bare feet, and she was already frozen near to death.

It was the sound of her phone that got her moving. She'd left it on the kitchen table and – thinking that it might be Richard, offering to pay her a visit – was enough for her to brave the journey.

The kitchen felt warmer. Wintry sun streamed through the rain-streaked window over the sink and Vanessa was grateful for it.

It wasn't Richard on the phone. It was Anita.

Vanessa groaned and considered rejecting the call. She didn't have the energy or the inclination for another lecture, but Anita wouldn't give up... may even pop back to the house... so she reluctantly accepted it.

'What?' she said, the word a sharp bark.

'Hello to you too,' Anita returned. 'Back in the land of the living, are you?'

Vanessa didn't immediately respond. She took the time to throw herself into a chair, swallow back on the ongoing feeling of nausea, then said, 'What do you want, Anita? I'm busy.'

'Forgive me if I don't believe that... not unless you're busy guzzling vodka.'

The thought of alcohol made Vanessa's stomach heave. 'Believe what you like,' she said. 'Just spit out whatever it is that you want, and please... no more pontificating on what a disgrace I am. I'm not in the mood.'

'Okay... fair enough. I've just got a simple question to ask you.'

'Fire away. I'm all ears.'

'I don't suppose you still have that forty thousand lying around?'

Vanessa's hand trembled. 'Forty thousand?'

'Pounds. The forty thousand pounds advance that The Publishing House so generously gifted to you. Well, I say *gifted* but we both know it's refundable."

'Why?' She cleared her throat. 'Why do you want to know if I still have it?'

'Because they're going to want it back.'

'Bullshit.' Even as she said the word, she knew that it wasn't a load of crap. If she didn't finish the book then, of course, they would want it back. She dragged in a breath, tried to find something to say to ward off the inevitable, then put her head in her hand and almost sobbed, 'I can't, Anita. I can't give it back.'

'They'll insist... get the lawyers onto it. You know what they're like.'

She didn't have the forty thousand. She didn't have anything close to that amount and she was certain that Anita was well aware of that fact. She thought she sensed a smile in the other woman's tone. She thought that she was enjoying the whole thing.

'What can I do?' she asked, hoping that Anita would have a solution to hand.

'Oh, I don't know. Oh, wait a minute... here's a thought... *finish the fucking book*.'

'I...'

'It's the only way.'

'Will they give me more time... six months maybe?'

'Jesus, Vanessa. What planet are you living on? Six months? You'll be lucky to get six days.'

A look of shock sparked across Vanessa's pale face. 'Six days? Are you having a laugh?'

'Do you hear me laughing?'

'No, but...'

'Look...' Anita let out a long slow breath. 'Send me what you have, and I'll see what can be done with it.'

What she had? She had nothing. Well, next to nothing. There were about forty thousand words formatted and on file, and another few thousand rambling notes, but every single word were shite.

'Okay, but I need some time to do some tidying up.'

'You have until Friday,' Anita was quick to return.

'But it's Wednesday already.' The whine in Vanessa's voice wasn't lost on her and she felt hot with shame.

'I'm impressed that you actually know what day it is. Well done you.'

'Do you have to be so facetious?'

'Pot and kettle, Vanessa. Usually, your tongue could strip wallpaper.'

After a pause, Vanessa said, 'Two days aren't enough.'

'You've already had nearly two years, Vanessa. I'm sticking with Friday.'

A pulse throbbed in her right temple. Her chest hurt. She had no choice but to agree. 'Okay,' she said. 'You'll have something by Friday.'

Four

Vanessa wasn't a lover of Facebook. She wasn't one of those people with hundreds of friends who she'd never once clapped eyes on. She also wasn't someone who was in the habit of posting pictures of what she'd had for dinner for everyone's amusement. The only reason she bothered with a social media account was so that she could spy on her husband. The only problem was that complete strangers kept sending her friend requests. Being the sort of woman who couldn't suffer the mundane prattling of a single human being, it wasn't surprising that she had no tolerance for any of the superficial shit found online. She neither needed nor wanted friends, particularly fake ones, so when her phone pinged with yet another friend request, she ignored it. Instead, she scrolled to Richard's profile, keen to have a nosey at his latest exploits.

Richard had an Avatar, and his profile was fake. He called himself Morgan, set his relationship status as single, and posted regularly. She'd been surprised to find that he had over six hundred friends but hadn't been surprised to discover that most of them were women. Although it pained her to read the posts and although it made her sick to her stomach to view the photographs, it didn't stop her visiting his page and checking out his timeline at least a dozen times every day.

Of course, Richard had no idea that she knew all about his fake account. He knew that she had one because she'd let it slip. She recalled that occasion and remembered how his eyes had narrowed in suspicion at the news. Knowing her as he did, he'd obviously found it a little weird. He'd had the cheek to ask her if she was going through some sort of a mid-life crisis, then asked if she'd opened an account as some sort of research for a book. He simply couldn't get his head around the fact that she – someone who had no interest in what she considered the tiny little lives of plebs – would invite those same people into her life. He knew that she would rather cut her tongue out than make small talk.

She'd had to be careful not to give the game away. If he ever discovered that she was following his every despicable post and scrutinising every photograph, he would close the account down and deny her even that small glimpse into his other life.

Anita was gobsmacked that Vanessa still loved her husband. Despite everything he'd put her through– continued to put her through – Vanessa's love for him had remained intact and Anita's opinion, although it rankled, was ignored. Deep down, Vanessa realised that she was a fool, but the vodka helped immensely with that. It helped to ease every humiliation, every slight, and every episode of extreme neglect. It helped her to continue to view her husband through rose-tinted glasses, but it also made her a lousy writer. When it came right down to it, she was willing to give up being an author if it meant she could hang onto her delusions about her husband, and that meant never going a day stone cold sober.

Every aspect of Vanessa's life had a double edge. Without the money her books brought in, Richard would wriggle off the hook. She was under no illusions that it was her money that kept him somewhat in her life. She needed to be perpetually pickled to accept what that meant, and keeping herself topped up with alcohol meant that, perversely, she couldn't write and therefore couldn't earn. The way she was going, she would end up with no Richard and no money.

She chafed to get at his recent posts but before she had the opportunity to open his status, her phone pinged again. It was a request to *like* something. Curiosity – and the desire to put off the moment when she would have to bite the bullet and head for her study and *that* manuscript – got the better of her and she opened the notification.

Zara, author page.

Another wannabe indie author. Vanessa sniffed at the notification with a certain derision. Hell would freeze over before she gave one of *those people* the time of day. They were all so... so desperate. It would be quite a catch to have a best-selling traditional author engaging with an indie. Zara, whoever she was, would think that she'd died and gone to heaven.

Vanessa had no intention of doing anything other than deleting the request, so it came as quite a shock when she found herself not only liking the page but swiping to open it, then viewing its content.

She hadn't really done that, had she? Had her brain really defied her and taken control of her finger, forcing her to open the damned thing? How was that even possible? Drunk, she'd done a great many things because her sozzled brain had dictated, against her better judgement, to do the stupidest of things but she'd slept off most of the effects of that morning's vodka, so that wasn't an excuse she could use.

She blinked, stared at the screen with an open-mouthed expression, then – before she realised what was happening – she had begun to read.

Blah, blah, blah. Utter shite.

Who gave a rat's arse about the trials and tribulations of formatting and editing and trying to promote and sell what was obviously a sub-standard novel? Didn't the silly cow realise that she was on a road to nowhere... travelling with tens of thousands of other wannabe indies, all with the same stories to tell?

She itched to say as much, and her finger hovered over the keypad before realising how much of a mistake that would be. Her advice, no matter how negative, was worth its weight in gold, and there was no way that she was about to give it away for free.

She dragged her finger upwards and shifted to Richard's profile. It was time to see what the bastard had been up to.

Instead, in the space of two blinks, she found herself tapping out a message on Zara's page.

Fuck a duck. She'd only just gone and introduced herself. Horror-struck, she made an attempt to delete the message. Then, she tried again, and yet again. The message stayed put.

It must be the phone, she thought. *Bloody thing was playing up.* She would have to delete it on her laptop.

The manuscript was on her laptop. She wasn't sure if she was ready to go anywhere near it.

Throwing the phone onto the table, she resigned herself to the fact that probably hundreds of the loser indie's Facebook friends would see her message, cream their panties, and hammer her with friend requests, but rather that than stumbling through to her study and facing the dreaded laptop.

Anything but that.

She knew that she was delaying the inevitable. At some point, she would have to pull herself together and at least attempt to meet Anita's deadline. If she didn't, then she was finished.

Being finished was a bitter pill for someone like Vanessa to swallow. She'd been successful, a force to be reckoned with, a woman who had carved out a name for herself, and one who was considered one of the greatest literary forces of the twenty-first century. She could be forgiven her psychological problems, her broken marriage, and even her excessive drinking. However, she would never be forgiven any form of lack-lustre writing. With two failed books to her name, she was definitely tottering on the brink of failure and even she – with her tendency to ignore the unpleasant – had enough sense to realise that she was about to see everything go tits up.

Sometimes, she didn't care, but those times were fleeting. When she examined those brief moments, she discovered that they were merely a means of excusing herself. If she pretended that she didn't care, then for a time, the pain of failure dissipated. She could carry on drinking, carry on ignoring the elephant in the room, and make herself believe that nothing mattered.

Who was she trying to kid? Nothing *did* matter. She'd already lost everything important to her – her son and her husband. Okay, she hadn't completely lost Richard. He still fucked her, still held her in his arms now and again. She had to pay for those fleeting moments, but the money didn't matter... or it *hadn't* mattered. Now, it did because she didn't have any – or not much. Once it was all gone, she wouldn't see Richard for dust.

Knowing that about her relationship was neither flattering nor fulfilling. Thinking about it drove her up and onto her feet and it had her moving to the fridge. Comfort came in many forms, but the only comfort that Vanessa craved came from the inside of a vodka bottle.

Half a dozen long slugs straight from the neck of the bottle and the room was suddenly spinning. It was like being on a jacked-up merry-go-round. That was the worst thing about too much alcohol, especially on an empty stomach – the woozy head reeling and the room revolving at a hundred miles an hour. It made thinking straight almost impossible. In such circumstances, she tried to lessen the effects by fixing her eyes and focusing on something in the room. It was a trick she learned from her mother and usually it worked. She chose the clock on the wall above the fridge.

It was a large clock with a white face and broad black hands. Her eyes swiped across it, not holding. Her head wobbled on her shoulders, and she swayed on her feet. The room spun faster.

She sat down and finally succeeded on locking on, but only for a second. Her eyes rolled up, she gagged and promised herself, for the thousandth time, that she wouldn't touch another drop. It was a promise that, once the dizziness and the nausea passed, she wouldn't keep. It was like the pain of childbirth... soon forgotten.

The nausea *did* pass, and she focused once more on the clock. Her eyes jerked in their sockets, then steadied. Something wasn't quite right and, at first, she thought it was her and not the clock. Blinking several times to clear her vision, she tried to make sense of what her eyes told her. She stiffened. She felt uneasy. Not for the first time, she wondered if she was heading the way of her mother – held fast in the grip of psychosis.

What, the good God, fucking hell, was going on?

She huffed in a breath and leaned back, but kept her eyes riveted on the face of the clock.

The hands were spinning at such an incredible speed that they seemed nothing but a blur. She blinked again – slow blinks that gave her the precious seconds required to try and reboot her brain – but, when she looked at the face of the clock once more, the hands were still spinning. She wobbled and almost tipped out of her chair. Another wave of dizziness swept over her, forcing her to grab hold of the edge of the table, bend over it, and rest her forehead on its cool surface.

She sat like that for long moments, determined that she wouldn't look at the clock again – not in any sort of hurry. She would do the sensible thing. She would avoid what she couldn't explain and hope for the best.

The vodka bottle slipped out of her hand and clattered to the floor, bouncing, and spilling the remainder of its contents. Vanessa was oblivious. Sleep had grabbed her once more and dragged her down into nothingness.

Sometime later, she woke with a start. Her whole body shook with cold. She was freezing, and when she tentatively raised her head from the table, her breath plumed out in front of her in a billowing, wispy cloud.

At first, she wasn't sure where she was. Disorientation on waking had become quite a thing with her. She refused to allow it to worry her. She took her time coming fully awake and let her surroundings sink in one slow moment at a time.

Finally, and with some trepidation, she glanced up at the clock, dreading what she would see. Everything seemed appeared perfectly normal and she sighed with relief. Now, all she had to worry about was the reason for the kitchen being as cold as a witch's tit. It was now as cold – perhaps even colder – than it had been on the landing, and she wondered if the boiler had given up the ghost and finally packed in. It was the only thing she could think of to explain the drop in temperature. Like most things in the house, the boiler was old and in need of replacement.

Her eyes lingered uneasily on the puffs of visible breath. Then she became aware of sounds she couldn't quite fathom – a rushing, gurgling sound and another noise blasting out in the background.

Turning her head towards the sink, she saw that the cold-water tap was turned on full blast and was spewing out water by the litre.

When had she turned the tap on?

To the left of the sink, the kettle boiled frantically. It boiled so hard that it juddered and spat out steam that was dangerous even looking at it from several feet away..

Vanessa was confused. Quite apart from the fact that the kettle should've clicked off when it reached the boil, there was the even more confusing question about who had switched it on. She was almost certain that – just like the tap – she hadn't been the one to turn it on.

She shook her head. Her whole body spasmed and she rubbed at her arms with frozen hands.

Now fully awake, she began to sense other things going on around her. There was a weight to the room, as if the air was saturated, and she could swear that there were eyes on her. Sometimes, particularly when she'd been drinking, she became a touch paranoid. It was only in her sober moments that she recognized that paranoia for what it was – the ministrations of a drink-damaged brain – and just then, she was far from sober.

It was a bizarre situation and one that she couldn't think her way through. She wasn't capable of a single rational thought, and she was tempted to lay her head back down on the table and ignore everything that was going on around her. She wanted to force it all from her mind, not think about it or consider any of it.

She just wanted to sleep.

Suddenly, her head snapped to the right and then over her shoulder. She was on high alert, all thoughts of pushing everything away, and succumbing to her exhausted confusion, exploding into nothing.

Someone was in the kitchen. She was sure of it. The hairs on the back of her neck told her as much.

'Anita?' she called out. 'Is that you? Where, the fuck are you hiding?'

She searched the room with narrowed eyes, turning in her chair to see into every corner, but spotted no one. It wasn't easy to hide in her kitchen. It was large but with no dark nooks or crannies. Despite that, nothing would convince her that she was alone.

The kettle continued its mad boil, and the water from the tap carried on gushing, the sound of both causing a rushing noise to fill her ears. She dragged her attention back to that end of the kitchen, snatched in a small breath and pulled herself to her feet. She wobbled, straightened herself, and moved across the room– her head swivelling on her neck – to turn off the offending kettle. It had almost boiled dry and, when she leaned over to switch it off at the socket, it spat hot steam at her. Startled, she thought that she saw a yawning maw in that steam. Swearing and jerking back in alarm, her gaze eventually settled on the dissipating haze. She'd been so sure that she's seen a huge mouth, set to swallow her, but as the air cleared in front of her, she began to doubt herself.

Just as the last of the steam disappeared, for an instant, she thought she heard an animalistic growl. It vibrated in her ears, but she put it down to the last spluttering of the kettle.

She turned to focus her attention on the offending tap. She had to shut the thing off. She wanted blessed silence. She would be able to think in silence.

Try as she might, she couldn't turn it off. Gritting her teeth, she squeezed and felt the strain in her wrist as she yanked her hand clockwise. Her knuckles showed white through her skin. Grunting with the effort, she finally gave up. It was stuck fast. It wasn't for shifting.

'Fuck it,' she said, backing off until her legs banged against the table. 'Fuck it to Hell and back.'

She stood trembling. Defensively, she wrapped her arms across her chest, and stared at the offending tap. The force of the water caused a spurting up the side of the sink to overflow onto the draining board and pour to the floor. It was soon lapping at her feet.

The only thing she could do was to turn the water off at the stopcock. But where was the fucking stopcock? She racked her brain, then suddenly remembered that it was in the cupboard under the sink.

She dropped to her knees and crawled through the water, all the while trying – without much success – to ignore the total weirdness of the whole situation. Perhaps it was the cold and the wet, but she felt a little less drunk. Being less inebriated had the effect of forcing her to begin to dwell on the things she'd been determined to ignore. She reminded herself that she hadn't been the one to turn the tap on. She was even more sure that it hadn't been Anita. So, who the fuck had it been?

Then, there was the kettle. Kettles weren't in the habit of turning themselves on. With her brain less befuddled, she had to admit that some creepy shit was definitely going on in her kitchen, but she was still drunk enough not to be terrified.

She pulled open the cupboard door, cleared away bottles of bleach and laundry detergent, and reached for the pipe at the back where the brass stopcock was. Before she had the chance to turn it, the sudden silence startled her. Of its own accord, the water had ceased its torrential outpouring.

What the...?

She scooted back and craned her neck to look up at the sink. Water still poured off the draining board and dropped down to add to her drenching.

She was so cold. Freezing water dripped from her hair and down her neck. Her whole body shuddered and jerked. The first sign of a dull throbbing in her temples warned her that a proper headache loomed.

Soaked to the skin, she forced herself to crawl her way back towards the table, sloshing through at least an inch of icy water on the way.

Her breath still plumed out in puffy clouds whenever she exhaled. The numbness in her bones wasn't just down to being drenched. The air in the room was frigid. She glanced at the window over the sink, believing that it must be wide open to the elements, but it was closed fast. Even if the boiler had died a quick death, there really was no reason for it to be so bitterly cold.

She wasn't one hundred percent sober but, with the help of the cold water, she was quickly getting there. Her thought processes were gradually shifting and switching themselves on and she found herself genuinely beginning to think her way through the confusion and the fucked-up weirdness of everything.

Four things had happened that couldn't be explained – the clock, the kettle, the tap, and the freezing cold. The image in the steam from the kettle and the growling sound in her ear could be explained away, so she gave those happenings no further thought. Deep down, she believed that there had to be a logical explanation for everything else. She simply had to come up with it.

She closed her eyes then gave her head a sharp shake. There wasn't anything wrong with her mind. *Fuck that for a game of soldiers*, she thought fervently. No fucking way was she going doo-lally-tap.

So, if it wasn't her mind – and it definitely wasn't – then that left two options. Either someone was fucking with her, or... She shook her head once more. Or, what... a ghost? Some sort of haunting? Despite how wretched she felt, she laughed. No ghost would dare mess with her... not that she believed in spirits or anything otherworldly. Belief in such things was for morons. She conveniently forgot her dealings with the Ouija board and her hope that Simon's spirit would come through. Like always, Vanessa remembered only what suited her in any given moment.

The house was over two hundred years old, and she knew that it had a certain history, but she had lived in it for eight years without a single bump in the night, or any ghostly goings on. If, over those eight years, she had heard or seen anything untoward, she would've shrugged it off. At no time would she have immediately jumped to an otherworldly explanation, so why was she even fleetingly considering it now?

Because it beat admitting that she was mental.

Common sense told her that it wasn't a ghost. Wishful thinking led her to surmise that she wasn't going off her rocker, so that just left the possibility of some arsehole trying to screw with her head. The obvious person was Richard. He wanted her out of the house. He wanted it on the market so he could line his pockets with his half of the proceeds, however her mind railed against that possibility. She couldn't help herself – she believed that he still loved her and that it was only a matter of time before they reconciled. Rather than believe that her husband would deliberately try to fuck her over, she suddenly realised that she would, after all, prefer to believe that she was losing her marbles.

Five

Richard fancied himself as a photographer. Adorning the walls of the room that Fiona permitted him to use as his study, were framed pictures of street people – youths begging outside Euston station, a tramp rummaging through a bin outside of McDonalds, and several depicting old men drinking wine straight from the bottle. None of them were very good and that was the main reason why he'd never made any money out of what Vanessa had always referred to as his *hobby*.

He'd never called her writing a hobby. Even way back, when she was struggling to write her first novel, he'd never disparaged her talent the way that she did his. He'd encouraged her, given her moral support, and put up with going to bed on his own because she just *had to* get that chapter finished. Not once, in all the years they'd been together, had she ever said a word of encouragement about his passion. Okay, she'd bought him a couple of expensive cameras, financed a showing at a local gallery, and even used one of his photographs on the cover of one of her books, but there was a difference between doing all of that and letting him know that she was proud of him, or that she respected his work.

She'd never said those words – *I'm proud of you, Richard.* She'd told him that she loved him, was mad about him, but never that he was her equal.

It was no wonder that he'd screwed around and ultimately walked out on her. A man didn't need a ball-breaker as a wife. No self-respecting man relished living in his spouse's shadow, and Vanessa had certainly cast a very long shadow. It was just a pity that he still needed her – at least until the divorce was progressed and he got half of everything. Only then would he finally be shot of her.

Pleased with the framing of his latest photograph, he hung it on the wall then stood back to admire it. It was black and white, and he thought it was his best work. As his eyes slowly took in the image, he frowned. The expression on the subject's face seemed a little off. Strangely, and suddenly, the woman's face seemed to be all eyes and teeth. He recalled the woman – a young girl, really, no more than sixteen or seventeen years old – as having an expression almost devoid of emotion. Flat featured, with eyes staring grimly out at a hostile world, she hadn't been smiling when he'd captured her image. In the photograph, she was grinning, and her eyes sparked with... something. He wasn't sure what, but it made him shiver.

There had been over thirty photographs in the sequence, and he wondered if he'd inadvertently framed the wrong one.

He closed his eyes, ran through what he could recall of that day - that few moments when the camera had run on burst mode and taken simultaneous shots all at once – then shook his head. It was an impossible scenario. There shouldn't be a hair's width of difference between one shot and another.

He opened his eyes, re-focussed, blinked again, then gasped. There it was – the emotionless face of a girl who'd given up on life. No teeth were visible. No grin. The eyes were as dead as the day he'd taken the photograph.

What had just happened? He leaned in, peered close, scrunched up his eyes, and tried to make sense of what he'd just witnessed.

There was no sense to be made and he eventually shrugged it off. It was an immaculate photo. The teddy bear clutched against the girl's chest was incongruent to the tableau presented of her circumstances. The photo spoke of ruined innocence, and he knew he could make good money off the back of its message. A print run of, say a hundred to start off with would mean that to make money, he had to *have* money up front, and the only one willing to give him any – or be persuaded to give him any – would be Vanessa.

Fiona, his latest squeeze, had more money than she could spend but getting a penny out of her would be like trying to prise a winkle out of its shell using only his teeth... an impossibility. Fiona had a great many things going for her, but generosity wasn't one of them.

It would mean another visit to the house, another couple of hours smarming his way into Vanessa's bed and then into her purse. It would mean another episode of closing his eyes and thinking only of how much he could charm out of her. Ultimately, the thought of the money was the only thing that would get him hard.... that and Viagra. It had been a long time since his wife had turned him on.

A couple of thousand should do it. He wouldn't be greedy. If he asked for two, then – sooner rather than later – he could go back for more. He'd recently made the mistake on insisting on five and, despite the frenzied sex and the cuddles afterwards, she hadn't parted with another penny for over three months.

He hated the cuddles far more than he hated the sex. Cuddles made him feel guilty because they didn't mean anything to him – not like he knew they meant to her. To Richard, they were nothing more than a means to an end. So was the sex, but it was easy for him to eliminate the intimacy of that act. He couldn't do that with spooning.

Turning his back on the wall of framed photographs, he picked up his phone from the desk in the corner. He would ring her, invite himself over for lunch, maybe take her a bunch of flowers – some roses, pink ones. They were her favourite.

The call went to voicemail. That was unusual. Vanessa always picked up for him. Even in the most drunken of stupors, she always picked up.

He decided against leaving a message, expecting her to notice the missed call and get straight back to him. When, after an hour, she hadn't called him back, he decided to go back to bed. Fiona was still asleep. She rarely got out of bed before midday, and he knew that she would welcome him with open arms. The thought of having sex with his nubile young girlfriend was ample compensation for having to wait a while longer for the next pay off from his wife.

VANESSA DIDN'T HEAR her phone ring. She was preoccupied with the need to get out of her wet clothes before they iced up and froze to her skin, but it wasn't the preoccupation with that, or the water flooding the kitchen floor, or the chatter of her teeth, which made her oblivious to Richard's call. The ringtone simply hadn't registered. If it had managed to reach her ears – which it hadn't – then it certainly hadn't got as far as connecting with her brain.

Getting to her feet proved to be easier said than done. The floor was slippery, and her legs couldn't quite hold her. Grasping the edge of the table, and summoning all her energy, she straightened, tested her balance, then made her way slowly towards the door. Twice, her feet slid out from under her, and she nearly did the splits, but she managed the journey without landing back on her arse.

She dripped all the way upstairs. She gave a silent prayer that the shower was still working and that the water was hot.

Earlier, Anita, the cheeky bitch, had mentioned that she needed to take a shower. Although it had rankled to hear it, Vanessa knew it to be true. She stank of sweat and stale booze. How long had it been since she'd shampooed her hair or had some soap on her body? *Too fucking long*, she mused. It had been six days since the last time her skinny body had been soaped and lathered. Six days of sitting in her own stink. It was all Richard's fault. If he had deigned to pay her a visit... take her to bed and make love to her... she would've been scrubbed and perfumed and creamed long before he showed up at the door. But he hadn't visited, and it had been weeks since she'd last felt him move inside her.

It was the lovemaking that continued to give her hope. It didn't matter that, after the deed was done, and she was floating in the afterglow of an orgasm, he always emptied her purse, or she was obliged to write him a cheque. She never admitted to herself that she paid dear for those orgasms. She never conceded to the fact that she was, in fact, paying him for sex. That had been far too sick a notion to even contemplate.

Of course, he had no clue about how skint she was. She'd been afraid to admit it to him. Subconsciously, she knew that if he ever found out, he would be off like a shot, but, consciously, she realised that he must know or why else was he hell-bent on selling the house out from under her?

He'd have to get the boiler fixed, she mused, a twisted smile playing across her lips – and the electrics, and the plumbing. All of that would cost a pretty penny. He was in for a rude awakening, that was for sure.

She'd forgotten all about the bedroom door being jammed and was forced to use the shower in the main bathroom.

Thankfully, the shower spat out a flow of wonderfully hot water. It took her a few minutes of standing beneath it before she felt warm enough to shampoo her hair.

She took her time in the shower – putting off the moment when she would be forced to go down to her study and begin to tackle the awful manuscript. Although the book could end up being the saving of her – that's if she managed to get her act together and turn it into something that was marketable – it was much too daunting a task to give her thoughts over to.

Fifteen minutes later, the long mirror over the sink reflected a sorry sight. Stick thin, pale yet blotchy, Vanessa looked exactly what she was – a fucking mess. Her curves were long gone and there was no longer anything pretty about her eyes or her hair. She poked at a rib. She could actually count them. Richard, when he'd last been on top of her, had commented that he could play a tune on her ribcage. When he'd said it, he'd tried to laugh it off as him being half-joking, but she'd known that he'd meant it to sound cruel.

A shiver ran the length of her spine. She was even thinner than before, and she had no doubt that Richard would be able to play the xylophone with his cock on her protruding bones. She smiled at that, but it was a cold, sorry looking, depreciating smile.

If only she could hate him. How much stronger that would make her feel. If she didn't worship the very ground he walked on, everything would be so much easier to bear and perhaps she would even get to like herself a little more.

But she didn't hate him. She could never hate the man who had given her their precious son. Without Richard, she would never have known what it was like to be on the receiving end of the unconditional love of a child. She wished that she'd been the one to die. She would give her life away in a heartbeat if it meant that Simon could live again.

A sharp pain stabbed behind her eyeballs. No matter how many years had passed since she'd lost him, the pain remained as acute and as devastating as that first dreadful moment when she'd realised that he was gone. It was something she knew she would never recover from.

She hadn't mentioned the Ouija board to Richard. She hadn't dared. He was funny about anything to do with spirits, and he would take her interest in contacting Simon from the great beyond as further evidence that she was cracked in the head. It wasn't that she believed in an afterlife, or in ghosts or spirits. She certainly didn't believe in God, however desperation wrapped up in grief ultimately had the consequence of making a naïve fool out of everyone.

Being drunk was the only way she could cope with the incessant grief, and she knew that she would brave the flooded kitchen again for the sake of grabbing up the second bottle of vodka sitting waiting for her in the fridge.

She now felt more sober than she'd been in weeks. She didn't like that feeling. Sobriety left her vulnerable and bare. She wasn't a maudlin drunk. She was more likely to suffer introspection and depression when she was stone cold sober and the only cure for that was to drink more. Richard had told her it was a sorry excuse for drunkenness and that she would never be able to cherish Simon's memory properly whilst pickled in vodka. He had a point, but it was a point she didn't care to take on board.

Her reflection now showed a slack expression. For a full minute, she stood and stared at the blankness in her eyes and at the downward cast of her mouth. She looked ugly. She was ugly inside and out.

Shaking herself from her dazed stance, she turned and grabbed up a pair of black leggings and an oversized T shir tout of the laundry basket in the corner. They smelled, were stained with God knew what, but she pulled them on, and headed back downstairs. Before she tackled the manuscript, she was definitely going to have another drink.

Back downstairs, she immediately noticed that the air wasn't quite so frigid and, when she passed the radiator in the hallway – the one just outside the kitchen – she felt the heat coming off it in comfortable waves.

Paddling her way across the floor to the fridge, even the water splashing over her bare feet seemed warm. She didn't give it much thought. Her mind was too preoccupied in imagining the burn in the back of her throat that would follow her first swallow.

People said that vodka didn't have a smell, but to Vanessa, it had a heady scent. As soon as she unscrewed the cap, it wafted to her nostrils and made them flare.

Licking her lips, she closed her eyes and raised the bottle to her mouth. The anticipation was almost as great as the actual taste and effect of the alcohol, and she dragged in a long sigh before tipping her head back, sucking on the neck of the bottle, and swallowing.

The burn was as good as she'd expected and, as it travelled down, she was already taking another gulp.

She told herself that was enough for the moment. She wasn't planning on getting sozzled. She still had work to do, and she had enough sense to realise that she couldn't do it whilst pissed.

She made for the study, but the ping on her phone caused her to halt mid step. It was on the kitchen table, and she turned at the door to look back at it.

Two things were registered on the screen – a missed call and another Facebook notification.

The missed call was from Richard. She noted the time and raised a brow. He hadn't called when she'd been in the shower. It had come through earlier than that, when she was on her knees on the kitchen floor. That she hadn't heard it ring was a mystery. Excitement bubbled all the way from her toes and brought colour to her cheeks. She disregarded her disquiet over missing the call. It didn't matter. A phone call might mean a visit and she was glad she'd had a shower because a visit always meant lovemaking. Her excitement made her breathless. She felt like a giddy schoolgirl.

Coffee. She needed coffee, and perhaps some food. She wouldn't return his call until she felt a little steadier, not until she'd settled her stomach. Sometimes Richard was too easily put off from visiting. One slurred word, one hint that she was under the influence, and he'd back off. He'd never liked seeing her drunk and he rarely initiated sex if she reeked of alcohol.

She was a little wary of approaching the kettle, and even more wary of turning on the tap to fill it, but the one thing Vanessa liked to believe she possessed, was backbone. She would never admit to being a coward.

Nothing untoward occurred. The coffee helped to cast off the last of her chills and it certainly settled her stomach. She began to think about food. She thought she might just about manage a slice of dry toast... anything that would help soak up the alcohol would do.

Sitting at the table, munching on her toast, she fingered her phone. The excitement at possibly seeing Richard had begun to wane. She had slowly reached the conclusion that it wasn't a good idea to call him back, or to ask him over.

The damned book. It had to come before Richard, before sex, and before everything else.

She knew that she couldn't put off the amendments – a virtual rewrite – of the draft for much longer, not if she was going to make some progress before Anita's Friday deadline.

Despite what Anita thought, deep down, Vanessa did have the sense to realise the precariousness of her position. She'd been skating on very thin ice with The Publishing House, and she knew that – if she continued to fuck-up – all of her past accolades wouldn't mean jack-shit. Her current work in progress was her last chance to redeem herself, and it might just be the thing that would bring Richard back to her. There was nothing like the smell of success to attract an errant husband back to the fold.

But first, she had a great deal of mopping up to do. the kitchen wasn't going to dry itself.

Six

The crash made her jump. The splintering of glass had her on her feet and staring at the window. Something had smashed into it, broke through the pane of glass and, when her eyes dropped down to the windowsill, she realised what that something was.

A small bird, its beak open, as if protesting its death, lay still and bloodied. It was a starling.

Vanessa had a fear of birds. When she was about six years old, one had got caught in her hair. Its frantic struggles had resulted in scratches to her face and neck and the experience had left her with a deep-rooted phobia. Richard had told her that she was a conundrum of phobias. In the early days, he'd found them quite quirky, quite endearing, but had soon come to use them as a stick to beat her with. Always an anxious person, there had been times when she couldn't face people, when she felt too panicky to go out to dinner or go on holiday and that had eventually pissed him off. The thing with the birds really got his goat because, for years, it stopped him from enjoying the garden. He had never been permitted to host a barbeque and she'd never sat outside with him and relaxed with a glass of wine in the cool of a summer's evening. Eventually, he'd spent hours out there on his own, not giving a damn about leaving her alone inside the house. Then, he'd taken to spending all day outside with Simon – denying her the company of her son. That had been hard to forgive.

Even though the bird was obviously dead, she couldn't bring herself to approach it. Anxiously, she glanced at the broken window and hoped there weren't any more kamikaze starlings poised to follow suit and fill her kitchen with their bodies.

Frozen to the spot, she contemplated how she could get rid of it. She couldn't touch it. The very thought made her feel faint. She couldn't leave it there. It would end up stinking the whole place out.

What to do?

She would have to ring Richard after all.

'SHE'S FREAKING OUT,' he said to Fiona. 'Some stupid bird crashed through the kitchen window, and she needs me to go over to dispose of it.'

'What are you... her janitor?'

Richard perched on the edge of the bed and avoided looking at her. 'She can't help being scared of the damned things. Why don't you cut her some slack?'

'Oh, hark at you... all knight in shining armour all of a sudden. I think you enjoy being at her beck and call.'

Her sarcasm rankled, but she did have a point. Vanessa had no right to expect him to simply drop everything and go get rid of a stupid bird.

He turned towards her. 'I won't go,' he said. 'Fuck her.'

'That's my boy.' Fiona leaned over and kissed him on the mouth, teasing him with her tongue. 'You show her who's boss. You've been far too soft with her.'

Now that he had refused to go, Richard could afford to inject a little magnanimity into his words without the risk of upsetting Fiona any further.

He hated having to tread on eggshells every time he mentioned his wife. For some stupid reason, Fiona was jealous of Vanessa and resented every mention of her and, for days on end after every visit he made to her, Fiona made his life hell. She wouldn't talk to him, refused to sleep with him, and disappeared with her friends without telling him who she was with, or where she was. He shuddered to think what she would do if she ever found out what they both got up to. It would probably be the end of them. Sometimes, he thought that wouldn't be such a bad thing... ending everything between them.

'I have to keep her sweet,' he said. 'She's still refusing to sign the divorce papers and it's dragging on far too long. You want it all over with, don't you?'

'She'll never sign them.' Fiona sighed and leaned back against the pillows. 'You'll have to do it the hard way.'

His brow puckered. 'The hard way?'

'Well, not hard, not really. I mean, she can't contest your petition... not anymore. The law changed. Didn't you know that?'

'You seem very well informed.' The words were clipped.

'Someone has to be.'

'I do happen to know all about the changes,' he said. 'But I *want* her consent. There's too much at stake to go to war with her.'

His eyes were drawn to the bedroom window. Outside, on the ledge, a bird sat staring in. He watched it for a moment, wishing he had his camera to hand.

'Go to war with her, Richard. I dare you.'

He dragged his eyes back to her. 'You dare me?'

She nodded. 'Absolutely.'

'Why?'

'Because I'm sick of watching you jump through hoops to... as you say... *keep her sweet*. It's sickening.'

He heard a *tap, tap, tap*, and turned back to the window. The bird, a starling, was pecking on the glass. Its eyes drew his gaze. They seemed to be looking directly at him.

Tap, tap, tap... louder, harder.

He got up from the bed, walked over to the window, and rapped a knuckle on the glass directly in front of the bird. He thought that the noise and the vibration would shoo it away. It didn't.

'Stubborn little fucker,' he said under his breath, rapping the glass one more.

The tapping stopped. The bird sat, motionless, staring up at him. Richard smiled, unperturbed, then leapt back as something quite phenomenal occurred.

What the bird did was, to Richard's mind, quite impossible. It had neither the size nor the strength to break the glass and, as it was standing quite still and didn't have the momentum of flight to add to its tiny weight, throwing its beak forward and crashing through was never going to be a conceivable feat, but that was exactly what it did.

'Jesus,' he uttered, stepping back in fright.

The bird hung by its neck on a shard of broken glass. Blood pooled on the window ledge. Its tiny chest fluttered as it died.

Fiona was suddenly at his side, pulling on his arm. 'What is it?' she asked. 'What did you do?'

'Me?' He shook his head. 'Nothing. I didn't do anything.'

VANESSA SAT AT THE kitchen table and waited for Richard to call her back. She'd asked him to come over to get rid of the bird – maybe bury it in the garden – and make the window secure by boarding it up, but of course, he had to run it past Fiona first. Recently, it seemed that he needed the bitch's permission every time he wanted to visit his own wife. Vanessa was sure that he even had to seek Fiona's permission to take a piss.

If it wasn't so tragic, it would be funny.

Lifting her eyes, she glanced nervously over at the sink and then up at window. She blinked, blinked again, then rocked back in her chair and gaped at ... nothing. There was no broken glass, no dead bird, no evidence of what had occurred just minutes before.

Something hammered her dead-centre on her chest. It felt like a blow from someone's fist, and it took the breath from her.

It wasn't a fist, and it wasn't a blow. It was her heart slamming against her breastbone. She dragged in a ragged breath. It stuttered in her throat before filling her chest and giving her the strength to jump to her feet.

Backing up, the water lapping over her toes, she panned her eyes frantically along the length of the windowsill.

Still, no bird and no evidence of it ever having been there.

It was a moment like no other. It was the only moment in her life when she'd really and truly questioned her own sanity. She'd had fleeting moments – like earlier – when she'd wondered if she was going off her rocker, but now... now, she really began to believe it.

Vanessa was no stranger to insanity. Throughout her childhood, she'd lived with a mother who saw giant spiders coming out of the walls, and who screamed well into the night, railing against a myriad of monsters. It wasn't unusual for her to arrive home from school to find her mother cowering in a corner, terrified of the aliens who had invaded the house. Of course, there were no aliens. There were never any spiders or monsters, except in her mother's mind. The psychiatrists – and there had been a few of them over the years – diagnosed alcohol induced psychosis and, later, Korsakoff's Syndrome... a form of dementia associated with years of alcohol abuse.

Vanessa knew that she ought to have had more sense than to look to alcohol for solace, but – just like the oncologists who smoked like chimneys – she chanced fate, hoping it wouldn't end up biting her on the arse.

She shook uncontrollably, the fear of madness overwhelming her. She couldn't end up like her mother... she couldn't. She would rather end it all right then.

Her eyes darted to the knife block standing next to the hob. Before that moment, suicide wasn't something she'd ever contemplated. Even after Simon was taken from her, she'd fought to survive the grief. Throughout every humiliation heaped upon her by a faithless husband, she'd turned to alcohol rather than a bottle of sleeping pills. Now, if she wanted to stave off a descent into the same hell her mother had endured, she wouldn't even have vodka to console her.

Before she could move towards the knives, a shadow darted in the corner of her eye. It was fleeting but dark enough to be noticed. She turned her head, expecting... she wasn't sure what to expect, but assumed that she would witness the flap of a dead bird's wings.

It wasn't a bird and, before she dropped in a dead faint, she knew that what she saw wasn't of this world.

The back of her head slammed against the floor. Beneath her, the water immediately turned pink.

She was out for the count for two long hours and, when she eventually opened her eyes – groggy and confused – she found that she couldn't move without inviting excruciating pain.

Soaked through, shuddering with cold, and with a head that felt as if it was ready to explode, she lay there until dusk began to settle outside, and the light in the room eventually faded.

Gradually, the confusion waned, and her head cleared. There was still pain – a lot of pain, mostly on the back of her skull and behind her eyes – but, as time passed, it became increasingly bearable.

At one point, she sobbed but the exertion raised the pain levels ten-fold, so she forced the tears back and stilled her body as much as she was able.

She dreaded what she would find when she finally got to her feet. It wasn't simply the agony of getting up from the floor that had her remaining flat on her back. She didn't want to see that *thing* again.

She didn't want to be faced with the proof that she'd tipped right over the edge.

But, when she closed her eyes, she saw it anyway. There was no name she could apply to it. Even with her extremely vivid imagination and her ability to conjure up descriptions out of thin air – something that helped immensely in her meteoritic rise as a bestselling author – she could find no words to describe it.

Except... it *seemed* like a giant mouth, similar to what she'd witnessed in the steam from the kettle... only bigger, blacker, more malevolent. In the split second before she'd fainted, it had seemed to come for her It intended to swallow her whole.

Behind her eyelids, it came for her again and, at last, she screamed.

Seven

Extract from the journal of author Vanessa Parker, discovered by her literary agent, Anita Sanderson.

Before this moment, I've never contemplated writing a journal, and I'm not even sure if I can call these scribblings an actual journal, but for want of a better description, for the time being, let's settle on that. If anyone ends up reading it, they can make up their own minds about what to call it. At the end of the day, it is what it is, and who gives a fuck anyway?

I have the headache from hell, feel as sick as a dog, and I don't mind admitting that I'm scared out of my wits.

It's Wednesday evening and, as usual, I'm on my own. I'm wishing that I had the guts to get in my car and get the hell out of here. Instead – coward that I am – I'm holed up in the downstairs loo with notepad and pen in hand trying to make sense of all the shit going on around me.

I want to believe that I'm simply imagining things. I don't want to draw the conclusion that I've turned into a nut job. We all imagine things sometimes, don't we? If we're stressed, depressed, drunk... well, it's not unheard of, under those circumstances, to have fleeting moments of what seems like insanity. But to be a complete nut job... that's pretty fucking scary.

What's more terrifying than being one slice short of a picnic?

It all being real, that's what. That it's not my imagination, and that it's not a drug fuelled psychosis.

That it's all fucking real.

It's NOT real. Jesus, it's mental to even think that it could be.

Get a grip, Vanessa!!!!!

I've decided that, after I finish the novel... IF I ever finish the novel... this journal is the last thing I will ever write. I'm only finishing the book because I can't return the advance. The money is almost gone. Some of it went on vodka, the rest on... well, let's just say that I screwed it away. I wish I could say that I got my money's worth.

There is a possibility that vodka fucked with my brain, fucked with my ability to write, and fucked with my whole life, but I can't admit – even to myself – that I'm an alcoholic. Would I get sympathy if I did? Would I want that sympathy? Hell, no. Screw that. I don't want anyone feeling sorry for me. Perish the thought.

But I will admit that alcohol is my curse. I'm quite happy to blame it for everything... the paranoia, the hallucinations, the whole sorry mess that is my life.

So, I'm going to try and knock drinking on the head. I'm not going to end up like my mother... God rest her rotten soul. I'm getting right off that particular path before it's too late.

If it's not already too late.

I'm going to try and make my final novel at least a half decent one. Not because I owe anyone anything. Everyone has already made a fortune out of me, so I owe them nothing. No, I'm going to do it for myself, and for my son. If there is an afterlife, then I want him to be up there, looking down, and being proud of me.

First, I have to get myself out of this toilet. Easier said than done. The house is quiet, freezing cold, and (I hope) empty. I'm praying that the presence I sense lurking in every corner is merely a figment of my fucked-up imagination. I'm hoping that, if I stay sober, the feeling of being watched, of being stalked in my own home, will disappear.

I don't want to emerge from the loo to see any more dead birds, or any more... Jesus, just thinking about it gives me the collywobbles.

Today has been a shitty day... one of the worst days of my life, and that's saying some-

thing. I never want to live through another day like it.

Now for another admission. Earlier, before I scuttled off to hide in here, I seriously contemplated killing myself. I'm not ruling it out. I'd be daft not to give myself that option. Death isn't the worst thing that could happen to me. Following my mother's path right to the end would be far worse.

I wish Richard was here. I don't think he would understand about the dead bird, or the screwy thing with the clock, and I'm sure he would want to bundle me off to rehab if I told him about the mouth, but I still wish he was here so I could confide in him.

I wish I didn't love him. I wish I didn't need him. I wish...

Enough.

SHE WAS STILL SOAKED through and so very cold. When she finished writing on the notepad – a sorry excuse for a journal – the tips of her fingers were turning blue and her whole body was a juddering, shivering wreck.

She swept her gaze up the length of the stairs. She had to go up and try to prise open her bedroom door, get to some warm clothes, and force some heat into her body.

It was dark at the top of the stairs. The landing light refused to click on when she pressed the switch. She didn't relish walking up and into that darkness, but she had no choice. There was a torch in one of the cupboards in the kitchen and her mobile phone had a light she could use to illuminate her way, but she wasn't ready to go back in there to make use of either one.

For the moment, she was determined that the kitchen was out of bounds.

One step and then two. She halted, bent her head to listen, satisfied herself that she was safe, then climbed steps three and four.

She reached the top and felt her way along the wall to her bedroom.

Startled, she realised that the door stood ajar. Inside the room it was grey, far lighter than the landing. Reaching in, she found the light switch and blinked as the sudden brightness momentarily blinded her.

There was nothing amiss. Nothing sat behind the door to suggest a blockage. Everything was as she'd left it.

She was too cold to consider what the open door meant. Rushing to the wardrobe, she hauled a long cardigan off a hanger, stripped out of her wet clothes and shrugged herself into it. She found a pair of woolly socks in a drawer and pulled them on, then sat on the edge of the bed, hugging herself and rocking backward and forward until she felt her body begin to thaw.

Her head still throbbed but far less acutely than before. The nausea had passed, leaving a hollow feeling in the pit of her stomach, a feeling that she recognised as hunger.

At first, the hunger displaced her anxiety, then it was the cause of increasing it. To eat, she would have to return to the kitchen. To return to the kitchen meant facing the fear that now sat malignantly, like a lump of cement, in her chest.

She couldn't do it. She couldn't bring herself to go anywhere near the kitchen.

Telling herself that she wouldn't starve to death for want of some supper, she made her way back downstairs and directly to her study.

She'd made herself a promise – two promises, actually – to stop drinking and to make something out of the messy draft on her laptop. She was determined to meet both promises with as much vigour as she could muster. The boiler could wait, the flooded kitchen could wait, and food could wait. First – the book.

Then, everything else.

Eight

Anita looked at her watch and made a tutting sound. She was running late, and it was all because she'd woke up that morning knowing that she needed to get in touch with Vanessa and maybe pay her another visit.

If she'd answered her phone, the journey to the house might not have been necessary. If she'd answered the door, then Anita wouldn't now be sitting in her car, fuming, cursing under her breath, and wishing that she hadn't bothered with the silly cow.

Up and out of the house early, Anita had arrived at Vanessa's just after eight o'clock. She fully expected to have to knock until she forced her out of bed. If she'd been too deep in sleep not to hear her phone, then Anita resigned herself to knocking her knuckles bloody in an attempt to get through to her.

She'd asked her numerous times to install a doorbell, but Vanessa had insisted that she didn't need one.

'Anyway,' she'd said, 'the house is old, has character, and I'm not spoiling it by putting in a stupid bell.'

Anita had countered that argument with suggesting an old-fashioned one – one that went *ding-dong*, instead of playing the William tell Overture.

Vanessa would have none of it, so that morning Anita had stood, hammering on the door, and turning the air blue with strong swear words.

Against her better judgement, she used the key Vanessa had given her for use in an emergency. The damned thing wouldn't turn in the lock.

Eventually, she had made her way around to the rear of the house. It meant shouldering her way through a rickety, six-foot, wooden gate that was rotted at the hinges, and then slipping and slithering across a weed-strewn path to reach the back door that led to the kitchen.

Before making her way to the door, she had peered in the window, didn't see anything to raise any concern, and then proceeded to make as much noise as she could by banging both fists on the window and then on the door.

Beneath her anger, Anita was worried, but she didn't have the time to do anything about that worry. She had a long drive ahead of her. Really, she ought to have taken the train. She wasn't sure what had possessed her to make the eight-hour journey to Edinburgh by car.

She gave the front door another hammering before giving up and leaving.

Now, she'd been on the road for over two hours, and she ought to have been on her way at first light. The A1 was being its usual nasty self. Roadworks were being thrown up every couple of miles, traffic was horrendous, and she realised that she would be lucky to arrive in time for dinner.

She frowned at the line of brake lights flashing in front of her. She could see at least a dozen cars ahead, and every one of them was quickly reducing speed. In the distance, she caught sight of the blue flashing lights of an ambulance.

Just her luck – a fucking accident. She looked at her watch once more. She could murder Vanessa fucking Parker.

Sweat trickled down the back of her neck and she turned off the blower and cracked the window. Cold air wafted in and quickly cooled her. Anita wondered if she could afford the time to pull into the next service station, grab a coffee and a burger, and strip off at least two layers of clothing. A third glance at her watch told her that she couldn't risk it. She could afford to miss dinner – although the thought of that almost broke her heart – but she couldn't be late for the keynote speaker at the evening opening of the conference. They would all notice her absence – her rivals, her enemies, those who would get the first crack at the new celebrity authors lining up for representation. Every one of her contemporaries would revel in her not being there for dinner and they would be cock-a-hoop to have her out of the way when the first of those would-be authors started mingling with the literary agents lining up to meet them.

She wished she had a drink. She'd guzzled the only can of coke she'd brought with her within the first half hour of being on the road. She reconsidered stopping. The sign ahead said the next service station was four miles further along.

She needn't be long, she mused. A quick in and out and she could be back on her way in under ten minutes.

Her mouth was so dry that her tongue stuck to the roof of her mouth. She would definitely have to stop. Anyway, she needed to pee, so she really had no choice.

Half an hour later, and the service station was still four miles ahead. Her car had been at a standstill for that full thirty minutes. It hadn't budged an inch and neither had any other vehicle except for a fire engine and two ambulances racing along the hard shoulder twenty minutes before. She surmised that the accident must be a bad one and reconciled to settling in for a long wait.

She spent some of the time listening to the radio, got bored, and searched in her bag for her laptop. If the police saw her using it, despite being stationary and stuck in a long traffic jam, she would probably get a fixed penalty ticket.

There was reading she could be getting on with. She'd managed to get her hands on the debut manuscripts of two 'B' list celebrities attending the conference. Both were on the look-out for an agent and, despite being mere reality stars on second-rate television shows,

Anita had seen promise in their books. Surprisingly, neither had used a ghost-writer, and for that alone, Anita was impressed enough to tout for their business. Vanessa was definitely on the wane, and she needed to grab herself another couple of budding best-selling authors to make up for the shortfall in income she knew was imminent.

She had no faith in Vanessa producing anything worthwhile by close of play the next day. She had no faith in her producing anything of worth ever again. She was too far gone, too deep in her own private hell, and too far up her own arsehole to accept advice or help.

A car horn sounded behind her, startling her. The traffic was moving. She put the car in gear and crawled forward.

Her bladder was fit to burst, and she didn't think she was going to get to a toilet in time. It was yet another thing to indirectly blame on Vanessa.

Although the traffic continued to move, it was extremely slow going and it took a full hour to travel the next four miles. With a huff of relief, Anita finally pulled off onto the slip road and, not caring who she inconvenienced, parked in a disabled space outside the main doors of the service station.

She got to the toilet in the nick of time.

Deciding not to immediately throw herself back into the traffic, she found an empty table and sat down with a bottle of water, a coffee, two burgers and an apple muffin. She was definitely going to miss dinner, so compensated by stuffing her face with as much grease and as many carbs as she had the time for.

Firing up her laptop, she went immediately to her saved files but, instead of opening either of the two manuscripts she was interested in, she decided to take another look at the draft Vanessa sent to her the week before.

She'd already read through it, hadn't been in the least impressed, and had all but decided to cut her loose then and there. Giving her the couple of days to at least try to make what was nothing more than a pile of steaming shit a little more readable was – in light of the fact that Vanessa had now gone off the grid – one of her less wise decisions.

Frowning, she clicked and searched, but couldn't locate the file. Had she been so disgusted with it that she'd deleted it? She would never have done that. Anita deleted nothing.

Nevertheless, she searched her trash folder. It wasn't there. Next, she searched her email folder. The file had come from Vanessa as an attachment on an email and Anita would be able to re-download the file from there, but there was no email with the expected attachment. In fact, she could find no emails at all from Vanessa.

That can't be right, she thought, her fingers clicking on the keypad as she searched further.

The missing emails confounded her, but time was marching on, and the morning would soon roll into afternoon, so she closed the laptop with a huff and got to her feet. She would worry about it all later. Vanessa had already made her late enough.

There was nothing worse than driving when the winter sun sat low on the horizon. Although a cold sun, it still dazzled and, because it sat below the visor, its blinding brilliance made a torturous journey north all the more unbearable.

Before Anita got much further, she was already contemplating turning at the next junction and heading back home.

Nine

Fiona stretched out on the bed, replete, her body half turned towards her lover. Richard looked down and, as his gaze settled on her, he frowned. He was going to have to tell her that he planned on paying Vanessa a visit, and he wasn't looking forward to her reaction. In his head, he calculated the chances of her not giving a shit and concluded that hell would freeze over before that ever happened. He couldn't understand her jealousy. Compared to his wife, Fiona was every man's wet dream and she had to know that there was nothing for her to worry about. Okay, so he fucked Vanessa now and again, but sex with his wife didn't mean anything to him and shouldn't be something that his girlfriend of two years ought to get worked up about.

But try telling her that, he mused. It seemed that even the most beautiful and sexiest of women could still come over all insecure and needy. After a while, it got rather exhausting. It took all the fun out of the relationship.

He considered not telling her but, if he was later caught out in the lie, she would make him suffer in ways he was scared to even contemplate. Fiona was a Class A bitch, but a bitch he couldn't get enough of. The thing was – the catch 22 – was that, although Fiona had plenty of money of her own, she expected him to match her pound for pound. He needed to be solvent to keep her happy, and to get the money to keep her at his side meant sleeping with Vanessa.

Sometimes, he felt a little bitter about the fact that Fiona refused to spend a penny on him, expecting him to pay for everything. She never questioned where his money came from, preferring to remain in happy ignorance, but there was one thing about Fiona that was never in any doubt – she could spend it faster than he could fuck it out of his wife.

The things you do for love... or lust... he thought to himself, a small grimace turning his mouth down at the corners. One, or both, of those women would be the death of him. Sometimes, he didn't even know which side was up.

Richard didn't consider himself a bad person. He knew that he'd been a lousy husband – was still a lousy husband – but he also knew that he'd been a great father and he believed the great father part of him cancelled out the fact that he was a cheat and a manipulator who was hell-bent on bleeding his wife dry.

If only Vanessa would allow him to put the house on the market. It would be a fresh start for both of them because he would have his own money and they could finally be rid of one another. However, she was playing hardball over the sale of the house. She had some sentimental notion that, because their son had been born there, she could never give it up. It wasn't that he didn't understand. It was more that he believed her attachment to the bricks and mortar was rather ghoulish. It was, after all, only a fucking house. Whenever he tried to tell her that, she'd screamed at him that he had no fucking clue and to do one.

He supposed, when he called round to see her later, that he would get more of the same, so he would have to tread carefully. He knew he would have to fuck her, but, more and more – if it wasn't for those little blue pills – he wouldn't be able to get it up. The very sight of her shrivelled his balls. He never had to depend on the pills when he fucked Fiona but, then again, Fiona wasn't a shrivelled up middle-aged hag who inhaled vodka by the pint.

He convulsed with a spasm of revulsion. Jesus, it was going to be a difficult few hours. He wasn't looking forward to a single minute of it.

Sighing, he rolled over and climbed from the bed. *No rest for the wicked*, he thought miserably, stretching out the kinks in his back and reaching for his trousers lying in a heap on the floor

'Where are you going?' Fiona asked, pouting, and tugging the duvet over to cover her naked breasts. 'I thought we were going to spend the afternoon in bed?'

'I can't, honey. I need to…'

'You're not going to see her, are you?' She pulled herself up onto one elbow. 'You are, aren't you? Well, let me tell you…'

He sighed and rolled his eyes. 'Don't start, Fiona. You know how it is. I need to keep an eye on her…. The thing with the bird…' He glanced over at the broken window. 'It's maybe a coincidence, but…'

'Of course, it's a bloody coincidence. Migrating birds do all sorts of weird shit. I don't know why you were so freaked out about it.'

'I should've gone over last night. If I was freaked out, imagine how she felt.'

'You're making a mountain out of a molehill. Anyway, it's not your job to keep an eye on her, Richard. She's not your responsibility.'

'That's as may be, but there's the house to consider. She's letting it go to wreck and ruin and soon it won't be worth shit. I have to go and do some repairs… get it ready for the agent to value, and we can't do that with a broken window, now can we?'

'You're wasting your time. You'll never persuade her to sell. Stay and fix *my* broken window, and never mind hers.'

'I'll fix this one later. I'll only be gone an hour or so.'

'I've heard that before.'

'I mean it… two ours, tops.'

She sighed, then asked, 'How much do you think you'll clear?'

'From the sale of the house?' He shrugged. 'My half should be around the half million mark.' Actually, he was expecting double that amount, but he didn't feel the need to tell her that.

'That doesn't sound a lot,' she said. 'It must be worth at least three million, and I know there's no mortgage on it.'

'Three million?' he scoffed. 'In your dreams, pet.' He hoped for two, but also kept that opinion to himself.

'Since you're hell-bent on doing the divorce the hard way, try and get her to sign the divorce papers when you're there.'

'I'll try, but you know what she's like.'

'Try harder,' she ground out. 'Make her sign the fucking things, or else...'

He rounded on her. 'Or else... what? You'll leave me? Go right ahead. I don't need this shit. I get enough of it from her, without you chipping in.' He dragged on a T shirt, already regretting his outburst. He lived in fear of her leaving him, and he knew better than to put the thought into her head. In a calmer tone, he said, 'Don't go breaking my balls over the divorce, Fiona. I'll get her to sign.'

She flopped back against the pillows. 'Just see that you do.'

He ran a hand through his mop of thick hair and sat back down on the bed. He reached for her, but she flinched and turned her back on him.

'Don't be like that,' he said.' If you'd rather I stayed...'

'I don't.'

'I can wait and go tomorrow.'

'Do what you want.' Her voice was muffled by the pillow. 'I'm past caring.'

He wished that *he* was past caring. Fiona had outlasted all of his other women – except Vanessa, of course – and he hoped that she would last at least a while longer. He appreciated the roof she put over his head, the warm bed she provided, and the even warmer body, and sometimes he really believed that he was in it for the duration. He was astute enough to realise that it was more the fact that he was getting old, rather than a love job, which made him want to stay right where he was. It was a terrible thing – getting old. He wasn't quite fifty, and on a good day he knew that he looked no older than thirty-five, but there was nothing quite like sex with a much younger woman to peel away the years. Once, he had lived for the hunt, but now he was happy in the knowledge that he had a warm and willing body waiting for him at home. The thought of starting again, finding a replacement for Fiona, filled him with a miserable dread. He couldn't start over – certainly not before he had that million in the bank.

A hollow feeling spread across his belly. Sometimes, he saw himself for what he was, and it didn't impress him. He'd had high hopes for his life. He'd had ambition, and then he'd met Vanessa. Her star shone much brighter than his. She had talent oozing from every pore and his wants and his needs had soon morphed into a lazy nonchalance. If he couldn't keep step with her, it was easier just to reap the benefits of being married to a bestselling author and stop trying to compete. His talent for photography paled into insignificance next to her talent as a writer.

He believed that his first affair was a means of punishing her for her success. Why not, he'd thought. She had her books and her adoring fans, so why shouldn't he have a bit on the side? Anyway, it served her right for ignoring him. He was her fucking husband and he deserved more than the crumbs from her table.

He'd finished the affair when the guilt had become too much to bear. Imagine that – a time when he'd actually felt some guilt. He couldn't help but smile to himself. The guilt had been short-lived, and he'd never suffered it again.

Of course, she'd forgiven him, and she'd carried on forgiving him, even after the fling with his therapist. If she hadn't...?

He shook his head. It was all her own fault. She should've kneed him in the balls and chucked him out on his ear.

Even now – after everything he'd done – she would take him back in a heartbeat. Didn't she realise how unattractive that made her? Didn't she understand how her attitude towards his infidelity made him want to stay away all the more? Women had no clue when it came to men. He didn't know many men who appreciated being tied to a whiney, insecure doormat. It was okay, for a while. It certainly bumped up the old ego, and stroked the manhood, but there were always the hurt expressions to contend with and who needed the subtle recriminations?

It was different with Fiona. She might have her moments – moments when she was almost as clingy and insecure as Vanessa – however, at least she was fiery. Fiona never had any intention of letting him off with a thing and, as tiring as that could get, he much preferred it to Vanessa's submissive acceptance.

But, for Richard, sometimes, a little bit of shame encroached. It often caught him unawares and, for the odd moment or two, he really didn't like himself.

It never lasted. He thought too much of himself to dwell on any fleeting self-recrimination.

Once, one of his lovers had described him – to his face – as a narcissistic arsehole. That was after he'd dumped her, so he didn't really blame her. She had to call him something, but *narcissistic*? He thought not. He could love himself, think that he was the bees' knees, and it didn't make him a narcissist. Some women simply didn't take rejection well.

'Are you going, or what?' Fiona said. 'Only I'd quite like to go back to sleep.'

Richard chewed on his lower lip. It was in the tip of his tongue to make a sarcastic retort – something like, *you've already been in bed twelve hours so isn't it about time you got up and tidied around a little bit?* But he had more sense than to say anything close to that. Instead, he said, 'See you later, then.'

As he walked through the door, he thought he heard her say, *fuck you*. He smiled. Typical Fiona... always demanding the last word.

He detoured to the kitchen and removed a bottle of chilled Chardonnay from the fridge, thinking it wouldn't do any harm to go and visit Vanessa bearing a gift. The wine, and the sex to come, would guarantee him something in return...hopefully, a gift of money.

He closed the door to the fridge and rummaged in a drawer for a plastic bag. Whistling to himself – feeling perkier now that the possibility of becoming temporarily solvent was imminent – his only concern was that Fiona would notice the missing wine. No doubt, she would have something to say about it, so he would have to make a point of stopping at the off-licence on the way back. It would be sensible to replace it before she noticed its absence. He didn't think he would react well to another pointed argument over the over-indulgence of his estranged wife and dragging out their earlier encounter wasn't something he relished.

With the bottle safely tucked inside the bag, and with car keys in hand, he made his way back into the hallway. As he passed the study on the way to the front door, his step faltered. His eyes drifted towards the firmly closed door. He wondered if Fiona had made her way downstairs whilst he'd been in the kitchen, because he had a sense that someone was in the study. It was just a feeling. He couldn't actually hear anything. For one mad moment he envisaged that one of the people in his photographs had come alive and was standing staring at him through the closed door.

He snorted, shook his head, and hurried out the front door.

Ten

Richard Arthur Parker (RAP)
Sample taken from PART ONE of recorded interview
Date: 21 January 2022
Duration: 61 minutes
Location: Wood Street Police Station, City of London
No of pages: 24 (total number of sample pages: 11)
Conducted by officers from the London Metropolitan Police
All police officer identifiers have been redacted as per Section 38 (1) (A)

Police: Now that we've got the preliminaries and the introductions out of the way, can you, for the audio recording, confirm that you have waived your right to legal representation.

RAP: I've already told you that I don't need a solicitor. Why would I need legal representation? Am I a suspect, or something? It's not as if I've done anything wrong.

Police: That's not the point, Mister Parker. I need to remind you that you're being interviewed under caution, and it is your right to have a solicitor present. So, I ask again – do you waive that right?

RAP: Yes... consider it waived.

Police: If, at any time, you change your mind, we will suspend the interview until your solicitor arrives.

RAP: Whatever.

Police: You don't appear to be taking this very seriously, Mister Parker. Aren't you worried about your wife?

RAP: Of course, I'm worried, but I'm always worried about my wife. What's new about that?

Police: What's new is that she seems to have disappeared. No one has seen her or been in contact with her for quite some time.

RAP: I don't know anything about that.

Police: Have you been in touch with her recently?

RAP: Not for a week, or so.

Police: Can you be more specific?

RAP: I can't remember... not exactly

Police: Okay. Have a think about it, and we'll come back to it. Meantime, have you any idea where she might be?

RAP: Nope.

Police: No recent phone calls, or text messages indicating if she's all right?

RAP: No. Well...

Police: Well?

RAP: She hasn't sounded right for a while. Her phone calls and texts were always a bit screwy.

Police: In what way?

RAP: In every way. It never helped that she was always six sheets to the wind.

Police: Drunk?

RAP: As a skunk.

Police: Every time?

RAP: Pretty much.

Police: Was she drunk the last time you saw her?

RAP: Now that you come to mention it... no, I don't think she was.

Police: And this was a week or so ago?

RAP: Maybe two weeks ago.

Police: Was that at her house?

RAP: I think you mean OUR house.

Police: Oh? But you aren't living there, are you?

RAP: You know I'm not. We're separated... have been for months.

Police: What was the reason for the separation?

RAP: None of your fucking business.

Police: Defensive, aren't we?

RAP: Well, I don't appreciate your line of questioning.

Police: So, it seems. Why is that? Don't you want to help us to find her?

RAP: Of course, but what has the reason for our separation got to do with anything?

Police: Maybe nothing but please bear with the questions.

RAP: Fine.

Police: Are you both on good terms?

RAP: We haven't been fighting like cat and dog, if that's what you're getting at?

Police: I'm not getting at anything. I'm simply trying to establish the facts.

RAP: We get on okay, I guess.

Police: You say no fights or arguments?

RAP: Are you married? If you are, then you'll know how ridiculous that question is. No fights or arguments? Are you fucking kidding me?

Police: Please be mindful of your language, Mister Parker. There's no need for profanity.

RAP: I'm sure you've heard worse.

Police: That's as may be, but it will make things run a lot smoother if you keep your language in check.

RAP: Whatever.

Police: So, there were arguments? What were they about?

RAP: Everything and nothing.

Police: Money?

RAP: Sometimes.

Police: Other women?

RAP: Of course.

Police: What else?

RAP: Her drinking, I suppose. As I said... she was always pissed.

Police: Was she an alcoholic?

RAP: With bells on.

Police: But she wasn't drunk the last time you saw her?

RAP: I think she'd been drinking, but she seemed pretty sober. Thing is... she had her paranoid head on.

Police: I'm surprised – considering your concern over her drinking – that you took her a gift of a bottle of wine that day.

RAP: How..?

Police: Fiona told us.

RAP: You've spoken to Fiona? She didn't mention it to me.

Police: We asked her not to. Now... you mentioned that Vanessa seemed paranoid?

RAP: What? Yes... imagining all sorts.

Police: Like what?

RAP: Things going bump. She thought someone was in the house.

Police: Was there?

RAP: No. Look... you have to understand something about Vanessa... she was brilliant, had a vivid imagination. Well, she had to have an imagination... to write all those best-selling books... but it could run away with her... her imagination.

Police: Would you say that she was depressed?

RAP: She'd been depressed ever since Simon. There was nothing new about that.

Police: You weren't worried about it... her depression?

RAP: Not any more than usual.

Police: So, that day... the day you took her the bottle of wine... did you argue?

RAP: Not that I recall.
Police: It was an amicable meeting?
RAP: You could say that, yes.
Police: Why did you go to see her?
RAP: I made a point of visiting her every few days.
Police: Your girlfriend couldn't have been happy with that?
RAP: I'm sure you made a point of questioning her about it, and I'm sure that you weren't left wondering just how mad she was at me.
Police: You got money from Vanessa every time you visited her, didn't you?
RAP: It was my money just as much as hers.
Police: Oh? You earned it, did you?
RAP: Fuck you.
Police: Moving on... I understand that Vanessa suffers from agoraphobia?
RAP: (inaudible)
Police: Can you repeat that, Mister Parker?
RAP: I simply said that it was something she alluded to.
Police: You think that she was making it up... the agoraphobia?
RAP: The thought had crossed my mind.
Police: It did?
RAP: I'm sure she could've gone out if she'd wanted to.
Police: Did she ever want to... go out? For example... did she go out shopping, visit friends, take a drive anywhere?
RAP: Not that I'm aware of. Not for a long time. If she did, then she never mentioned it to me. Anyway, she doesn't have any friends, and she isn't the sort of person who enjoys shopping. She has everything delivered.
Police: No friends?
RAP: Nope.... No one I would say were friends... no.
Police: Acquaintances, then?
RAP: Just her agent and I suppose, her publisher.

Police: No one else?
RAP: Vanessa didn't like people... couldn't tolerate them.
Police: What about friends on Facebook?
RAP: Facebook..? Vanessa..? Are you having a laugh?
Police: She had an account... a profile.
RAP: Yeah... to spy on me.
Police: She spied on you?
RAP: Too right, she did. She thought I didn't know. Pretty sad, really.
Police: She must've been pretty cut up when you left her.
RAP: I guess.
Police: But you still visit... still look out for her?
RAP: As much as I can.
Police: Did she ever go out anywhere with you?
RAP: Not for years..
Police: What about with anyone else?
RAP: Not to my knowledge.
Police: Her agent? Her publisher?
RAP: Maybe. I'm not sure.
Police: Is there any chance that she's simply taken herself off somewhere?
RAP: She must have.
Police: But her car is still in the garage.
RAP: Is it? I wouldn't know.
Police: How else could she have left? The house is pretty isolated.
RAP: Your guess is as good as mine.
Police: What would be your best guess?
RAP: Do you really want to know my best guess? Well, I'll tell you. I think it's all some sort of a publicity stunt. She has a new book in the pipeline, and this sort of thing... doing a disappearing act... well it'll bring a whole shitload of publicity, won't it?
Police: That's an interesting theory.

RAP: You asked for my best guess, and that's what I've given you.

Police: Do you believe that your wife needs that sort of publicity?

RAP: (inaudible)

Police: Her financial records suggest that she's in trouble.

RAP: That's news to me.

Police: It's not something you're aware of?

RAP: No.

Police: She gives you a great deal of money, doesn't she?

RAP: Only what I'm entitled to… Not that it's any of our business.

Police: In fact, she is your only means of income, isn't she?

RAP: What are you driving at? I'm owed that money. I didn't take a penny from her that wasn't my due.

Police: Do you realise that you were bleeding her dry?

RAP: Bullshit.

Police: No, not bullshit, Mister Parker. Bank statements don't lie.

RAP: You've been poking into her bank statements? Is that allowed?

Police: One interesting thing we discovered is that, since her disappearance, she hasn't withdrawn or spent so much as a single penny.

RAP: (inaudible)

Police: Very worrying, don't you think?

RAP: If you say so.

Police: Let's recap, shall we? Your estranged wife has been missing for more than a week. No one has a clue where she is and it's concerning that she suffers from agoraphobia, making it highly unlikely she left home of her own volition. She may be depressed, has an addiction problem, is on the verge of bankruptcy, and she hasn't used her bank card or credit card since leaving home. She's made no phone calls, sent no texts or emails, and has – quite literally – vanished off the face of the earth. That makes us concerned for her wellbeing. Tell me... has your wife ever expressed suicidal thoughts?

RAP: Now, hang on a minute... you think..? (inaudible)

Police: Then, we mustn't forget the threat of divorce. That might have tipped her over the edge, don't you think?

RAP: I've told you... she isn't suicidal. I'll grant you... she wasn't happy about the divorce, but I don't think she ever believed I would go through with it. For God's sake... the papers haven't even been fucking signed yet.

Police: Are you saying that you were considering not going ahead?

RAP: No, I'm not saying that. I'd had enough. It was time to draw a line under the whole marriage.

Police: Did you discuss the divorce the last time you saw her?

RAP: It was mentioned... yes. Look, can I go for a piss?

Police: You want a break?

RAP: Just long enough to go to the toilet, then we can finish this whole crapshoot up.

Police: Okay. Interview suspended at 11.16 a.m.

Eleven

In the study, her laptop sat open on the desk. She hovered in the doorway and, for long moments, simply stood staring at it. She realised that she now viewed that laptop as her enemy – something to be conquered – and was wary of approaching it.

She moved across the threshold and closed the door behind her.

The desk was Georgian, an antique, something she'd bought with her very first royalty cheque – a reward for her hard work and for the successful launch of her debut book. It was thick with dust and – like everything else in the house – terribly neglected. She'd had to let the cleaner go. The ten pounds an hour had suddenly become unaffordable. It had been years since she'd had to count her pennies, and if her royalty cheques *did* dwindle, and then stop completely, she'd be in a right mess.

The thought of bankruptcy terrified her. She couldn't let herself be poor.

She just couldn't.

Her blood froze at the very thought of it and fear stabbed a hole in her throat. Clutching at her neck, she swallowed back hard.

She'd been poor. She had bitter experience of worrying about how she would keep a roof over her head, or pay the bills, and she would do anything to prevent that from happening again. There was nothing noble about being penniless, nothing dignified about it. Maybe, in some epic tragedy it would be acceptable, but not in the stage play that was her sorry excuse for a life.

It would take courage to tackle the manuscript – a sustained courage. It would also take determination. When was the last time she'd been determined about anything other than getting pissed? Ruefully, she shook her head.

It had been years.

Getting her act together meant sitting at the antique desk, firing up the laptop, and being brutal with an edit she knew would probably wipe out most of her work. She wasn't stupid, and she hadn't needed Anita to tell her just how shite the book was. There wasn't a single sentence to be proud of because – in the writing of every sentence – she had been neither careful nor conscientious. Every line was unconvincing and ambiguous and, instead of the beautiful and satisfying prose her readers were used to and expected from her, every page was bland and insubstantial. Between the lines, the lack of proper research was glaringly obvious, so it definitely required more than a developmental edit to bring it up to scratch. It would require a total re-write. Even if she started right that minute – worked all day, through the night, and then rinsed and repeated – she would be lucky to make a dent in even a quarter of the total word count. To produce something worthy – a novel of exquisite perfection – usually took her more than twelve months, and all she had was two days.

It was never going to happen, so, surely, it would be better if she didn't even try?

I can't do it... I can't do it... she mentally whined, only for some other inner voice to add its two pennies worth by saying – *get a fucking grip... of course, you can bloody well do it.*

She argued back that, yes, she could do it, but only if she had a drink first.

But the drink was what had got her into such a mess in the first place. It was the reason the first book flopped and then the second. When the first book nose-dived in the rankings it should've been a wake-up call. Then, when it failed to earn the cost of her advance, she should've realised that she was at the beginning of a downward spiral but, instead of getting her act together, she'd drank even more, and now it seemed like Groundhog Day all over again.

Everyone thought it was the easiest thing in the world to stop drinking. They believed that all it took was willpower and desire. Vanessa thought that most of the time she had the willpower but realised that she'd never felt the desire. Who, in their right mind, would desire to give up the only thing that made living worthwhile, the only thing that numbed the grief and prevented her from slitting her throat? They said that alcohol was a depressant but, for her, it was the only thing that held back that depression... kept it at bay. Or so she thought.

She would have to force herself to stay dry, at least until she'd given the edit of the book her best shot, but she would have to mean it. There could be no more back and forth, toing-and-froing with the decision to hit the vodka on the head. The desire to finish the book, and finish it well, had to override the desire to drink.

Dragging in a breath, she sat down and booted up the laptop. *Here goes*, she thought, clicking on the Word file.

She blinked at the screen. The words on that first page seemed to wriggle like demented worms in front of her eyes. She focussed, and they all drew themselves into line.

She began to read.

Drivel. Unadulterated shite.

It was even worse than she'd remembered. To add insult to injury, it wasn't just the writing that was bad. As she scrolled through the first chapter, she realised that the basic premise of the story was utter crap.

She began to highlight and delete whole paragraphs. As she watched the word count drastically drop, she knew that, if she carried on the way she'd begun, she'd be left with nothing but a blank screen.

Would that be so bad?

Her finger hovered over the delete key. Perhaps it wouldn't be such a ridiculous idea to get rid of the lot of it... start again from scratch. She hesitated a full minute before highlighting the whole document and finally doing what she knew she must.

One click, and it was gone.

Jesus, Mary, and Joseph. What had she done?

She expected to feel a sense of panic but, instead, felt an immense relief. Before she changed her mind, she went into the back- up files and quickly deleted every version.

There. It was done. She gave a short laugh and hugged herself. She had courage. She had determination. Why had she ever doubted herself?

Leaning in, she typed Chapter One as the first header.

It was as far as she got. The sound of the front door opening and closing, and then the sound of familiar footsteps travelling along the hallway, had her on her feet and moving quickly to the middle of the room.

She knew those footsteps.

It was Richard.

She flushed and swiped a strand of damp hair from her face, tucking it behind her ear. There was no doubt in her mind that she looked a mess, but at least she'd showered. She silently thanked God that he hadn't arrived an hour earlier.

'Vanessa? Where the fuck are you?'

She jerked at the sound of his voice. He always sounded so angry. Even when they were in bed, and he was screwing her, his every grunt sounded furious.

'In here,' she called out. 'I'm in the study.'

The door opened, and there he was.

As she stared at him, she tried to keep an even expression on her face, but she knew her cheeks were flushed and that her chest was visibly heaving.

Casually but as always, beautifully dressed, his dark blond hair artfully tousled, and looking as if he'd just stepped off the front page of some posh magazine, he cut quite the figure. The very sight of him was enough to unnerve her.

His familiar scent made her nostrils flare. She gave a languid blink and tried to control the flash of desire that rippled across her belly.

He hiked a perfect eyebrow. She thought that he could sense her arousal and it embarrassed her. She didn't want him knowing just how much he turned her on.

'Are you okay? You look a little damp,' he quipped, smiling suggestively.

'I've just had a shower,' she said, by means of an explanation, but nevertheless wriggling in her skin at the innuendo.

'For you,' he said, holding out a rather limp bunch of flowers and the bottle of wine.

She gaped at them. She couldn't recall him ever bringing her flowers and the last time he'd brought wine was the night they'd brought Simon home from the hospital after the birth.

'You shouldn't have,' she said.

He shrugged, passing the gifts off as nothing of consequence.

She eyed the wine, her stomach folding greasily, and muttered her thanks. He handed them over and she turned and placed them on the desk.

Now what? she thought.

They stood facing one another awkwardly. Richard nodded at the wine bottle on the desk, and said, 'Why don't you find some glasses and I'll pop the cork on that little beauty?'

'Are we celebrating something?'

'No... not unless you want to celebrate your latest novel a little early?'

'And jinx it?' She shook her head. 'You know better than that, Richard.'

'Okay... no celebration, but we can still have a drink together, can't we?'

'Not for me, thanks. I'm not in the mood.'

The smile slid from his face. 'Something to eat, then?'

'I'm not hungry.'

'You look half-starved.'

She shifted self-consciously, then turned to ensure that the screensaver had kicked in on the laptop. She didn't want him noticing the huge blank space beneath the chapter one heading.

She said, 'I've been too busy writing to think much about food.'

'How are you getting on with it?'

'It's been a bit of a struggle, but I'm on the final draft.'

'What do you think my share will be?'

'Your share?' *Had she just heard right?* 'What is that supposed to mean?'

'Well, I don't expect half...'

'Half?' Her voice came out as a squeak. 'Are you mad?'

'Not mad, Vanessa... realistic. We really need to sit down and discuss my settlement. It's only fair.'

'Fair? What do you know about fair?' She was shouting now.

Richard bristled. 'If you're going to get all psycho on me, then I'll...'

'What? You'll what?'

'Leave and let the lawyers sort it out,' he snapped back at her. 'Is that what you want, Vanessa? Do you want me to leave?'

She didn't. Although his visits always ended up being about money, at least he visited. The bottom line was that she didn't care what his reasons were. Seeing him was better than not seeing him.

He took that moment to give her one of his lop-sided smiles, obviously thinking better of alienating her.

He said, 'I'm sorry that I haven't been around much.'

She clenched her hands into fists at her side. 'I guess that's Fiona's doing?' She wasn't quite ready to relax into congeniality. 'I'm surprised she gave you permission to come at all.'

Rolling his eyes, he said, 'Don't let's talk about Fiona. Don't spoil things, Vanessa.'

'But she's the elephant in the room, Richard. I can't simply forget what she did to us.'

He sighed. 'Blame me... not Fiona. I didn't leave you because of her. You know that. You know exactly why I left.'

The problem was, she didn't know – not really. Yes, they'd been unhappy, and Richard's womanising had taken a terrible toll on their relationship, however, she'd been prepared to struggle on because she'd loved him. She'd thought that – despite everything – he had also loved her, so him leaving hadn't made any sense.

He saw her confusion and looked at her with consternation. 'You can't seriously not know, Vanessa? You can't tell me that you really blame Fiona?'

She brought up her chin. 'We were muddling along just fine before she arrived on the scene. It's no coincidence that, when she spread her legs for you, you walked out on me.'

'Muddling along? Is that how you remember it?'

'Well, how do you remember things being between us?'

He shook his head, exasperated. 'I remember it being a living hell.'

That stung.

He reached for her. 'But things are okay between us now, aren't they? We get on much better now we're not living under the same roof.'

For him, maybe, she thought, a tad bitterly.

Richard tightened his grip on her arm and they both stood, awkwardly eyeing one another, neither seeming to know what to say next.

'Don't let's fight,' he finally huffed out. 'Let's try and be friends.' Another lop-sided smile. 'You'll always be part of my life, Vanessa, and you can take that to the bank.'

'Along with another cheque, I suppose?'

He ignored the barb and reached out with his other hand to stroke a finger lightly over her lips. He stared at her long and hard. 'You know that I want you. That will never change.'

She dropped her eyes. She didn't want to see the lie on his face. To see it, to acknowledge that he wanted her for one reason, and one reason only, was heart-breaking.

He closed the gap between them and dragged her into his arms. 'It is what it is, Vanessa. There's no point getting upset about it.'

She pressed her face against his chest and huffed in a breath. 'I'll always love you,' she said.

With his chin resting on the top of her head, he rolled his eyes at the ceiling. 'I know, but you really should stop... loving me, I mean.'

'Just like you having stopped loving me?' She held her breath. She needed to hear him deny it... just once. His arms went slack, and she was suddenly scared that she'd gone too far. 'I'm sorry. Forget I said that.'

'It's not that I don't love you,' he returned on a long sigh. 'It's just that it's now a different sort of love.'

Oh, God... not that again. He actually believed that she was willing to accept a watered-down version of his love. Didn't he realise that she didn't want the sort of love that was reserved for a pet dog?

She tilted her head back, looked up and into his face, and, swallowing back on every vestige of humiliation, said, 'Kiss me.'

He obliged, but it was no more than a brief and unsatisfying gesture. Vanessa felt her face flash with heat. He couldn't even make the effort to pretend. She closed her eyes tight and dragged in a breath, wondering if she could really go through with what was about to happen. Could she really offer herself up to him again, knowing the cost of their imminent coupling – a cost that was not only financial but personal?

She stiffened in his arms. He tightened his grip and waited until he felt her relax before saying, 'We don't have to. If you'd rather not...?'

His face filled her vision. She shook her head. 'No... no. I want to.'

'If you're sure...?'

'I'm sure.'

Pulling back, she took his hand, led him from the study, and then preceded him up the stairs and into the bedroom.

The room was a tip and she hoped that he wouldn't feel the need to comment on it. It wouldn't take much to kill what little anticipation there was between them.

'Why is it so cold in here?' he asked, pulling off his clothes and climbing into bed. 'Did you forget to pay the gas bill?'

It *was* cold. The house had warmed up before his arrival, but the whole house now seemed as frigid as it had been earlier that morning.

'I think the boiler is on the blink,' she returned, snuggling down beside him. 'Can you take a look at it before you leave?'

'Sure.' He felt her hand on him. He jerked, as if electrocuted. 'Jesus, Vanessa, you could've at least warmed your fucking hand. You've shrivelled my balls.'

'Sorry.' She removed her hand and flopped onto her back. It was already not going well.

'No, *I'm* sorry,' he said, grabbing her hand and placing it under his armpit. 'Here, I'll warm it for you.'

They lay quietly, each thinking about what was about to happen. For two people who'd had sex hundreds of times, perhaps even thousands, over a ten-year period, the uncomfortable silence was very telling. It was obvious that neither of them really wanted to be there – Vanessa because she knew that she would end up feeling dirty and used, and Richard because... well, because the last thing he wanted to do was fuck a bag of bones. The only way he would get through it was to close his eyes and conjure up an image of Fiona.

He prayed that he wouldn't call out her name at the moment of climax.

The sex was over very quickly. For Richard it had been an endurance and for Vanessa a reminder that she wasn't cherished. Both experienced emotions that they swallowed back on and both – in their own way – wished that it could've been different.

Half an hour later, after a stilted conversation about the temperature in the house, and after making herself a thousand pounds poorer, Vanessa stood at the front door and watched him leave.

He hadn't found anything wrong with the boiler or the radiators and neither of them could come up with an explanation for the cold. He didn't dawdle to find out, anxious to bank the cheque and get back to Fiona.

He left her without kissing her goodbye. A big part of her wished that she would never see him again, but within minutes of his car pulling off the drive, she was already pining for him.

The emptiness that Richard left in his wake was something Vanessa had never found a way to fill but, for the first time, she considered the possibility of simply accepting his absence. However, every atom of her being rebelled against such a thing. The thought of being completely alone for the rest of her life terrified her. For years she had believed that a bad marriage was better than no marriage at all, and she was no nearer to considering the alternative. Anyway, she loved him and, deep in the dark recesses of her soul, she believed that she didn't deserve any better than him.

On a sigh, she turned from the door, closed, and locked it before the outside encroached and sent her into a panic. But panic was set to move in anyway because she immediately began to worry about the very real possibility of the cheque she'd given him bouncing. She'd written more than one rubber cheque in her life – more so since Richard had walked out on her – but she'd always managed to cover any shortfall in her current account before those cheques had been presented to the bank. She didn't believe she would manage to do it again, not in time for Richard's latest cheque to clear, and she now ran the risk of him discovering the true state of her finances. She realised that, before long, she wouldn't have any choice in whether she was left alone. In the end – like everything else in her life – she had no control. Richard would find out that she was skint, and she would never see him again.

She couldn't afford to dwell on that eventuality. If she did, she knew that she would head straight back to the fridge and to the vodka. A slug of vodka had always been her default position after Richard left. That one slug always led to another, and then another. Drinking had been her failsafe. It stopped her thinking, and it somehow cleansed her – albeit temporarily.

But, not today, she thought. She would suffer the loss and the humiliation without the crutch of alcohol.

She walked back along the hallway towards the study. For the time being, she would avoid the kitchen.

Light glinted and her eye caught sight of an object sitting on the small lamp table next to the stairs. It wasn't a large object, and it was unfamiliar to her. It snagged her attention. Was it something left behind by Richard?

She picked it up. It felt almost warm in the palm of her hand and, as she peered down at it, her eyes were intrigued and confused.

What was it?

She turned it over, studied it from all angles, lifted it to her nose and sniffed. It had no odour and its shape – rectangular, with a round loop at one end and narrowing to a blunt point at the other – wasn't reminiscent of anything she'd ever seen before. She noticed some writing on its flat metal edge, but the lettering was so small and so faint that she couldn't make it out.

Confused, she put it back on the table and mentally shrugged. It wasn't important enough to keep her from her work and, dismissing it from her mind, she walked back into the study. Then, after half an hour of sitting and staring at the almost empty screen, she finally gave up.

Why had she been daft enough to delete the whole fucking thing? She shook her head at her stupidity. She'd given herself a mountain to climb and found that she couldn't do it. She couldn't even take the first step. It wasn't that her mind was a complete blank. She almost wished that it was. There were too many things ricocheting inside her head and competing for her attention to allow her to focus on the one thing that was paramount – that first elusive sentence.

One fucking sentence. How difficult could it be to string a dozen words together?

Her determination and desire were fading fast. Her head reeled from the effort of trying to think her way through a jumble of random rubbish. She was on the verge of throwing in the towel... again.

What about something to take the edge off... something to mellow her out a little? One drink wouldn't hurt... surely?

She stood up, pushed the chair back with her legs, and hugged herself.

She promised herself that she would stop at one.

It was a promise she wouldn't keep.

Twelve

Vanessa woke up frowning. Something had penetrated the layers of drunken slumber, but she wasn't sure what.

Her mouth tasted of dirt. Her tongue was like sandpaper, and her head throbbed behind her eyes. Rough didn't begin to explain how bad she felt and – even if she'd wanted to – she couldn't shift herself from the sofa.

She lay there with eyes scrunched closed against the late afternoon light splashing in through the window. The January sun was low in the sky and almost blindingly bright. She groaned and turned her head slightly, trying to get out from under its glare. The slight movement of her head made the bile rise to the back of her throat and she was forced to swallow it back. The thought of violent vomiting scared her. She didn't believe her aching head would cope with it. If a gentle movement made her sick to her stomach, she shuddered to think what throwing herself forward to spew on the floor would do to her – probably break her in two.

It was fairly quiet in the room. Except for her agonised groans, the only sound was the soft ticking of the carriage clock on the mantlepiece. Usually, the sound of a gently ticking clock was soothing, but not then. It jarred and stabbed and seemed louder than it actually was and, if she could summon the energy to get up and go to it, she knew that she would smash it to pieces.

'Oh, God,' she moaned. She'd promised herself that she'd only have the one lousy drink. One thing was for sure – there was no way she could trust herself around a bottle of vodka ever again.

She felt like a ping-pong ball being swatted from one end of the table to the other by a bat that was crafted from the circumstances of her shitty life. The trouble was, she was never the person wielding the bat and, because of that, she had no control. Back and forth, from one end to the other, from drinking to not drinking, then back to drinking again. Her life wasn't just a rollercoaster, it was a cross between a seesaw and a fucking merry-go-round.

The familiar stab of shame grounded her. There was now no escaping the fact that she needed help. It was just a pity that she could no longer afford a stint in rehab.

It was a Catch 22. To afford rehab, she needed the book, and to finish the book, she needed the rehab. If it hadn't been so tragic, she would laugh until she pissed herself.

Guzzling her body weight in vodka was no longer the answer. It wasn't just that it caused untold pain and misery... not forgetting the nausea... but also because she had no idea what it was doing to her brain. She hated to admit it, but she was a card-carrying alcoholic, just like her mother, however – unlike her mother – she would cut her own throat before she allowed it to send her totally mental.

Frustrated and dismayed, she grasped at the only thing she believed could save her. She had to do justice to that fucking book – prove everyone wrong and, more than that, take back the future she was owed.

The ticking of the clock reminded her how quickly time was passing. She wondered what had woken her. It hadn't been the clock and she didn't think it was the light filtering into the room from outside. Maybe it had been the smell? There was a damp whiff in the room that was difficult to define. She considered that her sleeping brain must have recognised it as being an alien aroma – not a smell associated with the inside of her house, but more akin to that which seeped from the walls of an underground cavern. She believed it was that smell that had jerked her to consciousness.

She scrunched up her face. *What was it?* She lifted her arms one at a time and sniffed beneath her armpits. The movement caused needles of pain to stab at her temples and all for nothing. All she could scent was a tinge of sweat breaking through the bodywash she'd used in the shower earlier. She would make a point of checking the toilets later just in case the plumbing problems experienced in the kitchen extended to the waste pipes.

Suddenly, she realised that the clock had stopped ticking and the room was now weighed down in silence. Then, from nowhere, she heard what sounded like a sigh. It only lasted a couple of seconds, not long enough for her to pinpoint where it had come from, but it had been loud enough to startle her. Cocking her head, she listened intently, waiting for the sound of the sigh to return. Long moments passed and she was just about ready to accept that she'd imagined it, when a louder, more guttural breath ripped through the air, followed by a stench so foul that it seemed as if it had come from the mouth of something either diseased or dead. It totally eclipsed the earlier odour in the room, and she gagged against its encroachment.

Head thumping, her heart feeling as if it wanted to break through her chest, she scrabbled along the sofa and pulled herself to her feet before stumbling her way to the door. Once through and in the hallway, she dropped to her knees and dry-heaved until, exhausted, she collapsed to her side in a faint.

Minutes later, regaining consciousness but still in that hazy moment before she was fully alert, a memory – or maybe the tail-end of a brief dream – flashed behind her eyes. She saw a drunken mother, deep in the throes of delirium tremens... the dreaded DT's... squirming on the floor and frantically brushing away at imaginary insects. She saw an image of herself as an impressionable ten-year-old, standing and looking down at her mother, watching as she screamed at her to knock the spiders and cockroaches away. She saw herself kneeling on the floor beside her and swiping at her body for all she'd been worth – swiping at those invisible insects and praying that she was doing enough to make her mum safe.

Her head lolled. Her tongue felt thick in her mouth. Slowly, she became aware of the stench-free air she was now huffing into her lungs and – just as there had been no spiders and no cockroaches on her mother's body – she began to believe that there had never been any foul smell or any frightening sounds. She had her mother's vivid imagination as well as her addiction and they were a toxic combination.

Pulling herself into a sitting position, she leaned against the wall. The door to the sitting room stood open to her left and it took a simple turn of her shoulders and a twist of her body before she was able to peer back inside. She scanned what she could see of the room and her eyes rested on the huge bookshelf taking up almost all of the far wall. Each shelf boasted a variety of books across many genres, and she'd always been proud of the fact that she'd read most of them from cover to cover. The books weren't for show – not that anyone ever got to see them because visitors were few and far between, and none were ever allowed into that particular sitting room. No, they definitely weren't for show. She loved them, had always cherished them, but she was now aware of their neglect. Dust coated their jackets. Dozens were piled one on top of the other haphazardly instead of standing in line, their spines pointing forward and upright.

Was that why her last two books had tanked? Her every spare hour had been taken up with drinking and not reading. She couldn't recall the last time she'd taken a book down from one of those shelves. It was another shame to add to the many that already plagued her.

She forced herself to stand. A wave of nausea roiled up from her belly, but she mastered it and managed to take a couple of faltering steps forward. She was going to make that moment the first one of the rest of her life. No more vodka, no more Richard, and no more prevarication. She would read and she would write, and she wouldn't end up like her mother. She knew that she'd made that promise to herself on more than one occasion previously. Only a few short hours before, she'd made the decision not to drink, and along came Richard and, when he'd left, she'd been left feeling so empty that her promise had died a sudden and painful death. How much simpler her life would be if there was no more going to bed with him, no more meeting behind Fiona's back, and no more being used as his own personal bank. As long as there was Richard, there would be vodka, and both would be her ultimate ruin.

But there would always be Richard. She couldn't imagine life without him. It was only a half-life... not even that... but she guessed that it was better than no life at all.

Straightening her spine and throwing her shoulders back, she said, 'Right. Let's do this.'

Back in the study, she sat down at the desk, adjusted her chair, and leaned in. One touch on the keyboard, and the file opened to the first page on the manuscript – the page with only two words, *Chapter One*.

Although daunted, she decided not to allow the enormity of the task to defeat her. Even if she only managed to write the first couple of chapters by Anita's deadline, she was determined to do those chapters justice. She would sink or swim off the back of the improvements she had the time to make.

Now, for the first sentence. Getting that first sentence right was critical. It would be the first hook. Praying silently that her earlier writer's block wouldn't rear its ugly head again, she leaned back and huffed out a breath. Like before, nothing was seeding in her brain – no words came to mind.

She sat there, straining to come up with something... anything. Nothing.

Dismayed, she felt tears prick behind her eyes. It really was over for her.

Her stomach rumbled. She was suddenly hungry. Apart from that slice of dry toast earlier, she hadn't eaten in nearly two days. Food might help. She had to feed her belly to feed her brain, and the last of the alcohol needed something to push it through her system. But she was loath to get up to go in search of sustenance. She knew that, if she left the study, it would take a miracle to get her back in front of the screen.

She leaned forward once more, her fingers hovering above the keyboard. 'Just one sentence,' she whispered. '*Please, please, please...*'

Her hands shook. She clenched her fists. Just one fucking sentence and the rest would flow.

Still nothing. Frustrated, she jumped to her feet and began to pace the floor. Her head still thumped, and her mouth still tasted as if someone had pissed in it, but she refused to leave the room for the kitchen. She had the sense to realise that it would be the worst thing she could do.

Time passed. The walls began to close in on her, then she heard a voice. It was nothing more than a mere whisper and it spoke directly into her ear. It said – *Lady Amanda Golding died for the first time on the seventeenth of September eighteen hundred and sixty-four. She was eighteen years old.*

Startled, she jerked her head all the way around on her neck. Had that really been a voice, or merely her own thoughts? Either way, she didn't care. She not only had her first sentence... she had her first two.

All thoughts of hunger evaporating, she turned back and threw herself down into her chair and immediately typed in the two sentences. Thereafter, and for the next six hours, she wrote non-stop, her mind racing ahead from one word and one sentence to whole paragraphs, pages, and chapters.

At just after ten o'clock, when the only light in the room was that emanating from the screen of the laptop, she stopped, utterly exhausted.

Every bone in her body – from those in her fingers to every single vertebra – screamed out in agony. She couldn't straighten her spine and her muscles refused to relax sufficiently to unclench her hands or move her legs. Even breathing was painful. All she could do was sit there and stare at the word count on the bottom left of the screen.

Sixteen thousand words. It took a great deal of believing.

Sixteen thousand perfectly formatted words. She lifted her eyes to read what was on that last page. Not a single error was highlighted. She laughed out loud. Her chest tightened in protest, and then her stomach gave out a huge growl. Her few reserves had been well and truly depleted, and she was famished, but she made no attempt to get up from the chair. The food could wait whilst she took another few moments to marvel at her achievement.

By rights, it should have been impossible. There was no way she could have sustained that amount of words per minute. In six hours, it meant that she had typed at a rate of forty-five words a minute. No, not typed – created forty-five perfect words every single minute. There was a big difference between simply typing and writing. On a good day, she could manage two or three thousand words, but they would've been words that required editing. Every author, no matter how disciplined, made errors – even if it was just the odd typo, or a mistake with the formatting.

Scrolling back through the last chapter she'd written, she immediately saw that no edit was required. The chapter was written without fault and, it was good. Actually, it was more than good. It was sensational.

Her jaw dropped and her mouth hung open. She couldn't quite believe it. In fact, she didn't believe it. Her eyes must be deceiving her.

She read some more. Although she recognised her style in and across the lines on the pages, there was something sharper, less meandering with the writing and, the more she read, the greater the feeling of disbelief.

As well as the obvious differences in the writing, she had introduced a completely different antagonist. She wondered where he had come from. Not from her imagination, that was for sure. She hadn't recognised him in any way, and she always knew her characters inside and out before introducing them into the story. Not so with Lord John Trollope. Even after sixteen thousand words, he remained a complete stranger.

Was she going to worry about it? Was she fuck. She wasn't going to question a damned thing about any of it – knowing that, if she kept up the pace, by the Friday deadline she could easily have the book finished, especially if she wrote for twelve or even sixteen hours a day.

She glanced at the clock on the computer. If she hurried up with feeding herself, she could manage at least another four hours. A nice round twenty thousand words would be a perfect end to a day that hadn't started so well.

She visualised the expression on Anita's face when she saw the result of her efforts. She would shit a brick.

Vanessa closed her mouth with a snap. A self-satisfied grin spread over her whole face.

Suck on that, you fat bitch.

So pleased with herself, and so completely caught up in her own self-congratulation, she hardly felt the gentle finger-like movement that fluttered through her hair. She wasn't aware of some invisible force brushing her hair to one side, but something made her automatically lift her hand to swipe at the top of her head, as if swatting at a fly.

Thirteen

Anita did, in fact, miss dinner, but arrived in time to have a quick shower and get changed before the evening speeches commenced. Unfortunately, afterwards, over drinks, there were more than a few of her fellow literary agents who felt inclined to waylay her with questions about the failing author she continued to have on her books. None of them could understand why she still gave Vanessa the time of day, never mind most of her time.

Anita had expected the unwelcome attention. The opportunity to put the boot in was an anticipated downside of getting together with some of the biggest bitches in the industry. Jealousy of Anita's good fortune in having the likes of Vanessa Parker as her client had morphed into gleeful celebration of the recent downfall of the once celebrated author. Anita's peers liked nothing better than to kick a competitor when they were down, and Anita didn't exactly blame them. Over the years, she'd done much the same to them because, after all, it was a dog-eat-dog business.

'I hear she's drunk all the time,' one said, leaning in and grinning. 'Too drunk to string a coherent sentence together.'

Anita thinned her lips but made no response. She made no mention of the fact that the person bad-mouthing Vanessa for being a drunk was, herself, three sheets to the wind, hammered on the free champagne. That was another thing about her contemporaries – they were all fucking hypocrites.

'I hear she's struggling with her latest book,' another said, hiking a brow. 'I hope you've told her to get her finger out her arse and finish it?'

'It'll get finished,' Anita was forced to respond. 'Don't you lose any sleep over that, Marjory. I'm certainly not.'

As soon as the words were out of her mouth, she wished that she'd kept her trap shut. They would all remember what she'd said. When Vanessa didn't deliver on Friday, every last one of them would remind her of her stupid, blind faith. Oh, they would couch their barbed comments in feigned sympathy and lack-lustre understanding, but – beneath it all – they'd be gloating.

'I'm surprised at you, Anita,' Martine Cooper, one of her fiercest rivals, piped in. 'Why didn't you dump her after her last book bombed?'

'That book you mentioned,' Anita returned, her face a stiff mask, 'probably still sold more copies than that silly excuse for a romance your golden girl published last year. What was it called?' She made a pretence of mulling over the title. 'Cowboy, something or other.'

'*A Cowboy for Me*,' Martine replied, glowering through thickly mascaraed eyelashes. 'And I think you'll find that Augustine's novel topped the best-seller's chart in *The Times*, whilst Vanessa's barely ranked at all.'

'How much did that cost you?' Anita snapped.

'I beg your pardon?' Martine drew herself up to her full height. 'Are you suggesting…?'

'Everyone knows you play the system, Martine. One of these days, you're going to be sussed and then let's see how many best-sellers you manage to get on that *Times*' list.'

'You cheeky mare.' Martine was livid. 'I'll have you know…'

'Save it for someone who cares, Martine. Everyone knows what you are.'

Defending Vanessa and humiliating Martine had just made her a bitter enemy. Although Martine had never been a friend, she'd not been a true foe. A rival, yes, but never an enemy. Now, when Vanessa's book bombed – as Anita had no doubt it would –her claws would be sharpened and, next time they met, she would go right for her jugular.

It wasn't only Vanessa's reputation that rode on that final draft being pristine. If she couldn't pull it together, and if it ended up never being published, then Anita could kiss goodbye any chance of keeping her crown as the best literary agent in the country.

Perhaps she'd been too hasty in giving Friday as the deadline? Perhaps she should have taken Vanessa up on her request for a developmental edit? Looking back on their meeting that morning, she realised that it must have taken quite a lot for Vanessa to make that suggestion for a developmental edit. She wished that she hadn't swatted it away, had, instead, agreed and set it up.

But it wasn't too late. She could still provide that lifeline. If she could just get one more best-seller out of her, she could then quietly dump her and none of those bitches still standing and looking at her would dare say another nasty thing. They would see that she had no qualms about getting rid of an author who was still up there with the best of them. They would wonder why, and she would leave them guessing. She would never admit to them that she knew Vanessa didn't have another book left in her. With any luck, the hapless Martine would snap her up, and learn the hard way that all that glittered, certainly wasn't gold. It would cost the stupid bitch thousands to turn around anything Vanessa produced in the future and probably tens of thousands to have her placed high in the rankings.

For the remainder of the evening, everyone avoided her, and that suited her just fine.

Before turning in for the night, she decided to call Vanessa with the news of her decision to pay for developmental support. She knew that she would have to play it down, tell her that it wasn't because she didn't have confidence in her ability, that she had every confidence in her, persuade her that a little help would speed things along. It wouldn't be too much of a problem because Vanessa had already intimated that she wanted help.

Gathering herself, she made the call and was a little relieved when it went to voicemail. If she was being honest with herself, she really wasn't that keen on talking to her, or discussing the edit. She imagined Vanessa answering the phone, three sheets to the wind and in a belligerent mood and ending up not getting anywhere with her. There was never any certainty when it came to how Vanessa would react. Over ten years of working with her had given her an insight into the author's many moods and, more recently, a nervousness around communicating with her when she was wasted. So, an unanswered call was, in fact, a blessing. She settled on leaving a voicemail message with the hope that Vanessa chose not to return it.

The hotel room was definitely a quality setting. One thing Anita always ensured was that any conferences she attended were held in five-star establishments, and if it had a well-stocked mini-bar, then so much the better.

In the morning, when she woke confused and somewhat frightened, she would wonder if her weird, almost hallucinogenic experiences during the night were down to making a raid on that mini-bar and depleting it of everything alcoholic. But she had yet to go through that waking nightmare, and the glistening little bottles of whisky soon had her grabbing for them and, when she'd slugged her way through the Scotch and then the bourbon, she reached for the wine.

Before getting too inebriated, she opened her laptop and searched for the missing communications between her and Vanessa. Believing there had been a glitch with her iPhone, and that the laptop would produce everything, including the file of Vanessa's abysmal draft, she was dismayed to find that wasn't the case. Everything was gone and, although she searched every nook and cranny of the computer, she found no trace of a single message or file.

She treated it all with a shrug and settled down with her drink. She would worry about it in the morning.

Fourteen

Considering the stiffness in her joints and the muscle pain, Vanessa rose amazingly easily from her chair at the desk. It was almost as if someone had given her a helping hand. It was a weird sensation, one that made her feel as light as a feather, but not one that she gave much thought to – just as she hadn't given much thought to the gentle brush of something through her hair, or the soft ping of her phone letting her know that she had a voicemail message.

She wasn't sure how many hours had passed since both Anita and Richard had paid her a visit earlier in the day. Considering how she felt and how hungry she was and considering that the shadows in the room had grown long, she believed it to have been many more than the four she'd planned on spending in front of the laptop.

The exact expanse of time was lost to her. That should've been worrying but it wasn't – not yet anyway. Her mind was as empty as her belly.

She wasn't simply hungry, she was starving. The hollow feeling in the pit of her stomach wasn't one she was used to – a full belly being something she'd usually paid scant heed to – but, at that moment, all she could think about was food. She couldn't remember a time when she'd felt so ravenous. It put everything else – the progress of the book, the strange almost weighty atmosphere in the air, the fact that there was something not quite right about almost everything – out of her mind.

Avoiding looking at the word count on the bottom of the screen, she turned for the door, telling herself that she'd check her progress later, then – drifting like a wraith from the study – she headed for the kitchen.

Despite refusing to think of anything other than what she was about to cook, she couldn't help but feel a little wary. *What if there was something behind the door? What if...?*

She gave herself a mental shake, telling herself that there was no need to be cautious... no need to be afraid. She'd gone almost the full day without guzzling on the vodka bottle and that meant her mind and her senses were clear for the first time in ages. It meant that she wasn't about to imagine one horror or another or conjure up some weird shit that she couldn't explain.

As soon as she pushed open the kitchen door, the aroma of freshly brewed coffee assaulted her senses. *Someone had made coffee?* Her nostrils flared and her eyes darted towards the French press sitting in the middle of the table, a jug of milk and a China cup placed close by.

She almost jumped out of her skin when the toaster on one of the granite worktops popped out two perfectly browned slices of bread, and when she became aware of a spitting, sizzling sound, her eyes jerked to the stove at the side of the sink to find two sunny-side-up eggs spluttering in oil inside a frying pan.

What in the name of...?

She staggered into the kitchen and turned full circle, the hairs on the back of her neck prickling in, if not exactly alarm, then confusion. Had someone... Richard or Anita... arrived whilst she'd been busy in the study? Had one of them decided to surprise her with a snack and coffee?

No. Anita was in Edinburgh. It couldn't have been her.

For a moment, her heart surged with hope. It was immediately obvious to her gobsmacked brain that Richard had come back to her.

'Richard?' she called out, her voice warbling with the first stirring of excitement. 'Where are you? Come out, come out, wherever you are.'

The silence thrumming in her ears was almost painful. Why wasn't he answering her?

'Richard?' She turned and walked back out into the hallway, peered along its length, and then went to stand at the bottom of the stairs. 'Richard, are you up there?'

There wasn't the sound of anyone else in the house – no footsteps, no opening or closing of doors. There was nothing but a heavy quiet.

If Richard was somewhere in the house, he couldn't be far. He wasn't stupid enough to go off and leave a frying pan and hot oil on the gas.

A dark thought entered her head… not unless he wanted to start a fire… burn the house down with her in it.

It was an evil thought, but one that – once in her head – she couldn't shift.

With a heavy tread, she made her way back to the kitchen and immediately looked across to the door leading to the garden. She could see it was still bolted from the inside. Her confusion began to slide into acute anxiety.

She didn't know what to do. The smell of burning focussed her thoughts and she turned to the stove. The oil was seconds away from catching. Perhaps a fire was exactly what had been intended?

Her stomach lurched at the sight of the now cremated eggs. She surprised herself by thinking of how difficult it would be to scrub the pan clean.

Once the gas was off, she reached down to the pocket in her leggings, expecting to find her phone. Then, she remembered that she'd left it on the desk in the study.

Shit, she thought. *Now what?*

The silence surrounding her was growing increasingly oppressive. Without her phone, she felt extremely vulnerable. To retrieve it meant another trek back along the hallway to the study – a journey she didn't relish, not with the possibility of a potential murderer in the house.

Maybe it wasn't Richard? Maybe it was some psychopath?

She was suddenly too scared to move. She'd read about burglars and rapists breaking into people's homes and cooking themselves a meal before doing what they'd come to do and then leaving. It made sense that a criminal would keep themselves very quiet. She jerked a look over her shoulder. Was someone already creeping towards the kitchen?

She eyed the housephone in a docking station next to the fridge. Relief flooded through her. She didn't need her mobile to call the police. She stepped towards it, screamed and nearly fainted when she heard an enormous thud on the ceiling right above her head.

The scream died in her throat, to be replaced by a series of small whimpers. Scrabbling forward, she grabbed the phone, punched in 999, and pressed it against her ear.

Silence. No ringtone. The line was dead.

Shit. She threw the phone down onto the worktop. Goose bumps exploded all up her arms. She was icy with dread. A dead phone was never a good thing. It meant there was premeditation involved.

Well, she wasn't about to simply stand there and await her fate. She was going to have to grow a pair and think of a way to save herself. The obvious thing to do would be to escape out the back door. She got as far as considering it before she was overcome with a terror so acute that it nearly drove her to her knees. She would rather face a rapist than venture outside into the dark night.

It was fucking stupid. Everyone would say that she was an imbecile. They would say – who would choose to stay trapped in a house when there was a perfectly good way out?

But at least she had an inkling of what was in the house. She understood that danger. She had no idea what she would have to face on the outside. The last time she'd attempted to cross over the threshold, she'd actually stopped breathing. She had absolutely believed that the sky was thundering down to crush her, and she'd only managed a few steps before she'd literally catapulted herself back inside.

No. She was staying put. She could tackle a rapist, even someone hell-bent on killing her, but she couldn't face what was behind that bolted door.

She needed a weapon. Her eyes searched and found the knife block. Five black-handled blades protruded from the block, all tipped forward at uniform angles. There should've been six.

He had one.

Fuck. Fuck. Fuck.

Propelling herself forward, she made a grab for the largest one. Clenching it in her fist, and holding it out in front of her, she immediately felt better, safer.

Now armed, she decided to make her way back to the study and her mobile phone. It was easier said than done. Both feet now seemed glued to the floor.

She tried to breathe, to gather herself for what she needed to do. There was no way she was going to be another fucking victim. She was already a victim to her mother's genetic make-up, a victim of a shattered marriage, a victim of dreadful loss, and there was no way she would allow herself to also be a victim of rape and murder. Whoever was in the house had a rude awakening coming. She had no doubt that she would use the knife to defend herself. Cutting off her assailant's balls wasn't something she would shy from doing. But first, she had to move.

Okay, she told herself, *get a fucking move on.*

Her legs obeyed her silent command, and she made steady headway back towards the door, the knife still held out in front of her. It swayed a little. She swayed a little, but she crossed the floor without her knees buckling.

At the door, she cocked her head and listened for footsteps. She had to hold her breath to prevent her whimpers from disguising the sounds in the house, and she stood for a full two minutes before being satisfied that no one was making their way from upstairs.

There was a breeze. She became aware of it when it wafted across her face and ruffled through her hair. She shivered, momentarily nonplussed.

There shouldn't be a breeze, not unless...

The front door stood wide open.

She blinked and eased herself to the side until her back was pressed against the wall. Her hands shook so violently that the knife almost jerked from her grasp. She couldn't lose the knife. She knew that her life depended on keeping hold of it, so she dragged in her elbows and clutched it to her heaving breast.

She heard the sounds of the encroaching night leaching in through the open door. She heard the thud, thud, thud of her heart hammering in her ears, and she heard something else. She strained to understand what the noise was, sitting behind all the other sounds.

Breathing, she thought wildly, her own breath stalling in her chest. The house was breathing.

Mad. I'm fucking mad.

Jesus.

She slid down the wall until she was hunched on the floor. The walls seemed to pulsate in time to the sounds of their every breath. Then, her eyes, growing wide and terror-filled, watched as the inky black of the night began to seep slowly towards her.

It looked like blood – dead blood, black and ominous. It puddled just inside the door and then began to seep across the floor. Soon, it would reach her and swallow her up.

It was difficult for her to differentiate between what was real and what was a figment of her terrified imagination, but there was one thing she was sure of – regardless of her terror, and regardless of what she was seeing, she had to close that fucking door and lock out, not only the night, but whoever it was that had just made his escape right through it.

That was the only explanation for the door being open. It seemed that her would-be assailant had got cold feet and bolted. She should've felt a modicum of relief but there was no room amongst her tumultuous emotions for such a thing as a let-up in her terror.

Getting to the open door wasn't going to be easy. For one thing, she would have to wade through the inky stuff making its way towards her. She could close her eyes, try to make herself believe that it was only the floor beneath her feet, but that brought about its own fair share of fear. She'd much rather see than not see. She would much rather know what she was dealing with than have all the danger be invisible.

Her body was all but cemented to the wall and her legs didn't feel stable enough to hold her. Nevertheless, she gritted her teeth and pushed up, getting traction by digging in her heels and pressing her shoulders back and lifting them one at a time.

It was so very cold. The air blowing in through the open door had ice in it and Vanessa took a moment to think about how it might snow.

Grunting back a derisive snort, she told herself off for prevaricating. *What did it matter if it was going to snow? If she didn't close the door, she might not be alive to see it.*

Did she want to be alive to see it? Fuck, yes!

The door to the study was on her left, just a few strides across the floor. Her phone was in there and her phone was the only way – apart from running from the house and screaming for help – that would enable her to summon the police. It might be better to forget all about closing and locking the front door and go straight for the phone. She thought that might make more sense.

She shook her head. *No, it fucking didn't.* What if he came back? He could storm his way back through that open door at any moment, get at her before the police had time to arrive, so she really had no choice but to bar his way.

Straightening her spine, and steeling herself, she peeled herself off the wall then, reassuring herself that she still had the knife, she took the first couple of tentative steps forward.

She didn't get far. Seconds later, she found herself pushed back and hugging the wall, her whole body jerking as if she'd been poked with a cattle-prod.

The door was no longer ajar. Of its own volition, it had closed with an almighty slam. The force of it had ruptured the air and catapulted her backwards, slamming her against the wall and knocking the air from her lungs.

At first, she thought it might have been the wind. When she got her breath back, she quickly dismissed that as being a ridiculous explanation. There was no way for the wind to have got itself behind the door and, anyway, it was a heavy door, made of thick oak, and it would have taken a force ten gale to shift it.

Regardless of the reason, she now had to get to it and turn the key. Wasting no time, she skittered across the floor on her hands and knees, reached up, and locked it. But that wasn't secure enough, so she pulled herself to her feet and drew the large bolt across the top.

Being behind the now secure door didn't immediately make her feel safe. There was no way to know if the intruder was still in the house. It wasn't as if she'd seen him leave. For all she knew, she might just have just locked herself inside with him.

As scary as that was, it wasn't as scary as the night rushing in through that open door. Nothing was as scary as that.

Without wasting another second, she went to the study, picked up her phone, and called the police. She waited, hunched in a corner of the room, her eyes glued to the door and praying that no one would burst through, and eventually help arrived.

Fifteen

Richard Arthur Parker (RAP)
  Sample taken from PART TWO of recorded interview
Date: 21 January 2022
Duration: 90 minutes
Location: Wood Street Police Station, City of London
No of pages: 19 (total number of sample pages: 8)
Conducted by officers from the London Metropolitan Police
All police identifiers have been redacted Section 38 (1) (A)

Police: Part two of the interview conducted under caution with Richard Arthur Parker. Interview recommenced at eleven thirty-five a.m. Now, Mister Parker, I would like to remind you that you are still under caution. You are not under arrest. You have the right to have a solicitor present during this interview. Do you wish to have a solicitor present?

RAP: I've already answered that.

Police: Please answer it again.

RAP: Okay. If you insist. No, I do not want a solicitor. Is it okay if we just get on with this? I've been here for ages, and I want to go home.

Police: You are free to leave at any time. Do you want to leave, Mister Parker?

RAP: What if I do? You're saying that I can simply get up and walk out? You won't try and stop me?

Police: No, we won't prevent you from leaving, however we would wonder why you weren't keen to assist us with our enquiries.

We would wonder why you didn't want to help us to find your wife. To us, it would look rather suspicious.

RAP: Oh, we can't have you suspicious of me now, can we? Not any more than you already are. No, I'll stay, but can you just hurry up and ask your questions? Stop all this faffing about? I mean... if you really think that something terrible has happened to her, shouldn't you be out there searching instead of wasting time with me?

Police: We're not wasting time. You were one of the last people to see your wife, or to speak to her. Any information you give us will help us to track her down.

RAP: Well, just get on with it.

Police: Before we move onto the last time you were at the house, can you tell us a bit more about your relationship with Vanessa?

RAP: We don't have a relationship... not the way you mean.

Police: You're still married. You visit her frequently. You take money from her. All of that suggests an ongoing relationship.

RAP: (inaudible)

Police: She gave you a cheque that day, didn't she? And the day after that, you paid it into your account at the bank. How much was the cheque made out for?

RAP: If you know about the cheque, then you know how much it was for.

Police: One thousand pounds?

RAP: Yes.

Police: Why a cheque? Why didn't she simply transfer the money into your account?

RAP: She always gives me a cheque. She gets off on making me wait for the cash to clear. She doesn't believe in instant gratification.

Police: Not a nice person then... your wife?

RAP: Not especially, no.

Police: That must've rankled... only giving you cheques?

RAP: Well, it was my money as much as hers. Not giving me cash was her way of giving me the finger, so yes, it rankled. Actually, it pissed me right off.

Police: Enough to hurt her?

RAP: No fucking way. I don't hurt women, and I resent the suggestion.

Police: You hurt her psychologically, though, didn't you?

RAP: I don't know what you mean.

Police: All the affairs. Before and after your son died...

RAP: Don't bring my child into this.

Police: After your son died, you had an affair with the therapist... the one that your wife paid for.

RAP: That was a figment of her imagination.

Police: Didn't she catch you in the act?

RAP: Who told you that? Whoever said that is a fucking liar.

Police: You deny it, then?

RAP: Too right, I do.

Police: Let me put you straight on something, Mister Parker. If you get caught out in a lie, it makes it impossible for us to believe anything else that comes out of your mouth. So, would you like to take a moment to reconsider what you just denied?

RAP: It wasn't an affair. It was one time... just one fucking time, okay?

Police: You had sex with your therapist one time?

RAP: A wham, bam, thank you ma'am.

Police: Very droll.

RAP: It didn't mean anything. Vanessa blew it out of all proportion.

Police: What was she... a bereavement therapist?

RAP: Not exactly.

Police: No, she was a sex therapist who your wife hoped would encourage you to be faithful. Am I right?

RAP: Something like that. Look, change the subject, or I'm out of here.

Police: Why is it such a touchy subject?

RAP: Because I know what you're getting at. You think I hurt her... had something to do with her going walkabout. Well, I'm here to tell you that you're barking up the wrong tree. If someone hurt her, then it wasn't me.

Police: Okay... moving on...

RAP: About fucking time.

Police: The last time you saw your wife, had you gone to see her specifically to ask for more money?

RAP: Amongst other things.

Police: What other things?

RAP: Well, to see how she was, I suppose, and to talk about the sale of the house.

Police: Vanessa hadn't agreed to the sale, had she?

RAP: No.

Police: Did you get around to talking about it?

RAP: Not really. I didn't get the chance to raise the subject with her.

Police: Oh? How long were you there that day?

RAP: I'm not sure. I guess, about an hour or so.

Police: Can you be more specific?

RAP: Let's say, ninety minutes.

Police: How was she? How did she seem to you?

RAP: A bit of a mess.

Police: Upset?

RAP: I suppose.

Police: Did she say what about?

RAP: Not that I recall.

Police: Did you have sex with her during that visit?

RAP: That is none of your fucking business.

Police: Everything is our business, Mister Parker. So, tell me... do you often have sex with your estranged wife?

RAP: I'm not answering that.

Police: You seem very touchy on the subject of sex. For someone who obviously enjoys it, you're pretty shy about talking about it.

RAP: Are you getting off on this? Is this how you get your jollies?

Police: Such a wicked sense of humour. That could get you into trouble.

RAP: Is that a threat?

Police: Hardly a threat, Mister Parker. Simply an observation. Now, moving on once more... That day, did she mention anything about leaving... about going anywhere?

RAP: No. I would've told you that already.

Police: You said that her disappearance might be some sort of a publicity stunt. Do you really believe that... considering the extent of her agoraphobia? You told us that you didn't believe she had that condition, but, on the other hand, you couldn't recall knowing if she actually ever went out anywhere.

RAP: Look, I'm no shrink, so what do I know? I don't think it's as bad as she makes out. She uses the agoraphobia excuse to get sympathy from me.

Police: So, if she ever felt threatened in her own home... say, if there was an intruder... you think that she would be perfectly fine escaping the house to get away? Her condition wouldn't hinder her escape?

RAP: I'm not sure I understand the question.

Police: let's put it this way... Were you worried enough about her to go back to the house that night... the night before you banked one thousand pounds of her money?

RAP: I told you... it was OUR money, and what's this about an intruder?

Police: Didn't you know? Didn't your wife tell you?

RAP: Know what? What didn't she tell me?

Police: About someone breaking into her house that night.

RAP: (inaudible)

Police: She could've got out, but she stayed inside. The police report said that she'd been too terrified to go outside. That sounds like agoraphobia to me.

RAP: What is this bullshit? If there had been someone in the house, she would've told me. And, as for the agoraphobia... who the fuck knows? She probably stayed inside because she knew there wasn't any threat. She probably made the whole thing up.

Police: Are you sure that you didn't go back to the house that night... fry her some eggs, make her some toast, brew her some coffee?

RAP: What, the fuck?

Police: Just so I've got this clear... you deny going back to the house that night?

RAP: Absolutely. Listen... I'm not going to answer any more of your dumb questions. I want a solicitor. Either let me go home or give me a fucking phone so I can get one in here.

Police: Are you now asserting your right to legal representation, Mister Parker?

RAP: Fucking right.

Police: Very well. Interview suspended at twelve thirteen.

Sixteen

She heard their heavy footsteps as they searched the house from top to bottom. There were two of them and, at first, neither seemed to doubt her story of an intruder. It was only when they spied the bin in the corner of the kitchen, filled to overflowing with empty vodka bottles, that the doubt appeared to set in.

She saw it in their eyes and then in their expressions which were a mixture of pity and scorn. She looked away, not able to bear the way they attempted to make their faces neutral... the way they tried not to judge.

A loud bang startled her, and she turned to see one of the officers flicking something off one of the worktops.

'Pesky fly,' he said. 'Can't stand the damned things.'

He obviously didn't wonder what a fly was doing in her kitchen in the middle of winter. She wondered, though, and then noticed that there were a few others, buzzing around the bin. Stranger still, was the fact that the officer, who so obviously hated them, hadn't seemed to notice. Why only notice the one fly?

She was sure that there was no discarded food in the bin, so what was attracting them? Mesmerised, she stood and silently watched as they dive-bombed, regrouped, and almost swarmed.

'There isn't anyone here, Ms Parker.'

Her head jerked to the side, and she responded to his words with a soft grunt.

'Of course, we'll search the garden... just in case he's hiding out in the bushes, or in the shed.'

She could quite clearly see that a perfunctory search of the garden would simply be him going through the motions. He didn't believe, not for a moment, that anyone was skulking outside. He was just humouring her. It should've made her angry, but all she felt was despair.

Not being believed, crushed her.

The wind whipped the door from his grasp as he pulled the door open. She heard him cursing under his breath as he stepped outside.

'Blowing up quite a storm,' the other officer said, pushing the door closed behind his partner. 'I wouldn't be surprised if it was the noise of the wind that spooked you.'

'Maybe,' she said, not believing it.

'I mean…' he went on, 'everything is locked up tight, and there are no signs of a break-in. These old houses are notorious for creaking and groaning, especially when there's a storm brewing and the windows are rattling, and everything. Are you getting a little disturbed…?' His eyes flitted once more to the bin in the corner. 'Well, it's perfectly understandable.'

One of the flies buzzed around his head. He didn't seem to notice. She watched and waited for him to swat it away, but he never did. Even when it alighted on his cheek and began to walk across his flesh, it didn't elicit any reaction from him.

'You're a writer, aren't you?'

The question surprised her.

He smiled. 'My wife has all your books. I recognised you from your picture on the dustcovers.' He frowned. 'She wasn't very enamoured of your last two.' Once again, his eyes rested on the empty vodka bottles overspilling the bin, seemingly putting two and two together and concluding that the drink was to blame for the decline in her writing.

'I hope she'll like my latest one,' she said, not really giving a fuck either way.

'Oh? You still writing, then?'

'Of course.'

'You authors must have quite the imagination?'

Her hackles rose. 'I didn't imagine someone being in my house.'

'No, of course not. I didn't mean...'

The door gusted open, and the other officer was pushed over the threshold by the wind. His partner looked mightily relieved to see him.

'Anything?' he asked.

'Not a thing. No one out there.'

The flies had left their incessant bombardment of the bin and, in a small black swarm, buzzed over both officers' heads. The noise they made was incongruent with their numbers and Vanessa found herself standing, open-mouthed and confused at the two men's lack of awareness.

'You all right, Ms Parker?'

Her mouth snapped closed. Both of their eyes were on her. Both were frowning.

'Fine. I'm fine,' she said, then, 'There was no one out there in the garden, in the shed? Are you sure?' She looked from one to the other, her eyes jerking in their sockets, then flicking across the dipping, diving flies. 'And there was no one upstairs?'

'No one. You're perfectly safe.'

There were even more flies. She stepped back, feeling a sense of abject horror as every inch of flesh on both officers' faces turned black. She could no longer see any of their features. Their mouths were two huge black swarming holes. No flesh was visible.

Her stomach heaved. Bent double at the waist, she retched.

One officer reached out a hand to steady her. That hand was crawling, undulating with wave upon wave of black insects.

Lurching back in horror, she stumbled and steadied herself before the hand could touch her. She couldn't bear the thought of that hand touching her.

The other officer coughed, and a splutter of flies erupted from his throat.

Vanessa fainted.

IT WAS DARK IN THE hotel room, but more of a velvety grey than an absolute gloom. Anita was a mere hump beneath the quilt and, apart from the rise and fall of her natural breathing, there was no other movement – not until there was.

A tiny chink of light from the streetlamp outside the bedroom window – a chink so tiny that there wasn't even a finger of illumination to bright the darkest corner – seeped in through the blinds. It was enough to show a flicker of movement – a dart of a small shadow – but nothing more.

Anita snored in a deep, drunken slumber. She was wholly unaware of the gradual increase in sound in the room. It was only when the drone became so loud and so strong that it vibrated the very air, that she was dragged from sleep.

'What...?' She pulled herself up onto her elbows, immediately aware that something was wrong, but not quite sure what. It took a few moments before her eyes grew accustomed to the dark and she could recognise the shadowy silhouette of the dressing table, the television, the wardrobe, and...

What the fuck was that?

She reached over and searched with her hand for the switch that would turn on the bedside lamp. It took a few goes, but she finally succeeded in turning it on.

At first, blinking the sleep from her eyes, she had no clue what she saw, or what she heard. When realisation dawned, she was immediately up and off the bed, arms waving frantically over her head in an attempt to thwart the flies and then staggering her way towards the bathroom.

It was like ploughing through a thick wall of shifting sand. Flies batted off her face, got stuck in her hair, crawled over every inch of her body. She was too terrified to open her mouth to scream, lest they swarm inside and clog up her windpipe.

She reached the bathroom but saw that the door handle was alive and moving. She would have to touch the insects, crush, and squish them before she could open the door.

She didn't hesitate, pushing down on the handle, she dragged the door towards her, but before she managed to close it once more – close it against the vicious onslaught – the flies seemed to shift into a sort of formation and the last thing she witnessed, before slamming the door closed, was a gaping black maw, with wicked teeth, made entirely of buzzing black flies, rush towards her.

VANESSA CAME TO AND was lifted gently from the floor and into one of the chairs at the table. One of the officers held a glass of water to her lips and she drank it down greedily.

She was relieved to see that all the flies were gone.

'You gave us quite a scare,' the officer holding the glass said. 'At least you didn't bump your head when you hit the floor. That's something to be grateful for.'

She swallowed the last of the water and found herself apologising. They already thought that she was drunk and conking out cold on them wasn't about to alter that opinion. Her own opinion of what was going on was muddy. It was obvious that they didn't see or feel the flies and that made the whole thing a figment of her imagination, and that meant that everything else that had transpired probably was as well.

'I think we ought to call an ambulance... just to be on the safe side.'

'What? No.' Vanessa jumped to her feet. 'I'm fine. I just need to get something in my stomach. I haven't eaten all day.'

'Too busy writing?'

Or, drinking, she imagined him thinking.

'Something like that,' she said, choking back on her growing dread and flopping back down into the chair. She let out what she hoped was a small and reassuring laugh but a laugh she knew sounded strangulated. 'Sometimes I don't realise where the time goes.'

'I still think that an ambulance isn't a bad idea.'

Vanessa emphatically shook her head. An ambulance, and perhaps a trip to the hospital, was the last thing she wanted. They would have to straitjacket her to get her out of the house.

'Okay, if you're sure?'

'I'm sure.'

'Then, at least go see your GP.'

See her GP? Was he having a laugh? Since Covid, her GP refused to do house calls, and there was no way she would contemplate forcing herself to visit him at the surgery. And, for what? To be told to cut out the booze, to be handed a prescription for some pills that would do nothing but zonk her? No, thank you very much.

'I will,' she lied. 'You can be sure of that.'

'Meantime is there anyone you'd like us to call?' the other officer asked, his expression showing quite clearly that he thought she was a danger to herself. 'A friend... a family member?'

She shook her head.

'What about a neighbour?'

Her nearest neighbour was over a mile away. *He ought to know that* she thought grimly. *How fucking stupid was he?*

She shook her head once more.

'Okay, then, we'll get off. Remember to lock up after us and get some food inside you.'

She suddenly wished that they would stay. She wanted to ask, to beg them to see the remainder of the night through with her, but she meekly rose from the chair and stood to the side as they walked to the door. They had to leave. That was obvious, and she had no choice but to let them.

One of them glanced up the stairs on the way to the front door. Vanessa cocked her ear, trying to ascertain if he'd heard something alarming, but apart from the wind whistling at the windows, there was only silence.

The house had been ominously hushed since their arrival. Even the sound of the impending storm, and the buzzing of the flies, hadn't taken away from the muted atmosphere. It was if the house held its breath, just waiting.

When the heavy oak door was pulled open, she stiffened, wondering if the shadows from outside would leech back into the hallway. They didn't, but she was nonetheless relieved when she pushed it fully closed and then locked and bolted it.

Huffing in a shattered breath, she leaned back, her hands clenched at her sides and her heart hammering in her chest.

Now what, she wondered, her eyes searching the length and breadth of the hall. Seeing nothing untoward, and hearing nothing but the wind, she eventually sagged with relief.

Everything felt normal and her fear gradually subsided. Perhaps she would try to see her GP. Even if it meant venturing out, it might be worth the agony of the journey. The thought of swallowing a few pills no longer seemed such an abomination – not if it meant she could rid herself of whatever fucked-up psychosis was tearing away at her mind and her senses.

ARMED WITH THE ONLY weapon she could find, Anita opened the bathroom door a crack. In her hand was a deodorant aerosol. She planned on spraying it right into the midst of the disease-ridden little fuckers. It might not kill them, but she was hopeful it would allow her to clear a path to the phone. She would get right on to reception, demand they give her another room, and woe betide the management if they didn't refund her stay. She might even manage to screw a free weekend out of them, knowing she could lose them a great deal of business if she decided to slate the hotel on TripAdvisor.

She pushed the memory of those little fuckers attacking her like some rendition of a giant mouth to the side, concluding that she'd imagined it. She'd been half asleep, still a little drunk, and her glasses were still on the bedside table where she'd left them. Fuck only knew what she'd seen, but one thing she was sure of... it wasn't a bastard mouth.

She wasn't exactly afraid when she pushed the door fully open. They were, after all, only flies. But she admitted to being a little anxious. They weren't the cleanest of things, flies, and Anita had an aversion to any form of germ. She was sure they were riddled with every germ known to man and they'd been on her, in her hair, nearly in her mouth. She felt sick at the memory. She should have stopped to wonder why there were no flies in the bathroom with her. She should have pondered a moment and took better stock of what had just happened. Instead, she went blindly back into the room.

The silence was the first thing she became aware of. No more buzzing. The second thing she noticed was that there were no more flies. Not a single one remained in the room.

Taken aback, the hand holding the aerosol dropped to her side. She looked to the ceiling, to the walls, to the bed, and saw nothing amiss. She walked to the window and was surprised to see that it was closed and locked. *The flies couldn't have escaped through there, so where were they?*

Nonplussed, she made her way back to the bed and slowly sat down on the edge.

Had she dreamt it? She was sure that she must have. There was no other explanation.

There goes my free weekend, she thought with some bemusement. She no longer had any cause for complaint.

After a long moment of sitting, calming herself and contemplating searching the minibar for any remaining spirits, her attention was drawn to the wardrobe. The door was open. She frowned, sure it had been closed before she'd sat down on the bed.

Anita had lost count of the many novels she'd read by authors who wrote in the horror genre. The one thing all those books had in common was the stupidity of their main characters. Every one of them always went down into the dark cellar, or peered into the cavernous wardrobe, knowing a monster or a demon lurked there. They couldn't help themselves or, better still, the writers couldn't stop themselves from making their characters do the stupidest of things.

But Anita felt compelled to do the stupid thing. She couldn't stop herself from standing up, walking to the wardrobe, and peering in. It was as if an invisible force dragged her there and made her crane her neck to see what was inside.

She hadn't brought many clothes with her, so the majority of the hangers were empty. There was nothing to obscure the view of the interior, but she squinted nonetheless because, right in front of her was a shadow she couldn't make head nor tail of. It was a shadow that shouldn't have been there. It rose to cover the backboard of the wardrobe. It had twin horns curving towards a peak atop a lumpy expression of a head and two glowing red dots that Anita immediately took for eyes.

Before her brain could make sense of it, thousands of flies – a thick blanket of them – swarmed straight for her face.

Seventeen

It took all her reserves and every little bit of willpower she possessed not to phone Richard. Being alone, frightened, and having no clue what had been happening since early that morning, was something she wouldn't wish on her worst enemy. The house might seem quiet, and there might not be anything going on now to alarm her, but that didn't mean that she wasn't alarmed. Call it instinct. Call it a sixth sense. Whatever it was that continued to cause the hairs on the back of her neck to stand to attention, it was scary enough to have her considering rousing the wrath of the formidable Fiona by ringing Richard and getting him out of bed.

Fiona was jealous of her. Vanessa had no doubt about that. The other woman would never be able to trust their lover because that lover had cheated with them and who was to say that they wouldn't do the dirty across them? She didn't believe that Fiona had an inkling that Richard continued to fuck his estranged wife. Vanessa couldn't imagine her putting up with that and – although tempted to land Richard right in the shit by informing the bitch of his shenanigans – she'd kept stum, mainly because she believed she would ultimately hurt herself far more than she would either of them.

What finally stopped her from calling him was the fear that he would think the same as the police – that she was cracked in the head. It didn't take a genius to work out what he would say. He would say it was the vodka. He would say it was all her own fault, that he had no sympathy for her, and he might... just might... take matters into his own hands and have her thrown into some locked-down rehab facility. He already thought that she was a sandwich short of a picnic, and God only knew what steps he would take, supposedly in her best interests. The events of the whole day might be the only excuse he needed to take charge of her, and not in a nice or caring way.

At that particular point in their ragged relationship, the worse thing she could do was to give him the ammunition to end it completely. Nothing would make her want to lose him... not forever.

So, she didn't call him. Instead, she went back into the study, found a blank notebook, and sat down to make a record of the strange happenings and how they had affected her. One day, Richard might read it, and he might feel a frisson of sorrow, or guilt. She hoped that he would end up choking on both.

Out of the corner of her eye, she saw the screensaver flit across the laptop. Although tempted to check on the progress of the book, she stayed well clear of it. She had a feeling she wouldn't like what the wordcount told her.

There goes that sixth sense again, she mused. The progress made on the novel was just as confusing and just as terrifying as everything else, and she would rather poke a nest of wasps with a sharp stick rather than go anywhere near the manuscript. Not yet anyway. She would wait until she was in a better frame of mind.

As she wrote – her handwriting much the worse for her ordeal – she grew calmer, more settled. She began to breathe easier and, now that she was immortalising everything on paper, she felt that she was retaking some of the control.

She was pleased with that first entry in what would become her journal. She was particularly pleased with the fact that she was thinking clearly enough to begin to put into words her suspicion that someone was playing mind games with her. She was honest enough to point out that everyone would blame her drinking, but she fell short of admitting that she was paranoid.

She was a writer and a damned good one and writing was the means by which she made sense of things. Just as a mathematical genius solved problems by putting down formula, she worked things out using words – by transcribing her thoughts onto the screen or transferring them onto paper.

Done, she huffed in a breath and made her way back to the kitchen, one ear tuned to any noise from upstairs and the other ear homing in on any sounds of movement ahead of her. Every sense told her that she was alone in the house, but she hadn't quite learned to fully trust her senses so remained on high alert.

The coffee in the French press was cold but she poured a cup anyway. Cold caffeine was just as effective as the warm stuff and the one thing she needed – apart from a stiff drink – was caffeine. She put a second cup in the microwave and warmed it. There was no point in denying herself that little bit of warming heat in her belly.

Steam wafted across her face, and she appreciated its warmth. Her body felt like a block of ice and her hands trembled with a combination of what remained of her angst and cold. She wrapped them around the cup before raising it to her mouth. Some coffee spilled over the rim and dripped down her chin, but she didn't notice. She took a small sip, closed her eyes, and swallowed.

It was now well into the small hours of the morning. Exhaustion made her limbs limp and overwhelming fatigue dragged her further down into misery. Whatever scenario proved to be the reason for everything that had occurred, she was lost within it. With no one to turn to for help – because who could she trust – how would she ever climb out the other end?

After a while, the coffee worked its magic, and she felt the exhaustion begin to seep from her body. She knew that she would suffer for it later. Coffee was a mere panacea. Once the caffeine wore off, she would feel as if she'd been hit by a lorry.

She was much too wired to sleep, and her mind kept jumping back to what was on her laptop. Come what may, she was going to finish the book, and she was going to do it sober. When it was done, she would take the credit for every damned word.

Her phone pinged. She frowned. It was four o'clock in the morning. Who would be messaging her at such an ungodly hour? She immediately panicked… thinking something had happened to Richard. The last time she'd received a message at that time in the morning it was to tell her a heart had been found for her son and to get her arse over to the hospital right away.

Simon had been in intensive care, his heart – diseased beyond repair – was failing fast. She'd only gone home for a change of clothes, hadn't expected that a donor would be found in time. The message was from Richard, from their son's bedside, urging her to be quick. She always resented the fact that Richard's face had been the last one Simon had seen before being wheeled into theatre. It should have been her face. It should have been her lips pressed to his hot brow.

He died without hearing her tell him how much she loved him, that mummy would be there waiting for him when it was all over. The guilt was something she'd never recovered from.

Blinking back tears, she glanced at the screen. It was just a Facebook notification. Nothing to worry about. No bad news. She sighed with relief.

Preoccupied, and not in the mood for any Facebook drivel – not even if it meant, for a time, she wouldn't feel quite so alone – she ignored it and threw the phone down onto the table before leaning forward and laying her head on her arms.

She wasn't tired, but she was weary. She needed a moment before getting back to the grind of finishing the book. She needed a moment to push the memories away, to quell the disquiet, and to shelf those dreadful memories.

As she sat at the table, eyes closed and her breath now coming in a steady rhythm, a feeling of wellbeing washed over her. She suddenly felt as if she'd been wrapped in a warm blanket, and it took quite some time for her to accept the absence of worry or fear. It was an alien feeling – that sense of peace – and it discomfited her. She couldn't help thinking that it was the calm before yet another storm.

After all the sensory overload, and after having to cope with everything from a clock's hands spinning, to believing there was an intruder in the house, and then all the weird stuff around the book, she could be forgiven for being utterly frazzled, however she felt as if she'd been injected with a new lease of life. Nothing ached, her eyes were no longer heavy, and the last of her exhaustion had dissipated. Her limbs felt as light as a feather and, for the first time in what seemed like forever, she felt herself smiling.

The urge to rush back to the study and the laptop was overwhelming. She could think of nothing else but getting up from the table and placing herself in front of her desk. Nothing else mattered but the book.

Hours later... she was unsure of just how many... Vanessa lurched awake. It took a moment for her to get her bearings before she realised that she was still in the study. It was morning. The light streaming in the window told her as much and a quick glance at the clock confirmed it.

It was gone ten. She couldn't have been asleep for very long as the last time she'd looked at the time it had shown six forty-five. *Unless*, she thought, *she'd slept through the day, and it was already Friday?*

The ache in her limbs, the weariness in her bones, and what felt like sand in her eyes, suggested that wasn't the case. Realistically, she'd probably been asleep for no more than a couple of hours.

Her senses registered nothing unnatural in the atmosphere. The house seemed still. There was no frisson of tension in the air. Everything felt perfectly normal, except... she hadn't woken up craving a drink. In fact, the thought of pouring a glass of ice-cold vodka made her feel nauseous.

It should have pleased her, but instead, it worried her. She was an alcoholic. She had no qualms about finally admitting that to herself, so she should want a drink. Why didn't she?

She heard the distant sound of her mobile ringing. It rang for the requisite four cycles before the person either disconnected the call or left a voicemail. She let it ring, feeling no desire to rush through to the kitchen to snatch it from the table and speak to whoever was on the line. She didn't care who it was. She had no interest in speaking to anyone. She was just so damned tired.

Her attention was drawn to a flash of pain shooting up her fingers and across her hands. When she looked down, she saw that every finger was bent. They resembled claws. When she tried to flex them, the agony took her breath away.

Only once before had her hands and her fingers pained her as much as they did at that moment and that had been years before, when she'd spent a full twelve hours at the keyboard. After that all-nighter, she hadn't been able to type for three full days.

She must have been hammering on the keys for hours and hours. And her body jolted at the thought of what not remembering a single minute of those hours meant.

It meant that something was still terribly wrong.

Her eyes flicked across to the laptop. The screensaver wasn't on, and she could clearly see a page of manuscript.

Pins and needles travelled the length of her calves, all the way up her thighs and into her groin and she heard the bones in her neck crack as she leaned forward in the chair. Biting down hard on her bottom lip, she dragged her eyes across the page before swivelling to the bottom left of the screen.

Her jaw dropped. Her eyes bugged in her head.

Seventy-five thousand words.

Holy fucking shit!

Eighteen

'I don't know why you bother,' Fiona said, her pretty face full of sleep. 'I wish you'd just leave her the fuck alone.'

Richard pushed himself up onto his elbows and shook his head. 'Well, she didn't pick up and I must've tried phoning her at least a dozen times this morning, and every time it's gone to voicemail.' He sighed and ran a hand through his bed hair. 'So, I guess leaving her the fuck alone is exactly the message she's sending me loud and clear.'

Fiona had overcome her previous pique and Richard felt safe enough to talk about Vanessa again. It was like that with Fiona. She was a hot and cold kind of girl. One minute, mad as Hell, and the next either indifferent or supportive.

'She's probably too drunk to hear the phone.'

'Maybe.' His brow furrowed. Usually – drunk, or not, Vanessa always picked up. 'I wish I knew what she's playing at.'

'She's a right fruit-loop... that wife of yours.'

'Tell me about it. I deserve a medal for all I've had to put up with. I had fucking years of it... never knowing whether I was coming or going.'

'Let her stew in her own juices for a while.'

'If it wasn't for needing those papers signed, I would.'

'She can't hold out forever.'

That was one of the problems with Fiona – she had no fucking clue as to how stubborn and pig-headed his wife could be. He had a feeling that hell would freeze over before Vanessa signed anything.

'Poor baby.' Fiona leaned forward and brushed her lips across his mouth. 'You're trying so hard. You'll eventually win her around, I'm sure.'

'It can't come soon enough.'

'I can't wait to be Mrs. Parker.'

Oh shit. His eyes shifted to the side. She actually thought that he would put himself from the frying pan and back into the fire. He wasn't that stupid. A second marriage was definitely not on the cards, but he kept that fact to himself. *So, why bother with a divorce?* he wondered. For several reasons – it would keep Fiona sweet, and it would give him access to half of the equity in the house, as well as being able, through the divorce court, to put a raid on Vanessa's bank accounts. He even hoped that she would be obliged to pay him spousal maintenance – which was another reason he wouldn't marry again. The goose would stop laying its golden eggs if he was stupid enough to do that.

In some ways, Richard knew that Fiona wasn't going to end up being his life partner, but for the moment, being with her came with certain benefits. For a start, she provided him with a roof over his head and a warm bed. Then there was the use of her body, and what a body it was.

He looked down and pulled back the duvet, exposing her breasts. Just the mere sight of them gave him a hard-on. Compared to Vanessa's almost boyish figure – much too thin from years of drinking and an exceptionally poor diet – Fiona's tits were far superior.

He had committed himself to those breasts, at least for the time being, and to keep them and her, he'd had to be prepared to lie. Not that lying was particularly difficult. He'd lied throughout most of his life, especially to women.

'Want to snuggle?' she asked, reaching for him.

'Sorry, babe. I have to go and pay in the cheque she gave me. I didn't manage to get to the bank yesterday.' He spoke reluctantly.

There was nothing he wanted more than to snuggle, but the sooner he paid the cheque in, the sooner it would clear.

He dragged himself to the edge of the bed, kicked his legs over the side, and stood up. He heard Fiona sigh in irritation and scrunched his eyes closed.

'You could come with me,' he said, bending to pick up his discarded clothes from the floor. 'Perhaps we could grab some lunch, do some shopping?'

'How absolutely boring.'

He swung around. 'Since when did you think eating out and shopping was boring?'

'Since about the time you started expecting me to pay.'

She had him there. He couldn't recall the last time he'd paid for a meal or bought her something nice.

'I'll treat you to dinner soon, I promise.'

She eyed him suspiciously. 'I hope you're not planning on going back to see her to ask her for more money. I know you're entitled to it, but I hate to imagine you begging.'

He wondered just how much she'd hate what he actually had to do to prise a few lousy pounds from his wife's hands.

'Uh, huh.' He shook his head. 'I'm not that much of a glutton for punishment.'

'I wish you didn't have to go anywhere near her... ever.'

'Well, my little spendthrift, I don't really have any choice, do I?'

He wished that he'd taken the trip to the bank the day before. Leaving it until that morning meant, because the weekend loomed, and the banks didn't do business at the weekend, it would be later the following week before it cleared.

It had been folly to wait the extra day. His car was running on fumes, and he didn't think he had enough cash to put in even a litre of fuel. His credit card was maxed out, and his wallet was empty of everything but a photograph of his son. There were a couple of pound coins in the pocket of his jeans, and that was all he had to his name.

'You couldn't spare a few quid, could you... just to tide me over?' He asked the question already knowing what the answer would be. Fiona was even stingier than Vanessa.

She threw him a look of incredulity and he dropped his eyes. He couldn't bear to see the scorn in them.

'Forget I asked,' he said. 'I'll do without.' In fact, he had another idea on how to get some cash. He would pawn his wedding ring. He'd taken to not wearing it, so he certainly wouldn't miss it and, since it was heavy and twenty-two carat gold, he ought to get at least a couple of hundred quid for it – enough to tide him over.

He dragged on his jeans and pulled his jumper over his head, trying to remember what he'd done with the damned thing. He recalled throwing it on the kitchen table a few weeks before in response to Fiona's snide remarks that it had remained on his finger but couldn't think where it had ended up.

He could ask Fiona, but knew that in doing so, he would probably start a cold war between them. it was already a little frosty.

Over his shoulder, he said, 'Forget I mentioned the money. I'm sorry. It was crass of me.'

She made a snorting noise, not immediately accepting his apology. That was another thing about Fiona – she never made saying sorry easy.

'Come on, love,' he said. 'Don't be such a misery guts.'

She stared up at him but said nothing.

He turned back around fully, blinked down at her, sighed, and shrugged his shoulders. 'Suit yourself. Be a fucking bitch.'

On those final words, he stormed from the room. If he hadn't needed somewhere to stay, he would fuck her right off... marvellous tits, or not.

He had time for a coffee and, whilst he waited for the kettle to boil, he decided to try calling Vanessa again. He didn't normally take the time to ring her once, never mind numerous times a day, but a niggle of worry tugged at his mind. He had a feeling that she needed to hear from him. There was no real reason for his disquiet. He left her the day before in much the same state as he had on numerous previous occasions, and there was nothing to suggest that she was in any sort of trouble – not any more than usual, with the drink and all that – and the only tangible concern he had was that she hadn't answered any of his calls and hadn't rung him back.

It surprised him that he was worried. He didn't love her. He believed that he didn't care if she lived or died, however she'd been the mother to his one and only child – a child who he had most definitely loved – and that had to mean something. He owed it to Simon's memory to at least be a little bit bothered.

Once again, the call went straight to voicemail, and once again, he left yet another message.

He didn't have time to do any more than that and put her temporarily from his mind.

Later, when Richard handed over the cheque along with a paying-in slip, the bank clerk gave him a funny look before tapping away on her computer and shaking her head.

'Is something wrong?' he asked.

'Wrong?' She looked at him, startled. 'No, sir... nothing's wrong.'

'You were shaking your head,' he said.

'Was I?' She dropped her eyes back to the computer screen and said nothing more.

For an awful moment he thought she'd been about to tell him that Vanessa didn't have enough funds to cover the cheque. He wasn't sure why he would think such a thing. His wife was rolling in money and was certainly good for a measly grand.

The clerk handed him the stub from the slip and her eyes, dismissing him, went automatically to the customer standing behind him.

He hated being so unimportant to a mere bank clerk. In her eyes, he was a nobody. If he had control over Vanessa's funds, she wouldn't have looked at him as if he was no better than... than... he looked to the side... no better than the old biddy handing over some money to pay her electricity bill.

Once he sold the house, he'd have at least half a million and then he would see how everyone looked at him.

He folded the receipt and put it in his wallet, eyeing the few pound coins in the palm of his hand and contemplating whether he should use it to pay for a taxi to take him to the pawn shop. He hadn't brought his car to town. It had truly been running on fumes and, until he had some cash, he had no chance of filling it up with petrol.

He didn't think the three-pound coins and the fifty-pence piece was enough for a taxi, so he was forced to walk.

The pawn shop was about a half mile from the bank and, like most establishments where the patrons were down on their luck – patrons who preferred not to be goggled at when they entered the shop – was hidden out of sight behind a large department store.

It wasn't his first visit to that particular shop, and Richard was well acquainted with the owner. To date, he had pawned the wristwatch that had been a gift from Vanessa following the birth of their son, a gold tie pin that had been one of many birthday gifts from her, and an antique snuff box he'd admired in a shop window in Venice and had later received as a Christmas present.

He'd always meant to buy them back, but time was fast running out on all three items and now, to add insult to injury, he was adding to the pawnbroker's stock by offering his wedding ring just so he could put petrol in his car and have some pocket money until the cheque cleared.

When he pushed through the door and stood in front of the counter, he had the good grace to feel embarrassed. Feeling embarrassed made him really despise his wife. She was the reason he was there, scrabbling for pennies, and she was the reason that he didn't feel too good about himself. It was all her fucking fault.

The counter was high, and the shop owner stood behind a Perspex screen. Even before Covid – when every sneeze and every cough seemed like a death sentence to the person standing opposite – the pawn shop already had that screen. Richard didn't think that it was bullet-proof and believed that it wouldn't be worth shit when it came to protecting anyone. If he'd been so inclined, he knew that it would take mere seconds to get behind it and reach the cash register with all that lovely money inside.

When he caught himself actually contemplating robbing the place, it frightened him. That's how low Vanessa had brought him. She had a lot to answer for.

'Just a week left on the wristwatch,' the shop owner said, bringing Richard's mind snapping back to why he was there. 'I have a buyer already lined up, so fair warning, Mister Parker – if you want it back, you had better make me an offer for it pretty soon.'

'Oh? How much was the buyer offering?'

'Now, that would be telling, wouldn't it? If you don't mind, I'll keep that information to myself.'

'Suit yourself.' Richard shrugged. 'I'm not interested in retrieving the watch, so do what you want with it, but – since it sounds as if you're set to make a healthy profit on it – how about giving me a good deal on this ring?'

Just as he reached into his pocket to pull out the ring, a loud groan seemed to escape from the wall behind the counter. It was such a strange sound, so unexpected, that it made the hairs on Richard's neck prickle.

He looked up, spooked. 'What was that?' he asked.

'What was what?' The man followed Richard's gaze and looked behind him.

'Didn't you hear it?'

'Um...?'

'That groaning sound?' He suddenly jumped in his skin. 'There it goes again.' He had an immediate impression of something almost alien in the sound. 'What is that?'

The man cocked his head, listened, and then shrugged. 'Maybe it's the pipes. This is an old building. There's always one weird noise or another rattling the walls.'

Richard narrowed his eyes. 'It doesn't sound like any pipes I've ever heard.'

'Can't say that I noticed anything out of the ordinary. Maybe I'm just used to the creaks of the old place?'

Richard felt a faint vibration below his feet. It was as if a huge animal had expelled a fierce growl under the floorboards. He made a little cry of alarm and stepped swiftly to the side, nearer to the door. He had an irrational feeling that he might have to flee the shop.

The man cocked an eyebrow and looked at him in puzzlement. 'Are you okay, buddy? You need a drink of water, or something?'

'No... no.' He peered at the floor and sighed with relief when the vibration suddenly ceased. 'I'm okay.'

'Glad to hear it. I was worried about you for a minute.' His expression showed that he was still a little worried. 'I've not seen someone spooked like that since the day my dear old granny stripped off, jack-naked, right outside the shop. Dementia... poor old duck. She scared some schoolkids half to death.'

'You don't say?' Richard moved tentatively back towards the counter. 'Must have been some sight.'

'You can say that again. Now, you mentioned something about a ring? You want to show it to me?'

'Sure, thing but, mind you, it's worth a few quid.' He reached into his pocket and drew it out. 'I'm expecting a good deal on it.'

From his position behind the Perspex screen, the man carefully eyed the ring in the palm of Richard's hand, and said, 'Not many folks care for second hand wedding rings. They think they bring bad luck.'

'Just as well I'm pawning it instead of selling it then, isn't it? I don't want you melting it down for its scrap weight.'

'Sentimental value, huh?'

'I wouldn't go as far as to say that.' Richard handed the ring over. 'I just think that it's worth keeping.'

'Uh, huh?' He examined the hallmark, nodded to himself, and then placed the ring on a small set of digital scales.

Richard eyed him closely, willing him to offer at least two hundred for it.

Just as he was about to hear the offer, a strong gust of wind blew the door open. As it slammed back against the wall, the sound it made was like a gunshot. Such was his fright, Richard almost pissed himself.

The wind got behind the screen and papers flapped and swirled up from the counter to spin low off the ceiling. Richard feared that he would be blown off his feet and, as the shop owner made feeble efforts to grab the papers, he pressed himself up tight against a wall. After a count of three, he pushed forward and grappled with the door until he was able to force it closed.

Once all was still, the man said, by means of an explanation, 'We catch the draughts here, but that was one hell of a big blow, wasn't it?'

'I'll say,' Richard walked back towards him, flattening his hair with an unsteady hand. 'Now, what will you give me for the...' His eyes widened. 'Where is it?'

'Where's what?'

'The ring?'

The man searched the scales and then the counter. 'You must've put it back in your pocket.'

'How could I have done that? There's a monster of a screen between us.'

'Okay, but check your pockets, just in case.'

Richard patted both trouser pockets, then searched those in his jacket.

'Not there?'

Richard shook his head. 'Look on the floor behind the counter.' Although he knew it would be a waste of time, because of the screen, he added, 'I'll search around my feet.'

Despite an extensive search, neither of them found the ring.

'Now, don't you go thinking that I lifted it,' the shop owner said, pulling himself up to his full height and bristling. 'I'm no thief.'

Richard bristled right back at him. 'Well, it didn't just evaporate into thin air, did it?' He frowned. Truth be told, he didn't quite know what to think. The man had played more than fair with him in the past, and he couldn't see him stealing a ring that was worth only a few hundred pounds. The thing was, he was now in a bind. Without the money from pawning it, apart from a few measly pounds, he was totally skint.

'I'm sure it'll turn up,' the man put in. 'As you said... it didn't just disappear.'

'I suppose so,' Richard relented, visibly sagging. 'You mentioned that you had someone interested in buying the watch?'

'Maybe. Why?'

'I just wondered... well, how about you splitting the profit with me? You didn't give me much for it, and I know how much it's worth.'

'That's not how it works, Mister Parker, and you know it.' He thought a moment, then said, 'I tell you what, if you let the snuff box go as well, I'll give you one hundred crisp new notes. How does that sound?'

'It sounds like you're trying to rip me off. Make it one-twenty and you have a deal.'

'Done.' He opened the cash register and handed the money over. 'And don't you worry about the ring. I'll find it. Come back tomorrow and there will be another two hundred waiting for you to collect.'

Richard had a feeling that he would never see that two-hundred pounds. He had a strange premonition that the ring would never allow itself to be pawned. He shook the thought off, gave the man a thin smile, and hastily left the shop.

Nineteen

'Housekeeping!' The voice was high and thin, almost world-weary. 'Anyone here?'

The door swung open and Anita, bleary-eyed and disorientated, lifted her head from the pillow to stare at the woman carrying a vacuum cleaner and pushing her way into the room.

Anita had no idea where she was. Her brain seemed stuffed with cotton wool and her head thumped cruelly.

'You should be long gone,' the cleaner said, putting a hand on her hip and glowering impatiently. 'You were supposed to vacate the room by ten.'

Anita grunted and prised open an eye. 'What time is it?'

'Time you weren't here. It's gone twelve.'

'In the afternoon?' Anita hauled herself up from the pillows. 'It can't be that late.'

'I can assure you...'

'Yeah, yeah... Okay.'

Anita shifted her heavy bulk across the bed and draped her feet over the edge. She looked confused. 'Remind me where I am.'

The cleaner looked as if she wasn't quite sure that she'd heard correctly. 'Where you are?' Her Scottish accent was anything but lilting and it grated on Anita's raw nerves. 'Are you telling me that you don't know?'

'I wouldn't be asking if I did.'

'Edinburgh.'

'Oh, that's right. I remember now.'

'Look, I'm sorry, but I have to get the room ready, so...'

The events of the previous night went crashing across Anita's brain. The flies... the thing in the wardrobe. Her eyes jerked to the side, searching.

'Are you okay?' The cleaner placed the vacuum on the floor and stepped closer to the bed. 'Do you need a doctor?'

'No... No, I'm all right. Just give me a minute, will you?'

'I'm really in a bit of a rush.'

'I'm only asking for a minute. Isn't there another room you could be cleaning?'

'This is the last one on this floor.'

'Go and have a fag break then.'

There must have been something in Anita's expression that gave the cleaner pause for thought because, after a moment, she turned and left, closing the door quietly behind her.

Anita hunched her shoulders and looked nervously around the room. It was as if she was expecting an ariel assault at any moment, but the air was still and quiet and nothing darted across her periphery.

She eyed the empty miniature bottles of alcohol on the dressing table, swallowed back hard on a dry mouth, and wondered if she was sober enough for the drive back to London. She'd hit the drink pretty hard the night before and either a horrible nightmare or a period of vivid hallucinations had been the outcome of imbibing a little too much.

But it had all seemed so real, and she couldn't convince herself that she hadn't actually lived through it. She even thought she could still taste the fetid evidence of those flies in her mouth.

Her eyes flicked across the carpet, moved towards the windowsill, searching for dead flies, and she was shocked not to see a single one. There should have been at least one, maybe a couple, and it beggared belief that there weren't any.

'Fucking hell,' she spluttered out loud, pushing herself up from the bed and then staggering to the mirror. 'That was some trip you had, old girl.'

Her reflection wasn't pretty, but it never was. She looked a little green around the gills, and it was obvious that she needed to take a shower. She hoped she would be given the time to make herself presentable before she was turned out on her ear.

She felt such a fool but that would've been nothing compared to how she would have felt if she'd made a fuss to the hotel management. How would she have explained disappearing flies and... and, what...? *What was that she'd seen in the wardrobe?*

Shivering, as if someone had walked over her grave, she hung *a Do Not Disturb* sign on the handle outside the door, then closed and double locked it, before stripping off and stepping under the shower. She turned it as hot as she could stand and, ten minutes later, still standing under the rejuvenating cascade, she ignored the incessant knocking on the door.

The would probably charge her extra – probably as much as another full day – but that was the least of her worries. The trip back was what worried her most – that and the flies.

ANITA SANDERSON (AS)
Sample taken from PART One of recorded interview
Date: 22 January 2022
Duration: 90 minutes
Location: Wood Street Police Station, City of London
No of pages: 16 (total number of sample pages: 6)
Conducted by officers from the London Metropolitan Police
All police officer identifiers have been redacted (Section 38 (1) (A)

Police: Thank you for making the time to see us, Ms Sanderson. I am Detective Sergeant (redacted), and my colleague is Detective Constable (redacted). As you know, we are looking into the disappearance of Vanessa Parker and I want to say, straight off the bat, that you aren't, at this point, a person of interest in that disappearance. I must add, though, that that position might change. Do you understand?

AS: I do.

Police: We are making a digital recording of this interview and you are quite at liberty to have a solicitor present throughout its duration.

AS: Is that necessary? I mean... should I call my solicitor?

Police: That's entirely up to you. You're not being interviewed under caution. Although we are recording this interview, it is, at this stage, informal, and nothing said can be used against you in a court of law.

AS: What's the difference between an informal interview and one done under caution?

Police: If we believe that there are grounds to suspect that you have committed a criminal offence, then we would proceed with the interview under caution and your rights would be made clear to you. This wouldn't mean that we believed that you were guilty of anything or that we would automatically prosecute you. It would simply mean that the evidence we'd obtained to date indicated that you might be involved in an offence, and we would hope that you would be able to assist with our enquiries. An interview under caution would give you the opportunity to provide an explanation of the events, and, if we found any evidence during the interview that you had committed an offence, you might be prosecuted.

AS: I see.

Police: We are at a very early stage in our enquiries, and we're grateful that you provided us with Ms. Parker's journal. Today's interview is merely to check all the background stuff and to see what we can determine from the entries in that journal. You seem best placed to help us with that.

AS: I'm only too pleased to help, and I'll forgo a solicitor for the moment.

Police: Okay... kicking straight off with something we're all anxious to know the answer to. How did you happen to find yourself in Vanessa Parker's house, going through her things, and ultimately stumbling across her journal?

AS: She told me to. I mean... she said that if anything happened to her, I should find her journal. I had no clue that she kept one and was surprised to realise that she meant a handwritten one rather than one done on a file on her laptop. I remember asking her if she was worried that something was going to happen to her, and she said... it already had.

Police: Did you know what she meant by that?

AS: Not at the time, and I can't say that I was unduly concerned. Vanessa had a habit of saying all sorts. It wasn't unusual for her to be a little paranoid, and I'd learned to take everything she said with a pinch of salt.

Police: But there was a time when you became concerned?

AS: Yes, but not until she seemed to go off the radar... not answering my calls or messages. She'd just completed the final draft of her latest novel and her going all silent on me was a tad inconvenient.

Police: You were inconvenienced but not worried at that point?

AS: Not until quite a bit of time had passed and I hadn't heard back from her.

Police: You had a key to her house?

AS: Yes, for emergencies.

Police: Did anyone else have a key?

AS: Richard, of course, and Vanessa used to have a cleaner. She may have given her one.

Police: Do you have a name?

AS: For the cleaner? Sorry... I haven't got a clue.

Police: Was she hired through an agency?

AS: Again... not a clue.

Police: You said – used to have a cleaner?

AS: She let her go some weeks ago. I think she struggled to pay her.

Police: You were aware of her financial difficulties?

AS: Well aware.

Police: She confided in you?

AS: No, not really, but it was obvious that she was struggling. She gave most of what she earned to Richard, and her royalties were quickly diminishing, so it didn't take a genius to work out how the land lay in that regard.

Police: But I'm guessing that her latest novel would've brought her in a few bob?

AS: Not for a while. She'd already had the advance and wouldn't earn anything until that was recovered.

Police: Okay, let's get back to the journal. Did you read all of the entries before handing it in to us?

AS: Most of them. I would've read them all, but I was anxious to hand it in to you and to report her missing.

Police: Were you surprised that her husband hadn't been the one to file the missing person's report?

AS: Not in the least bit surprised.

Police: Why was that?

AS: Me not being surprised? He didn't give a shit, that's why.

Police: Strong words.

AS: But true. The only person that Richard cares about is Richard.

Police: You don't like him?

AS: Never have.

Police: So, the journal... the bits that you read... what did you make of them?

AS: They were a bit whacky, but...

Police: But?

AS: You're going to think that I'm a sandwich short of a picnic.

Police: There's nothing you can tell us that we haven't heard before, Ms Sanderson. We hear all sorts in this job.

AS: That's as may be, but from someone like me? Have you ever heard a sensible, intelligent, and stone-cold sober person tell you that they believed in demons... that they believed everything they'd read in that journal? (inaudible)

AS: (inaudible)

Police: Miss Sanderson? Miss Sanderson, are you all right?

AS: (inaudible)

Police: What's happening? Are you all right, Ms Sanderson? Miss Sanderson, can you hear me? Quick... help me get her on the floor and get an ambulance.

OUTSIDE THE DOOR, ANITA heard raised voices. With the huge white towel barely covering her nakedness, she checked that the door was double-locked and continued to ignore the knocking.

She recognised one of the voices – the cleaner's – and she surmised that the other voice was the manager. She supposed that, at some point pretty soon, she would have to face them.

It was the low growl from behind the wardrobe door, and not the incessant heckling from the corridor, that got her moving with haste. Luckily, all of her belongings were either strewn across the floor, on the bed, or the wooden contraption that pretended to be a dressing-table. There was no way she was about to investigate the source of the growl, and, in less than ten minutes, she was dressed, packed, and confronting the hotel manager.

The drive back to London was hellish. She kept ten miles an hour below the speed limit, terrified that she would be pulled over for speeding and discovered to be still half drunk, and – what with the slow crawl through numerous roadworks – it took her the best part of twelve hours to get home.

Twenty

Seventy-five-thousand-words. Two blinks later and Vanessa saw the word count miraculously rise to a few hundred words short of the one hundred thousand mark.

The increased count had simply appeared on the screen. Out of nowhere and her first thought was that it must be a mistake, that her laptop was playing up but, when she scrolled through the whole file, she saw that it was true. The word count was accurate, and the book was finished.

Jesus, Mary, and Joseph, she thought, leaning back in her seat, and scrubbing at her eyes with her knuckles. *What the fuck is going on?*

She hoped that an explanation would come to her, would resonate within her – an explanation that would have a ring of something other than a supernatural event.

It was the first time that she'd considered the supernatural. After everything that had gone on, she realised that she should have contemplated that possibility. It was far-fetched, but maybe not as far-fetched as imagining that she was slowly going off her rocker, or that someone was out to get her.

People *did* believe in such things, even clever, sophisticated people. Jesus, even *she* had toyed with a Ouija board.

Was that it? Had she summoned some demon instead of her Simon?

She shook her head. No. there had to be a more rational explanation.

The cursor on the screen blinked at her. There was only one thing to do.

Using the mouse, she directed the cursor and saved the manuscript, then – before she changed her mind – she emailed a copy to Anita.

Although she knew that she hadn't finished it – although she realised that she wasn't that far gone to imagine that she had – it didn't stop her from sending it to Anita. It was her way of getting rid of it, to distance herself from it, and to draw a line under the whole thing. It was done. She could wash her hands of it.

Immediately on pressing *send*, her mobile pinged.

She opened the message.

Good girl. I'm so proud of you, love Zara.

Zara? Who the...?

Something clicked. She was the woman from the Facebook Group.

EXTRACT FROM THE JOURNAL of author Vanessa Parker, discovered by her literary agent, Anita Sanderson.

There are so many things in life that we take for granted... the air we breathe, the break of dawn, and the warmth of sunlight on our skin. Most of us never give those things a second thought. We might worry about having no money, but we never worry about having no air, or no sunlight. We might worry about dying, or losing someone we love, but how often do we worry about evil being present in our own homes? And, by evil, I mean pure, unadulterated malevolence – the sort of malicious presence that frightens you so much that it has you pissing yourself?

I'll bet, never – not unless you're me.

Don't ask me why I didn't tell anyone. I guess it took me far too long to accept what was happening and, by then, it was too late. If things had been different with Richard, then perhaps I wouldn't have minded looking like such a complete lunatic in his eyes but, if I'd told him, it would've been all the excuse he needed to have me locked up in the nearest crazy house. And can you imagine the glee on Fiona's face? I can. She would lap it up, the bitch.

I don't know what's going to happen to me. All I know is that I'm scared.

I think that I've always been scared. As a child, I was scared for my mother – not BY my mother but FOR my mother. I was scared that she would hurt herself, would die, would do something so crazy that she would be locked up. As an adult, I was mostly scared of failure – failure as a writer, as a wife, as a mother, and as a friend. For years, I've been terrified to go out my own front door. I can't recall a time when I wasn't scared, but all that fear pales in comparison to how I'm feeling now. THIS fear is all consuming.

I have to focus all of my wits on getting myself out of this, but what is THIS? Is it a conspiracy to send me loopy? Is it the degeneration of my brain? Is it something otherworldly? I don't know what would be worse – my husband doing his level best to take my sanity and everything that I own, dementia and psychosis rendering me a vegetable, or some entity putting me through a torturous experience for its own ends.

I haven't found the courage to strike back... not yet. How is it possible to strike at something you can't see or don't understand?

I have to wait until I understand and then I'll do something about it.

I sent the finished book off to Anita today. I think she's going to love it. What's not to love? It's well written, perfectly formatted, and without a single error.

Trouble is... I'm sure I didn't write it. Oh, I may have tapped out a few thousand words... maybe as many as sixty or seventy thousand of them (though, God knows how) but I sure as hell didn't create very many of them. It's not my story on the pages. They're not my characters.

Something possessed me, forced me to write what IT wanted, then It finished it off without my help.

Okay... Okay... Okay... as mad as that sounds, it's true. Don't ask me why I know it to be true, I just do.

Suffice it to say, I wish I'd never agreed to do another book. I wish I'd cut my losses and settled down to be an average person, living an average life, with no pressure to live up to something I no longer am. There are plenty of things worse than being broke. I've been broke before and survived it. I would've lost Richard, of course. It's only the money... or the thought of my money... that keeps him coming back. Without it, I won't see him for dust.

I've been sitting counting my mistakes. Richard was my biggest. I should never have married him. It would've meant never having Simon, but my child was born into a world of pain, and I could have saved him from that. Oh God, how I wish I could have saved him... my precious boy.

Another big mistake was joining the Facebook group. It brought Zara to me. Zara is...

I'm not sure what she is. She says that she's my friend... my special friend... but that's bullshit.

Why do I always attract weirdos? In school there was this girl who always followed me *around like a pet dog. No one liked her. Everyone avoided her and not only because she had a strange way of looking at you. I can't remember her name, but I remember how she made me feel every time I turned around and saw her at my back.*

Creepy ... that's what she was. Once, she told me that she loved me. Imagine being told by a fourteen-year-old crackpot that she loved you. At the time, my mum had been shipped off to hospital and I was living under the radar at home on my own. Social Services hadn't twigged, and I'd hoped to see the course out without being dragged off to foster care, or a children's home, but my creepy admirer very nearly ruined it for me.

Then, there was Jason... another weirdo if ever there was one. I guess you could call him my first boyfriend. He wasn't a proper boyfriend. We were both too young for all that serious stuff, but he wasn't too young to have de-

veloped that jealous, possessive streak that turns a perfectly normal person into an out and out nutter. Between him, my schoolgirl stalker, and my crazy mother, I don't have fond memories of my formative years.

Now, there's Zara. I didn't realise that, once you reply to a direct message, the person has a hold of your phone number. I can't remember messaging her, but I must have. Now, unless I change my number, she can text me, WhatsApp me, call me.

At least she doesn't know where I live.

GOOD GIRL. I'M SO PROUD *of you, love Zara.*
What, the fuck, did that mean?
Vanessa had the good sense not to text back, but that didn't stop the Zara person from bombarding her with more messages.
I'm your number one fan.
Oh, God... Annie Wilkes reincarnated. The Steven King novel, *Misery*, came immediately to Vanessa's mind. She shuddered.
Thank you for accepting me as your special friend.
When did she do that?
Your next book is going to fly off the shelves.
Did she mention the book on Facebook? She couldn't recall.

Her eyes swam out of focus, and she turned off the screen and put the phone down.

She'd had enough of Zara.

The phone immediately began to ping manically, and she was tempted to turn it off, but that would mean she wouldn't hear back from Anita. She was keen to discover what she thought of the manuscript... keen to find out if she'd sussed out that the work wasn't hers to own.

Her heartbeat quickened. How much trouble would she be in for trying to palm the book off as her own? Would she be forced to return the advance? *How, the fuck, could she afford to do that?*

A dull pain pulsed at both temples. She began to really ponder how it had been possible to have produced the novel. *Had she really been possessed by some demon she'd conjured up through the use of the Ouija board?*

Suddenly lightheaded, she thought she was about to pass out. She was exhausted, starving, and in desperate need of a drink. That desperation scared her far more than anything else. If she succumbed to the craving, she would lose her wits, and she had a feeling that she was going to need all of her faculties intact. Vodka would rob her of her senses. It would cause her paranoia to increase, and God only knew what she would end up hearing, or seeing, or doing.

She decided to go to bed. Really, she ought to have plucked up the courage... found the strength from somewhere... to leave the house – simply get in the car and go. Either that, or she could get in touch with the police again. She could say that she thought someone was in the house again. They would come back and maybe she would ask them to take her away... maybe to a hotel, or someplace else far away from whatever was lurking within the walls of her home.

Instead, she wrote a few notes in her journal and took herself upstairs.

The bedroom was as she'd left it. The door opened with the merest gentle push.

The bed was rumpled but inviting. She sank down into the mattress and dropped like a stone onto the pillows. She closed her eyes, but sleep eluded her.

It began to rain. She was aware of the sharp patter on the window, but it wasn't that that kept her from sleep. It was her mind. It wouldn't shut down. Flashes of the past whipped behind her closed lids, and memories – the sad and the happy ones – tormented her. Thoughts she recognised as paranoid messed with her painfully sought equilibrium and she was forced to get up and pace the floor in an attempt to further exhaust herself.

The rain got heavier. It battered against the glass. It was a distraction that she welcomed, and she walked over to peer out across the vast expanse of farmland beyond the border of the house. Looking out the window at a world that terrified her wasn't as uncomfortable as it had been. She was even tempted to open the window to the elements and stick her head out to feel the lash of rain on her face and got as far as pressing down on the latch before common sense prevailed. Cold water to the face was the last thing she needed, not if she wanted to eventually sleep.

Another message pinged on her phone. She recognised it as yet another Facebook notification, but thankfully not from Zara.

Why the hell not? she thought. She had nothing better to do – not until she felt ready to get back into bed.

She saw at least a couple of dozen notifications from the author group she'd recently joined. She read them with a growing sense of amazement. Praise had been thrown at her in almost sycophantic abandon. Once members of the group had realised she was one of them, they'd been quick to comment on their love for her books. Some begged advice. Some merely wanted to gush over her talent. Some wanted to know when her next book was due to be published.

She wasn't in the least tempted to reply to any of the comments. It was one thing to read what everyone had to say, but quite another to fully engage. She'd learned that lesson by having to suffer an invasion of her privacy by the Zara woman.

She turned away from the window and approached the bed once more. She was going to have to force herself to lie down and try to sleep. There was a great deal of shit about to hit the fan. Once Anita read the manuscript, she would have a lot of questions and, before long, she would have to answer them, and there was no way she would be in a fit state to do so... not without some shuteye.

But it wasn't any good. She couldn't sleep, not that in itself was surprising. Vanessa would have to be completely devoid of any anxiety, any fear, any macabre curiosity as to her situation, to be able to drift off into slumber.

The only thing that would help would be a couple of drinks... well, maybe a whole bottle... and, as the minutes ticked by, and she became increasingly restless, the desire grew.

The familiar thirst grew unbearable. She was sorely tempted to go downstairs and drink straight from the neck of the bottle. She saw herself sozzled and slobbering all over the place. She pictured herself snoring the sleep of the drunkard. She wondered how many functioning brain cells would be depleted by giving in to the incessant craving for alcohol. She wondered if she even cared.

Yes, you fucking care. Do you want to be at the mercy of that fucking vodka bottle... end up like your mother?

Although the thoughts were hers, it was as if an alien voice had spoken them in her ear. On hearing them, she actually lifted her head from the pillow and glanced to the side, looking for the owner of the voice.

Get a grip.

Those words sounded exactly like her own voice. She felt a modicum of relief. She really needed to get a tighter grip on her imagination.

There was nothing worse than trying to sleep and sleep eluding you. No matter how hard Vanessa tried to keep her eyes closed, and no matter what effort she put into relaxing, every nerve in her body jerked and her brain remained wide awake. Counting sheep did no good. Imagining herself lying on a deserted beach just made her feel anxious. Counting backwards from one hundred had her stumbling over the numbers. After an hour of struggle, she gave up. There was no point in beating a dead horse.

Downstairs, she made straight for the kitchen. Halfway along the hall, she almost jumped out of her skin when a loud knock on the door startled her. Turning, she saw a shadow behind the glass. It was much too small an image to be either Richard or Anita and her first thought was to ignore whoever it was, knowing they would probably knock another couple of times, then give up and leave.

The person on the other side of the door called out, 'Vanessa.' It was muffled but easily understood yet wasn't familiar to her.

She wasn't expecting anyone. She never expected anyone. Visitors were few and far between and, in the past few months, had consisted of – in addition to Richard and Anita – the cleaner, the police, the man who wanted to read the gas meter, and a gaggle of Jehovah's Witnesses. The person at the door knew her name. That, in itself, was weird, particularly as the voice wasn't known to her. Hearing her name being called out should have reassured her, but it had the opposite effect. It put her immediately on her guard.

She took a couple of tentative steps back, still determined on ignoring the visitor. She had no business to conduct with anyone and, therefore, no one had any business being at her door.

She would wait them out.

But... but... it was better not to be alone, even if it meant merely a few minutes talking to someone on the doorstep. Before she could make for the door, the voice said, 'I can see you standing there. It's wet out here. Please let me in.'

A bizarre thought zipped across her mind. What if it was a vampire? Vampires had to be invited in.

Don't be so fucking stupid.

She marched to the door, shoulders back, arms pumping at her sides, and stopped a little short. Pushing her head forward, she said, 'Who is it? What do you want?'

'To meet you. To talk. Please... I'm getting soaked out here.'

'You haven't said who you are.'

There was a short silence, then, 'Gosh, Vanessa, don't you know who I am?' She sounded almost peeved. 'I'm your biggest fan, your special friend.'

'What? Who?' Then it struck her. *Zara!* 'How did you know where I lived?' Her voice came out in a soft squeak.

'Haven't you heard of Google?' Again, with the peeved tone. 'Are you going to open the door, or what?'

'Sorry.' *She wasn't sorry.* 'I don't meet fans at my home. You'll have to leave. I'm busy.'

'Busy?'

'Yeah.' Vanessa held her breath.

'Doing what? You've finished your book.'

Her voice cracked. 'How... how did you know that?'

The sound of the rain increased, and Vanessa didn't catch Zara's reply. When she finally heard her words above the battering of the rain, Zara's voice had grown high-pitched and breathy.

'You're not busy, Vanessa... not really. You can spare a few moments to autograph the copies I have of all your wonderful books. I've got copies of them all... every last one of them.'

Vanessa was still trying to digest the fact that Zara knew about the completion of the novel. It was information that only Anita knew.

'No. I'm sorry,' she said, the words quivering at the edges. 'Please leave.'

Suddenly, the shadow behind the glass disappeared. Vanessa didn't hear any footsteps on the gravel but felt sure that Zara had heeded her words and left. Huffing in a breath, she turned, relieved.

Her breath lodged in the back of her throat. Her eyes grew as wide as saucers. There, right in front of her, standing not three feet away, was the figure of a small, almost elfin-like woman.

Every bit of blood in vanessa's body drained to the soles of her feet. Her knees buckled as she lurched backwards, causing the figure before her to leap forward, grab her with a surprisingly strong grip, and save her from what would've been a painful tumble.

A huge smile split the woman's face. 'Hello, Vanessa,' she said. 'I'm Zara, pleased to meet you.'

Twenty-One

Richard hesitated at the bottom of the stairs. He could hear Fiona moving about but he made no attempt to call up to her to let her know that he was home. He was still a little shaken up by the events at the pawnshop. Something about the strange noises, the vibration under his feet, and the sudden blast of wind – not to mention the sudden loss of his wedding ring – had left him feeling more than a little spooked. He certainly wasn't looking forward to a return visit and, if it hadn't been for his desperate need of the money the ring would bring him, he would've given it a full swerve.

'Is that you?'

He tilted his head back at the sound of Fiona's voice. 'Yeah. I'm back.'

'Put the kettle on, will you?'

He was relieved to hear none of the earlier rancour in her voice. He really wasn't in the mood for any further hostilities. All he wanted was a cup of coffee and a quiet moment to think.

Before walking through to the kitchen, he checked his phone. Still nothing from Vanessa. Her continued silence was disconcerting. He must really have pissed her off. He would have to go round, find out what was up, and try to smooth her ruffled feathers. But that would cause yet another argument with Fiona and that was the last thing he wanted.

One day, he told himself, he would rid himself of both of them. There was certainly something to say for a string of one-night stands and he could see himself going through the rest of his life meeting a different woman every night and never again getting entangled.

Women were just too much like hard work.

He wasn't sure what drew his eyes to the far end of the room. He thought it might've been the sun shining through the window above the sink and glinting on something lying on the worktop next to the kettle.

Then, he blinked and tried to deny what his eyes were telling him.

It must be a different ring, he said beneath his breath. *My ring is…*

He walked forward, further into the room, and approached the offending item. He reached out and picked it up. It *was* his wedding ring.

He glanced towards the ceiling, trying to work out if Fiona was still upstairs or if she was on her way down, expecting her coffee to be ready.

He couldn't be caught with the ring in his hand. She wouldn't understand. She hated any reminder that he was still married. He would have to explain things but how could he explain what he didn't understand?

He turned the ring over in his hand. It felt warm where the sun streaming through the window had kissed it. It also felt…

Wrong.

It seemed to throb in the palm of his hand, as if it was a living, breathing thing.

'What have you got there?'

'Jesus.' Startled, he swung around to face the door.

Fiona stood there, her gaze glued to his clenched fist, her hands on her hips.

Richard went immediately on the attack. 'Fuck's sake, Fiona, you almost made me shit myself. Did you have to creep up on me like that? You're always creeping about the place. It really pisses me off.'

He surreptitiously slipped the ring into his trouser pocket and immediately felt heat radiating down his leg.

He knew that he looked unhinged. His eyes were bugging out of his head, and he was sure that he was as white as a sheet. Rubbing absently down the length of his thigh, he turned back to stare out of the window, preparing himself for the barrage of questions he was sure that Fiona was just about to launch his way.

But, at his back, Fiona remained silent. That silence was even worse than the questions would've been. Fiona's silences were legendary and never boded well.

Finally, he heard her say, 'I saw it, Richard. I saw you looking at it.'

'You saw me looking at what?' He kept his back to her. 'I don't know what you're talking about.'

'The ring, Richard. Your fucking wedding ring... that's what.'

'Oh, that?' He shrugged. 'So what? What's the big deal?'

'Look at me when you're talking to me. Don't be so bloody ignorant.'

He huffed in a breath, turned, and put on his best game face. He forced a smile but imagined that it made him look like something deranged.

'Why are you wearing it?'

'What?' He glanced down at his hand, saw the gold band on his ring finger, and staggered back in fright.

'I... I...' He couldn't form a sentence. The words wouldn't come. He was so shocked that he believed he might pass out in a faint. He literally tingled with astonishment. The ring shouldn't be on his finger. It shouldn't be in the house. It was lost... on the floor somewhere back at the pawn shop.

What the fuck was it doing on his finger? What the hell was going on?

'Is all that talk about a divorce just some bullshit you've been feeding me to keep me sweet?'

'No... No... I...' His head swung from side to side in denial.

'At least be honest with me. I deserve that, at least.'

He felt a pulse of dread thunder in his ears. His heart was battering all the way to his temples. He couldn't concentrate to listen to Fiona's tirade, because all he could think about was that the ring shouldn't be on his finger.

He tried to screw it off.

'No point in taking it off now,' Fiona sniped, her eyes like flint. 'Don't do it on my account. Wear the fucking thing and see if I care.'

It was obvious, even to Richard in his state of utter bewilderment, that she really *did* care, but he wanted the ring gone from his finger for his own sake and not for hers.

'I didn't put it there. I didn't... I didn't...'

She rolled her eyes. 'Oh, spare me the bullcrap.'

'No. No. I was going to sell it. I lost it at the pawn shop. You have to believe me.' Even to his own ears, he sounded crazy, but he carried on, regardless. 'It just turned up. Somehow...'

'Jesus, Richard, are you for real?' She stepped forward, placed her two hands on his chest, and pushed him back on his heels. 'Instead of being honest with me, you give me some ludicrous story?' She gave him another push. 'Well, fuck you. I'm not putting up with this shit.'

Richard carried on twisting and pulling at the ring in an attempt to work it over his rapidly swelling knuckle.

He said nothing to prevent her storming from the kitchen, merely followed her departure with half-crazed eyes.

His whole finger was now beginning to swell. He would have to use some washing up liquid to lubricate it and prise it off.

Ten minutes, and copious amount of washing up liquid later, and still the ring wouldn't budge.

It had never been a tight fit. In fact, over the years, it had often slipped off his finger. He'd lost count of the number of times he'd nearly lost it, so there was no logical reason for it getting stuck. Okay, his finger had swollen after all the pulling and twisting, but that didn't explain why it had got stuck in the first place.

He gave up and ran his whole hand under the cold-water tap. Getting the swelling down now seemed to be his only option. The knot in his chest tightened with every breath. His finger and his head throbbed, and he felt sick. He dropped his chin and gnawed on his lip, all the while turning his brain inside and out in an attempt to try and understand his situation.

'Here... Let me try.'

He jerked back from the sink. He hadn't heard Fiona re-enter the kitchen.

'It's pretty stuck,' he said.

'I'll see what I can do but don't think that means you're off the hook.'

'I didn't put myself *on the hook*, Fiona. I know you don't believe me, but I didn't lie to you. I really did lose the ring back at the pawn shop.'

'Well, you're either raving bonkers, or you still think I'm an idiot.' She made a grab for his hand. 'I hope this hurts.'

He yelped then gritted his teeth as she repeated the twisting and pulling motion he'd spent ages trying to perfect.

'That won't work,' he said through teeth so clenched he thought they'd splinter. 'Don't you think I fucking tried that?'

'Well, now it's my turn. Hold still and stop being such a baby.'

Yanking his hand free of her ferocious grip, he backed away. 'Just leave it. I need to let the swelling go down.'

'*I need to let the swelling go down*,' she mimicked cruelly. 'How about I take a hacksaw to it?'

'Very funny.' He cradled his hand against his chest. 'Haven't you got a cauldron to stir, some bats to eviscerate?'

'Now who thinks he's being funny?'

'Do you blame me? You've just threatened to saw my finger off.'

'The ring, you stupid man. I meant the ring.'

'I'm not risking it. Knowing you, you'd saw all the way to the bone.'

Amazingly, Fiona let out a loud guffaw. She had begun to see the funny side. She said, 'Vanessa probably cursed that ring and that's why it's stuck on your stupid finger. It's one way of keeping her claim on you.'

Richard surprised himself by not immediately swatting that idea away. Then, he shook his head. It was too ridiculous to even contemplate.

'Give me your hand again.'

He shook his head once more and backed further away.

'Trust me,' she said, reaching out and gently taking his hand in hers. For a moment, she held his gaze and then pulled the ring finger into her mouth.

'That must taste horrible,' he said. 'I used a lot of washing up liquid.'

She nodded and began to suck.

Normally, having her mouth anywhere on his body would've been a giant turn on, but all he felt was the persistent stab of apprehension and fear. Richard was unaccustomed to fear or any form of anxiety. Like most people with a narcissistic personality, he was much too sure of everything to be affected by a nervous disposition. He left that sort of thing to the likes of his neurotic wife, but at that moment, there was no emotional defence mechanism that could shift his sense of growing dread.

His finger slithered in and out of Fiona's mouth and, in any other circumstance, it would've been an extremely erotic moment. When he heard a gentle moan escape from her softly sucking lips, he suddenly realised that she found the whole situation highly sexual as he did.

My God, he thought, *we're both horny.*

Despite his angst, he felt himself harden. Fiona must have sensed his arousal and she worked one of her hands down to his crotch and squeezed.

He gasped. He wanted to do her right there, on the kitchen floor, and he wanted to do her hard. He wanted to punish her for doubting his story about the ring and he wanted her begging him to stop.

Jesus, he had never felt so turned on. She kept up the slow, erotic sucking movement, all the while squeezing his cock through his trousers. Her moans grew louder, and Richard had to bite down on his lip to stop himself from letting out a groan.

Suddenly, Fiona reared back. His finger popped out of her mouth with a plop. It took a moment for him to realise that she was choking.

'What the hell, Fiona?'

He made a grab for her shoulders and immediately noticed that the ring was gone. It was no longer on his finger.

Shaking her head violently, and clawing at her throat, Fiona's state of high panic wasn't helping, and Richard didn't know what to do. When it came to a medical emergency, he was clueless.

Afterwards – when the crisis was over, and Fiona had lived to see another day – Richard would wonder if he'd imagined the rumble of laughter that had filled his ears. In saner moments, he would put the sound down to the mad rush of panicked blood, but in moments when other things happened to catch him unawares, he would find that his imagination took him to places he really didn't want to find himself.

Twenty-two

Vanessa felt the effects of her heart stopping. It only lasted a few seconds, but it was enough to have her swaying on her feet, almost crashing down again, and reaching out for something to grab – anything to take a hold of but Zara.

Her whole world tilted on its axis and there was black behind her eyes. *It was her. It was Zara. She was in her fucking house.*

'Hey, steady on there, Vanessa.'

The hand on her arm was ice cold, the fingers all bone and no flesh.

'There's no need to be a scaredy cat. Buck up, girl.'

Buck up girl... buck up girl... the words came as if from a great distance.

She eased herself against the wall, tentatively pulling free from Zara's grip. The wall felt solid at her back, but it meant she had no way to escape. Someone had once told her to always sit facing a door but to never trap yourself against a wall. *Did someone tell her that or was it something she'd written in one of her books?* She took a moment to puzzle over it, the puzzlement making a grand excuse to avoid the situation unfolding in front of her.

She drew a shallow breath and marshalled her thoughts. Zara's presence suggested some sort of climax to all the shit that had been happening. The fact that she had somehow materialised straight through a locked door, not to mention her unexpected knowledge about the completed novel, was certainly suggestive of a climax.

'You're scared,' Zara said. 'Really, there's no need to be.'

Zara was a diminutive woman, so in normal circumstances a grown woman at least a foot taller than her, ought not to be scared. There was nothing about her appearance that suggested danger. She stood in a puddle of rainwater, her hair hanging in wet strands to her slim shoulders and smiling benignly up at her.

But those weren't normal circumstances and Vanessa had no doubt that she had every reason to be terrified.

'Who are you?' The words came out in a near whisper. 'What are you doing here?'

'I told you... I'm Zara.'

Vanessa wondered why she wasn't screaming for her to get out of her house. Through the layers of confusion – and, yes, fear – she wondered why she hadn't grabbed her by the scruff of the neck and bodily ejected her back through the door? Maybe because she hadn't entered through the door in the first place?

'Look, what the fuck is going on?' she managed to choke out. 'What are you doing here, and don't tell me that it's to get some books autographed. I know bullshit when I smell it.' She refrained from addressing the elephant in the room... namely, how she simply appeared in the hallway. 'I don't know you. I don't want to know you,' she went on. 'So...'

'Friends visit friends, don't they?' Zara cocked a brow. 'It's not all that strange and really shouldn't be questioned. It's quite insulting, actually... you questioning me.' Her voice had lost its friendly tone. 'You're making me feel very unwelcome.'

'Well, I sure as hell don't want to make you feel unwelcome.' The sarcasm was laid on thick, Vanessa having grabbed back a little of her spunk. 'Perish the thought.'

Zara tutted, shook her head, causing rainwater to fly everywhere, and took a step closer. She said, 'You don't know what you've done, do you?'

'Done?'

'In bringing me here.'

'I didn't...'

'Oh, but you did, Vanessa, and a little gratitude for all I've done wouldn't go amiss.'

She wanted to ask what she meant, but dreaded the answer, so bit down on her tongue and said nothing.

'You're not ready. I can see that. It was remiss of me to visit so soon.' She dragged in an impatient sigh. 'No, you're definitely not ready. Pity, really.'

Vanessa's brows furrowed. 'Ready? Ready for what?'

'The truth, I suppose.'

'The truth about what?'

'Everything.' Her eyes sparked. 'I think you're going to be blown away by the truth.'

There was something patently ominous in Zara's words. They caused a cold finger of dread to brush down Vanessa's spine.

'Just tell me how you got in here. Have you been here before?'

Zara refrained from answering. A smile returned to her lips. It was the coldest, most terrifying smile that Vanessa had ever witnessed. It didn't reach her eyes and it hovered tauntingly on her beautiful face as a silence grew between them.

Vanessa soon realised that neither of her questions would receive a reply and, in the encroaching silence, another question popped into her almost paralysed brain. She asked it without taking a moment to consider what she would do if the answer turned out to be in the affirmative. She said, 'Did you have anything to do with the novel getting finished?'

This time, Zara answered. She said, 'Of course.'

Vanessa closed her eyes. She needed a minute to digest the admission, to understand what it meant... what it could *possibly* entail. When she opened her eyes once more, Zara was no longer in front of her.

She was gone.

The floor came up to meet her. She crashed to her knees, feeling no pain, and had to fight to prevent herself from passing out. Her only coherent thought was that it being a woman was worse than the bogeyman she'd already conjured up in her mind. That it was a female who'd been in her home, causing, havoc, tormenting her, was an ugly thing for Vanessa to accept and all the more frightening because women weren't supposed to do that sort of thing – not unless they were utterly deranged.

And she *was* the bogeyman. There was no doubt in her mind about that. It hadn't been Richard or Anita, and it hadn't been her mind playing tricks on her. It wasn't grief, or the booze, or even her mother's diseased genes.

It had been Zara.

What the actual fuck?

Get out... run... her mind screamed at her, only for an answering internal voice to immediately ridicule and squash any notion of escape. *You'll die out there*, it said. *You're too chicken shit to even try to save yourself.*

Nevertheless, she did get up and stumble to the door, and she did pull it open, intending to leave, and – although the outside seemed to rush in at her, taking the breath from her body – she did bravely keep it ajar long enough to at least give the appearance of meaning it.

The cold air nipped at her, but she barely felt it. Then she heard something that had her stomach roiling to her throat. It was a simple giggle, a girlish laugh, nothing immediately frightening, but it was so incongruous, so unexpected that a sudden terror paralysed her.

She was still in the house. She hadn't gone.

Still, she couldn't take that giant leap of faith and step over the threshold. As terrifying as the whole situation was, she had no choice but to move towards the danger and not away from it. She had no alternative. For her, the outside was simply unreachable. There was no sanctuary to be found beyond the confines of her home. She was trapped and there was nothing to be done about it.

The giggling echoed from the study. When it suddenly ceased, there were other sounds – unearthly, otherworldly sounds. They turned Vanessa's blood to ice and caused a low, keening to leak from her mouth. She didn't want to face what was in the study. She'd had enough. She wasn't built to face such things... things that, except for her imagination informing her writing, had no basis in reality.

Vanessa hovered between a fight or flight response and a complete state of catatonia. Her brain's indecision and its inability to choose between one or the other caused a misfire... a short in its circuitry... and finally, blessedly, she fainted.

THE DOOR STOOD OPEN. Night entered and bathed Vanessa in a heavy blanket of damp. Her body trembled beneath the weight of it. Hours had slipped by and there were no echoes of life remaining in the house beyond the steady rhythm of Vanessa's breathing. That steady rise and fall of her chest was the only evidence that a live person lay sprawled on the floor as opposed to a corpse.

The rain had ceased but the air remained sodden. The silence was deafening in its intensity. The house, the grounds, the very heavens seemed to wait, as if poised in anticipation of some marvellous, hideous, event.

An unseen force pushed at the door, and it slowly closed. The night was finally shut out.

A sigh. A flutter in the air, stirring Vanessa's hair and warming her cheeks.

She jerked into consciousness. At once the terror returned.

Eyes wide, mouth trembling, she peered into the gloom.

Twenty-three

It was late and Anita was absolutely shattered, but she had to see her. She had to hear with her own ears that the wonderful, magnificent, heart-stoppingly brilliant book was all Vanessa's own work.

Moments after arriving home, she'd booted up her laptop and seen the attachment on an email.

She hadn't meant to read the whole thing, just skim through the first few chapters to get a feel for it, expecting it to be crap and to then head for bed as soon as she'd drained a cup of hot chocolate, but she'd become completely engrossed and had ended up reading the whole thing.

Not only had Vanessa delivered the completely revised novel early, but she had also surpassed herself in the quality of the finished book. It was unlike anything Anita had ever read before, and – after five hours of being glued to her laptop screen – she had been left feeling completely dumbfounded because there wasn't a single error. The impossibility of such a thing – the delivery of a completely error-free manuscript – wasn't lost on her and, pairing that with the fact that the last draft was so awful, gave Anita significant pause for thought.

It would've been remiss of her not to run the whole thing through the plagiarism tool that she routinely used, particularly for new authors who thought it perfectly reasonable to steal the words of others, and that's exactly what she did.

It was the small hours of the morning when she climbed back into her car and headed for Vanessa's house. She'd considered ringing her to warn her that she was on her way but had the sense to realise that Vanessa would do her best to put her off. Well, she wasn't going to be put off and she would stand on her step, hammering on her door, until she was allowed inside.

For her own peace of mind, she had to know. She had to know by what miracle she'd managed – whilst drunk as a skunk most of the time – to pull off the book of the century.

There were no lights in any of the windows. Anita glanced at the clock on the dashboard. Five am. Of course, Vanessa would be in bed. It had been madness to drive all the way out there at such an ungodly hour. What had she been thinking?

ANITA SANDERSON (AS)

Sample taken from PART One (CONTINUED) of recorded interview

Date: 22 January 2022

Duration: 90 minutes (TOTAL)

Location: Wood Street Police Station, City of London

No of pages: 16 (total number of sample pages: 5)

Conducted by officers from the London Metropolitan Police

All police officer identifiers have been redacted (Section 38 (1) (A)

Police: For the recording, Ms Sanderson has agreed to continue with the interview and confirms no ill effects from her fainting fit. DS (redacted) and DC (redacted) are in attendance. Ms Sanderson, do you feel well enough? You're sure?

AS: I'm fine. I'm sure.

Police: Thank you. We'll continue where we left off.

AS: About me believing in demons? Are you sure that you really want to hear this?

Police: I want to hear why you decided that these so-called demons were relevant to Vanessa's disappearance... why you believed what she wrote in her journal.

AS: I don't want you thinking that I'm off my head.

Police: At this stage, what we think is irrelevant. It's what *you* think that we're most interested in.

AS: Well, don't say I didn't warn you.

Police: Just tell it as you see it. We'll draw our own conclusions.

AS: Okay. Where to begin? Probably when I got back from Edinburgh and went to see her.

Police: When was that?

AS: About two weeks ago. It was late... too late, really. I'd got back around ten at night, meaning to have a hot drink and go straight to bed, but Vanessa had sent me the final copy of her book... emailed it to me... and I found myself reading through the whole thing and then, hours later, I went to see her.

Police: What time was that?

AS: I got there just on five o'clock.

Police: In the morning?

AS: Yes... not one of my better decisions. I went to the house. I didn't notice that the door was open until I went up the steps. That was very unusual. In fact, it was downright wrong. Vanessa was scared of the outside and she always had a feeling that, when the door was open, the outside would creep in. She only ever opened it a crack, and never, in all the time I've known her, left it standing open unattended.

Police: Vanessa wasn't at the door?

AS: No. The house was pitch black and there was no sign of her. I should've called the police right then and there.

Police: Why didn't you?

AS: Phone you? Well, before I could really think about doing just that, a light went on in her bedroom window. I looked up and saw her peering down at me. She looked okay, so I went in.

Police: Was she pleased to see you?

AS: I'd say she was more relieved than pleased.

Police: What happened? Why was the door open?

AS: As best as I could make out, she'd left it closed and locked and had no explanation as to why it now stood open. She said... she said that maybe her visitor had come back.

Police: Visitor?

AS: Someone from a Facebook author group Vanessa had joined... Zara something or other. She just turned up out of the blue. She mentioned Zara in the journal. Did you catch that? I only saw the one mention of her, but, then again, I only read a few pages. Did she mention her much... further on?

Police: Yes. She's currently a person of interest to us.

AS: I suppose she mentioned that she thought Zara wasn't human?

Police: Why don't you simply carry on, please, Ms Sanderson. Leave your questions for later.

AS: Oh, so you ask, and I reply, but not the other way around? Suit yourself. As I was saying... I went into the house and Vanessa seemed relieved at the sight of me. She wasn't drunk, which was a miracle in itself, but she was wired to the hilt, all jittery and out of sync with the world. Know what I mean? No, maybe not. Suffice it to say... she was climbing the walls and hadn't a clue what day of the week it was.

Police: She hadn't been drinking?

AS: Not that I could tell. She acted weird but not drunk and I couldn't smell alcohol on her... not that vodka has much of a smell. Vodka was her favourite tipple. Anyway, she began to jabber on about her visitor... about how she materialised in the house out of thin air and how she'd then disappeared right in front of her eyes but that she thought she'd turned up again in the study. I thought she was mental... you know... imagining things? But the visitor was real enough. She didn't make her up.

Police: How do you know that?

AS: Because I met her. Not that night, of course, but the day after. But, let me get back to the demon bit of the story. That night... into the small hours of the morning... Vanessa kept insisting that the house was haunted. She told me about all the strange things that had been happening – those things she mentioned at the beginning of the journal – and I still thought she was either making it up or her imagination was playing tricks on her. Then, she described flies.

Police: Flies?

AS: She told me about the time your lot went round and there were flies in the kitchen that only she could see. It brought back to me something that went on in my hotel room in Edinburgh the night before and I found myself believing her.

Police: What happened in Edinburgh?

AS: I'd rather not say.

Police: If it's important...

AS: It's only important because it made me take her a little more seriously.

Police: About the demons?

AS: Yes.

Police: Go on.

AS: I remember that there was a terrible smell in the house... a stench of something dead. Vanessa said that it came and went, and I can tell you right now that it was insufferable. It made me feel physically sick. I don't know how Vanessa suffered it. Then, it just disappeared but what came in its place nearly had me wetting my knickers. (inaudible)

Police: Can you repeat that for the recording please?

AS: Yes. Sorry. This bit is difficult.

Police: Take your time.

AS: Okay but hear me out. Don't jump to any conclusions.

Police: Sure.

AS: I don't want you to think that I imagined it.

Police: We won't judge you.

AS: I saw something. It was... it was... I can't really be sure, but I think it was a face.

Police: At the window?

AS: No, coming right out of the wall. (Inaudible) Sorry... this is hard for me. I don't scare easily and I'm ashamed of myself. I remember screaming. I'm ashamed because I ran off. I left her on her own because I was shitting myself. I don't think I'll ever forgive myself for doing that... running away.... but I plucked up the courage to go back the next day and that's when I met Zara.

Twenty-four

Richard was banished to the sofa. Fiona wouldn't allow him in her bed. The choking incident of earlier the previous day had really frightened her, and she blamed him.

He didn't know who the fuck to blame. Or what to blame. His musings had prevailed throughout the night. He'd tossed and turned on the lumpy couch, his mind refusing to quiet down and allow him to sleep.

After Fiona had finally managed to dislodge the ring from her quickly closing throat, it bounced off the floor and then disappeared. Poof, and it was gone. Not that Fiona believed it had gone. That was one of the reasons she'd kicked him out the bedroom. She was adamant that he'd secreted it, that he was determined to hang onto it despite her hope that he wouldn't.

He wanted fuck all to do with the damned thing. He would be glad if he never clapped eyes on it again. If it turned up on the floor of the pawn broker's shop, then the man would be welcome to it. The money it would bring no longer mattered. For the first time in his life, he realised that there were more important things than money – like his sanity for example.

Good riddance to bad rubbish, he told himself, meaning it.

He hadn't dared any further attempts to reach Vanessa again, and there was no way he could risk any further wrath from Fiona by paying her a visit. Truth be told, he was glad of the excuse not to bother either ringing or visiting. There was still a niggling nub of concern about her, but not enough to piss Fiona off by doing anything to assuage it.

Vanessa would just have to look out for herself.

Grimly, he thought what salacious glee she would derive from the current state of war between him and Fiona, and all because of the wedding ring she'd pushed onto his finger at the alter all those years before. She would love the drama of it all. She wouldn't be able to help herself from deriding him. She would be merciless in her condemnation of him leaving her for a woman who was jealous of a stupid ring.

But it wasn't the ring... not really. It was the fact that Fiona believed that he'd lied to her and that he had carried on lying to her. There was no convincing her that he was much too smart to make up such a ridiculous story. That, more than anything, annoyed the hell out of him – that Fiona thought he was that stupid.

How fucking dare she.

He felt the crush of a virile man denied the chance to be top dog. Between them, Vanessa and Fiona had his balls in a vice.

He pulled himself up off the sofa, grabbed his pillow, and headed upstairs. If Fiona didn't like him in bed with her, then she could take the couch. It had just gone six, and he was determined to have at least a couple of hours of sleep.

Before he reached the top stair, his phone rang. He answered it quickly, lest it wake Fiona up. He had a feeling he knew who it was and, before he said so much as, hello, he made his way back down to the lounge, closed the door, and retook his position on the sofa.

'Richard?'

'Who else, Vanessa? It's my fucking phone. Do you have any idea what time it is?'

'Six o'clock, I think. I'm not sure.'

'Yeah, six o'clock... in the fucking morning. Jesus, don't you ever sleep?'

'I need to talk to you.'

'Well, you should've answered your phone. I must've called you at least a hundred times, and you ignored every fucking one of them. I was beginning to think that you'd died.'

'Sorry.'

"Yeah, well, what do you want to talk about? I hope it's the divorce, or the sale of the house. Those are the only two things I'm in the mood for.'

'Don't start on that again.'

'Then, don't phone me at this ungodly hour.'

A silence was eventually filled when Vanessa said, 'I finished the book.'

'Good for you. Is it as shit as the last two?' He knew that he was being mean, being unforgivably cruel, but he was in such a foul mood with no one to take it out on but her. 'Sorry,' he said on a long sigh. 'I'm tired. I shouldn't have said that.'

'No, but it's okay.'

What was it about her voice that bothered him? She sounded so calm, definitely not drunk, and she hadn't had a go at him when he said that about her books.

'Are you all right?' he asked.

'Not really.'

'Was that a stupid question?'

'Yeah. When have I ever been all right?'

'Once, maybe.'

'Before Simon.'

'Before we lost Simon, yeah.'

'I miss him.'

'Me too.'

'Would you do anything for him, Richard?'

'What do you mean... do anything for him?'

'Do anything to help him.'

He grew cold. It wasn't just the chill in the air. Her words spooked him, caused him to shiver.

'What are you talking about? Simon is beyond help. You must know that?'

'Yes. You're right. Forget I said anything.'

'Look, what's brought all this on?'

'Nothing. I'm just... oh, I don't know.'

'His birthday is coming up,' Richard said, attempting to lighten the mood. 'Do you remember the snow on the night he was born? I think it was the coldest night of the year.'

'I remember.'

A beat, then Richard said, 'Sorry. I shouldn't reminisce like this.'

'Why not? It's nice... to talk about him. Why do we never talk about him?'

He stated the obvious. 'Too busy arguing.'

'I suppose.'

Still, that calm almost detached voice. He barely recognised her. He asked, 'Is it because of his birthday?'

'Is *what* because of his birthday?'

'This.'

'No... maybe... I don't know.'

'He's on your mind more than usual?'

'He's *always* on my mind.' Her voice was suddenly short, clipped. 'I wonder how often *you* think about him?'

Richard closed his eyes. He didn't want the conversation to continue. They were getting into deep waters.

'Do you dream about him, Richard?'

'What? Sometimes.'

'Is he in hell... in your dreams?'

'Of course not. What a thing to ask.'

'I can't bear the thought of him being in Hell.'

'He's not. Jesus, Vanessa...'

'You don't know that. You don't know where he is.' Her voice began to sound panicked. 'I know...'

He cut her off. 'What *I know* is that little boys don't go there. Anyway, there's no such a place as Hell. Surely, you know that Vanessa?'

'I...'

'Just drop it, will you?' He rested his head in his free hand. 'You need to get some sleep. This conversation is stupid.'

'Talking about our son is stupid?'

'When you put him in Hell? Then, yes. It's more than stupid... it's sick.' He huffed in a breath. 'I'm not coming back. I've made that perfectly clear. If this is some ploy to...'

'What? Are you fucking kidding me? You think..?'

'I don't know what to think.'

'That I'd use Simon? That I'd make all of this up to get you back?'

'I think you'd use anything.'

'You bastard.'

'Sticks and stones.'

'There are things I could tell you.'

'I don't want to hear them.'

'What if..?'

'No, Vanessa... enough.'

Silence stretched out long and heavy. Richard was just about to break it when she asked, 'Do you believe in ghosts?'

The question took him completely unawares. The mention of ghosts conjured up thoughts of the incident in the pawn shop, the strange issue with the ring, the weird feeling about the photographs in his study, and he had to choke back on a gasp. He didn't believe in Hell, but it was more difficult to deny the existence of ghosts, especially considering his recent experiences.

Vanessa's question gave him pause.

'Do you?' she prompted.

'No. Of course not.' His reply came too quickly.

'I do,' she said.

His hand holding the phone shook as he held it to his ear. Her words, and the tone in which she said them, scared him. She wasn't herself. He'd known her for close to fifteen years, and he felt as if he was talking to a stranger. He said, 'How much have you had to drink?'

'I'm stone cold sober.' He heard her sigh. It sounded world-weary. 'I promise you that none of this has anything to do with being drunk.'

He returned her sigh. 'I wish I could believe that.'

'I'm not drunk, Richard. Ask Anita if you don't believe me.'

'Anita?'

'She was here earlier. She saw something. It scared her.'

'Saw something?'

'Coming out of the wall.'

Oh, man. 'Okay. That's enough. I can't believe you're bringing Anita into this... making all this shit up and involving her.'

'I'm not. I...'

'I've had it with you. You need to seriously think about sorting yourself out.'

'And you need to take your head out of your arse.'

He made a face. She couldn't see it but that didn't matter. He was sure that his derision would be clear in his tone. 'You've got some nerve saying that to me. You're the one with the delusions.' He began to pluck at his lower lip with his fingers. His anger was mounting, and he was on the verge of saying something really hurtful... something he would never be able to take back. He waited on her response. He was sure that it would be a doozey so was surprised when all he heard was another sigh and the sound of the call being disconnected.

Shit. He squeezed the phone until his knuckles turned white. He wished that his life wasn't so complicated. He didn't deserve to be plagued by fickle women. Women were turning out to be the bane of his life.

An unfamiliar feeling clutched at his belly. Any normal man – a man who wasn't devoid of the milk of human kindness – would have recognised the feeling as dread. He threw himself back down onto the sofa and, despite his total lack of empathy, and despite it being a contradiction, he began to worry.

His intuition kicked in. Just because – where relationships were concerned – he was a bit of a moron, he *did* have a nose for trouble, and his intuition told him that Vanessa was knee deep in it. Whether she was going off her rocker, or simply drunk, she needed help. There was no way he was about to admit to the alternative, that it was all true, every scary bit of it, but did he want to be the one to help her?

Hell, no.

And yet...

Fuck. Fuck. Fuck.

She was still his wife.

He swallowed, tried to come up with an excuse to leave her be. Fiona wouldn't be pleased. That should've been excuse enough, but it wasn't. Vanessa had hung up on him, made it clear that the conversation was over, and that fact gave him a way out. He very nearly convinced himself to climb the stairs and crawl into bed beside Fiona rather than make the trip to the house. He very nearly pushed all thoughts of his wife from his head but an image of Simon – their darling boy – intruded and he knew that he had no choice but to go. He could take her money, cheat on her, divorce her, but Simon's memory wouldn't allow him to abandon her all together. He owed it to him to at least check up on her.

Being banished to the sofa now seemed like a Godsend. Fiona would have no clue that he'd left the house, and what she didn't know wouldn't hurt her. He was sure he would return before she stirred.

Shrugging on his jacket and slipping into his shoes, he grabbed his car keys and let himself out of the house. When he started the car, he glanced up at the bedroom window, expecting the light to go on and was relieved when it didn't.

The roads were deserted. The journey took him less than twenty minutes – too short a time, he hoped, for Vanessa to have done anything stupid.

There was only one light on in the house – the one to their... *her*... bedroom. The drapes were open, but he couldn't see even the flicker of a shadow.

He had a key and he used it. She'd bolted the door on the inside, so the key ended up being useless.

He knocked, quietly at first, and then hammered with his fist, calling out her name and thanking God that there were no close neighbours to hear him. The last thing he wanted was to explain himself to the police.

When the incessant banging on the door elicited no response, he tried ringing her. He rang her mobile and then called the house phone. She answered neither.

He considered summoning the police himself. Someone needed to batter down the door and he was absolutely positive that it wasn't going to be him. He could just hear her divorce solicitor – when she got around to engaging one – lambasting him for harassment. In the long run, breaking into the house would probably cost him. There was no way he would do anything to turn her into his victim.

She's already your victim.

Oh, fuck off, he snarled at his inner, frustratingly truthful, voice.

He aimed a kick at the door, went back to the car, started the engine, turned it off, then sat and watched the windows. His patience paid off and he eventually saw movement at the window on the upstairs landing. It had been a mere shadow but was convincing enough to reassure him that Vanessa was okay. At least that was what he told himself as he drove away.

Twenty-five

Extract from the journal of author Vanessa Parker, discovered by her literary agent, Anita Sanderson.

When I heard Richard at the front door, I was relieved. I thought, my God, he cared enough to come and check up on me. I can still feel the sensation of hope blossoming in my chest... hope that lulled me into thinking that, at last, he'd come to his senses. I was warm with anticipation. There was suddenly a promise of something.

I battered my way downstairs but didn't get as far as the door. Suddenly she was there... in front of me... a ghoulish apparition. I froze. I wanted to punch her hard on the face, wipe the smirk off her mouth, but I didn't. I did nothing. I still wonder why I did nothing. Perhaps it was the quietness of her stance, the look in her eyes as she smirked up at m, or because she didn't physically prevent me from going downstairs and to the door. She didn't put her hands on me or restrain me in any way. I think, if she had, I might have fought, but she just stood there, hands on hips, a smile on her face, and told me NO.

How can I explain the power behind that simple word? It's such a tiny little thing. It wasn't a word I'd paid much heed to in the past. No one said NO to me with the expectation that I would take any notice. Even when the word had been accompanied by a hard stare, it never fazed me. Anyone who told me No could go fuck themselves.

But this was Zara and that tiny little word resonated in the air and sucked every bit of courage and defiance out of me. So, I froze and all the while, Richard hammered and called out my name over and over again. He didn't give up and I sensed that he realised something was wrong.

She was amused. Her eyes dared me to answer him, to scream, to beg for help. My tongue felt huge in my mouth. I was so fucking scared. I suddenly realised that I was more scared for Richard than I was for myself. I began to silently will him to leave... to get back in his car and drive away. I felt that the danger to him was very real. I knew that Zara wanted to hurt him.

I don't know how long I stood there on the landing before Zara gestured for me to return to the bedroom. Richard was still at the door but there was now a half-heartedness about his knocking. He was giving up. It wouldn't be long before he abandoned me. For once, I was glad. Leaving me was the right thing do.

She told me to sit on the bed. She told me to listen without interruption. I was tense. All of a sudden, she looked so serious, almost sorry. The glint of mockery had gone from her eyes, and I wondered if I'd imagined the evil that I'd wit-

nessed in their depths. I wondered what else I'd imagined.

Then, she told me about Simon.

My Simon.

I didn't believe her. I remember laughing right in her face. Who would ever be stupid enough to believe such unadulterated crap? Not me. I'm too smart for that.

My derision washed over her. She was patient. She allowed her words to fester and sink in. She smiled when she saw my conviction waver.

She told me that it was all my fault. There was no reproach in her words. She wasn't blaming me, just stating facts. I think it was her cool, almost blasé tone that finally got me to really listen to what she'd said.

'My fault?' I said. 'Why is it my fault?'

'You summoned me,' was her curt reply. 'You wanted Simon, and you got me instead.'

The Ouija board. My eyes darted to the wardrobe and then slid back to her face. What was she telling me?

'There's a fine balance,' she said, reaching out and patting my knee, as if to give me solace. 'Bringing me here shifted that balance.'

I wanted to get up and run. I didn't want to hear the rest. I got as far as pushing myself to my feet before I realised that there was no escaping the truth. I had to know. I had to know it all.

'Tell me,' I said, dropping back down onto the bed. 'Tell me everything.'

And she did.

Earlier, she'd told me that my son was in Hell. I hadn't believed her. What child ever goes to hell? Simon had been an innocent. The souls of the innocent don't fuel the fires of Hades. That wasn't how it worked. God wouldn't allow that.

Would He?

But Zara spoke to me about balance. She explained that summoning a demon had consequences. The gap had to be filled and it was always filled by the soul of a loved one.

I had Zara... my special friend... and Satan had my Simon.

My nightmares had been testament to that.

HER WHOLE BODY WAS numb, her brain a mere vessel that harboured thoughts of delusional proportion. She was, at last, alone. There was no great relief at being alone. There was simply no relief to be had.

The house was unusually warm. It had been cold for days and the sudden rise in temperature seemed surreal. Despite the heat, she shivered. Despite the sweat pooling beneath her arms and popping out in small globules on her forehead, she was stiff and numb with cold.

Zara was gone. Vanessa was alone with her thoughts. The journal lay on her lap, open at the last entry. Only, it wasn't the last entry. There was more to tell, more to share. Zara hadn't ended the telling of Simon's story with a fate accompli, because, it seemed, that Simon's destiny wasn't set.

There was a way to save him.

Vanessa had gone through the past few years believing that there was no agony to compare to the death of one's child. People told her, in their cack-handed way, that at least he was at peace, at least he was free from pain, that she should be glad he was no longer suffering.

She'd tried to believe them – finally *did* believe them – and, although she still agonised, she eventually found some comfort in their words. There had been no heaven, not then, but she had come to accept that he was resting somewhere beyond sickness and pain. She hadn't managed to take herself beyond all grief – no mother could – but the vodka had helped.

Vodka wouldn't help her now, nothing would, but it was the thought of the anesthetising effects of alcohol that roused her from her stupor.

She had a sudden gut-clenching, ugly thirst. It was a thirst that couldn't be denied. Once quenched, it would obliterate everything — even thoughts of her son. Before guilt could grab a hold of her, she was on her feet. A wave of vertigo almost had her dropping like a stone, but she caught herself with her hands before her face slammed to the floor. She had a fleeting thought that she'd fractured one of her wrists. There wasn't any pain, but she was sure she'd heard the crack of a bone. It didn't matter. As long as it didn't interfere with her holding a glass, a broken bone was neither here nor there.

Unsteady – the floor undulating beneath her feet – she made her way downstairs. The house was eerily silent. At the bottom of the stairs, she had to clench her eyes tightly closed to prevent the images of Simon, hanging battered and bruised above the licking flames of Hell's fire, from overwhelming her.

Zara had been very descriptive. She had left no detail untold. Even her worst nightmares hadn't prepared Vanessa for the truth of Simon's purgatory. She was sure that no one would blame her for wanting nothing more than to drink those images away.

She passed the strange object lying on the hall table. She now knew what it was and shuddered at the sight of it. It didn't, after all, belong to Richard. It was Zara's device — a device that would be the means of freeing Simon... if Vanessa permitted its use.

Of course, she would permit it.

She would do anything for her son, but not before the vodka gave her the necessary courage.

The closer she got to the kitchen the steeper the gradient of the floor seemed to become. Vanessa suddenly felt as if she was walking uphill. Her breathing became ragged. The air seemed much too thin to sustain her lungs. She found herself tilting to the left and had to reach out to steady herself against the wall.

A great weight pressed against her chest, pushing her back. Something didn't want her reaching the kitchen, the fridge, and the vodka.

Fuck you, she said, bending forward and straining against the invisible force.

When the walls began to leak blood, she didn't allow it to affect her. When it dripped onto the top of her head from the ceiling, she struggled on, indifferent. The only fear that affected her was the fear that there would be no vodka in the fridge.

At last, the door was within reach. It was closed to her, and she would have to press down on the handle to open it. There was nothing difficult about doing that, or so she thought. Try as she might, her hand – like the hand of a ghost – swiped over and through the handle as if it wasn't there. *Swipe, swipe, swipe.*

What the..?

She threw her shoulder against the wood and bounced back as the door rejected her attempt to force it open. Tears of frustration spurted from her eyes.

Enough with the games, she screamed.

Zara's tittering laughter was the only reply she got before the door swung open of its own volition and the kitchen welcomed her in.

'You look like shit,' Zara said, sliding her feet to the floor and standing as tall as her five-foot frame allowed. 'You look as if you could do with a stiff drink.'

Vanessa licked her lips. She tasted blood. She must have bit her lip. Wiping the back of her hand across her mouth, she nodded, her eyes going immediately to the bottle of vodka, sweating with frost, sitting in the middle of the table.

'It won't help,' Zara said. 'It won't change anything.'

Vanessa wanted to tell her to fuck off. She wanted to tell her that there was nothing else she could do to her that would touch her in any way but decided that she wasn't worth the breath it would cost to say the words.

She weaved towards the table, changed her mind, and turned for the fridge. She didn't trust the bottle on offer, believing it tainted in some way.

Something in her wrist popped when she yanked the door open, and she gave a little yelp of pain.

Inside were at least a dozen bottles of vodka. She didn't remember bringing them from the garage and placing them there. She grabbed one and immediately unscrewed the lid. She didn't stop swallowing until a third of the bottle had been downed.

'You're only delaying the inevitable,' Zara said from behind her. 'And you'd been doing so well. I'm tremendously disappointed in you.'

Vanessa choked, coughed, and swallowed a little more. She was desperate for the effects to kick-in.

'You said I could do with a stiff drink,' she said, the vodka burning a track down her throat.

'Someone like you...' Zara returned, 'the queen of the sarcastic comment, should've recognised the irony in my statement.' She hiked a beautifully plucked brow. 'You make an ugly drunk.'

'Fuck you,' Vanessa spluttered, vodka spraying from her mouth. 'Fuck you all the way back to hell.'

Without warning, the bottle exploded in Vanessa's hand. The shock was so great that it stupefied her and, for what seemed like endless moments, she stood and stared at the large shard of glass sticking out the palm of her hand. It was an alarming sight, one that mesmerised her. It took nearly a full minute before she plucked up the courage to yank it out.

The blood welled and then ran, slick, along her forearm. Its colour nonplussed her. It was too red. *Surely, blood wasn't supposed to be as red as that*? She wondered if she would bleed to death and wasn't shocked to discover that she didn't care.

The glass shard dropped to the floor. Vanessa immediately reaches into the fridge for another bottle. She knows that the only way she is going to get through the next few minutes, the next hour, the rest of her life, is by being so sozzled that nothing would touch her.

'I want you sober,' Zara said, in her sing-song voice. 'I don't want you all fucked-up and senseless. What would be the fun in that?'

Vanessa shrugged and huffed out a *huh*. She clutched the precious bottle to her chest, protecting it. Her wrist ached, her hand throbbed, even her teeth hurt, but that didn't prevent her from keeping a tight hold of the bottle.

Zara laughed. Vanessa felt something shift and became aware that the bottle was no longer pressed against her chest. *Had it ever been there*?

'It matters... what I want,' Zara said, matter of fact. 'What I want is the *only* thing that matters. The sooner you accept that, the sooner we can move on.'

'Move on?' The words were forced out from between chattering teeth. 'Just do it. Just get it over with.'

Zara took a step towards her. Vanessa held her ground. She was done being intimidated and simply wanted it all to be over.

'It's not time,' Zara said. 'We have the book to consider first.'

'The book?'

'It's going to make you a very rich woman... far richer than you could ever imagine.'

'I don't...'

'Oh, I know, Vanessa.' She reached out and stroked a finger along her cheek. 'I know that money no longer matters to you, and fame..? You're no longer interested in that, are you?'

Vanessa shook her head. She became aware of a sharp sensation on her cheek. When she cast her eyes to the side, she saw that Zara's slender fingers now resembled scaly green claws.

She stifled a scream, remained perfectly still. One of the claws drew blood.

'Your sacrifice has to mean something. We don't want a washed-up has-been of a failed author. The soul of your son is worth more than that, don't you think?'

'I don't...'

'You don't know what to think?'

'No.'

The claw scratched its way down to the corner of her mouth. Vanessa winced as more blood was drawn. It seemed as if her cheek was opening up like a ripe tomato pierced by a sharp knife.

To the side of her, every bottle in the fridge exploded. The noise was deafening. Glass flew everywhere. Despite her determination not to move, Vanessa ducked and hunched. Death by a thousand cuts seemed imminent.

Stomach clenched in terror Vanessa forced herself to take a step back. She expected Zara to grab her, prevent even the semblance of escape, but she merely dropped her hand – a hand that was now actually a hand and no longer a monstrous appendage – and allowed her to put distance between them.

As she stepped further away, glass ground beneath her slippered feet. The floor was awash with vodka. She was sure that there were shards in her hair, clinging to her skin. She was certain to be bleeding from many tiny wounds as well as the gash in her palm and the scratch on her cheek from Zara's claw.

'What now?' she asked, her voice breathy with terror.

'Now?' Zara tipped her head to the side, thought a moment, then said, 'We get tidied up.'

In the blink of an eye, every trace of glass was suddenly gone. The floor miraculously dried and Vanessa felt the uncanny sense of her skin healing. Everything was suddenly pristine, and Vanessa was whole once more.

'Just in time,' Zara said, as the sound of knocking echoed from the hall. 'You have a visitor.'

Twenty-Six

Anita guessed who she was. She couldn't be anyone else other than the woman Vanessa had mentioned the night before. In the open doorway, she looked harmless and certainly not someone who could appear and disappear at will. It eased her a little – seeing her in the flesh. She'd spent a sleepless night conjuring up all sorts of crazy things in her mind. She couldn't quite reconcile with what had gone on in Vanessa's bedroom the night before, and she was still a little embarrassed and ashamed of running out on her and abandoning her to… well, she really had no idea what she'd abandoned Vanessa to. She had no explanation for either the horrid stench or what her rational mind now tried to reinvent as a shadow on the wall.

She wasn't prone to fanciful thinking. She didn't share the same imagination as her authors and, therefore, didn't possess the level of ingenuity required to accept what, to her, was absolutely impossible.

Seeing the young woman standing before her, her face open and friendly, belied everything that Vanessa had implied about her. She was obviously not a threat, and certainly nothing remotely close to a ghost.

Yes, a ghost was the word Vanessa had used to describe her.

'Thank goodness you're here,' the woman said, her voice high and full of concern. 'I'm Zara.' She held out a slim hand. 'I'm very pleased to finally meet you.'

Anita took the small hand in her pudgy grip and returned her smile. 'You know who I am?'

'Of course. Vanessa told me all about you. She didn't say that she was expecting you this morning, but I'm so glad that you're here.

Vanessa has got herself into quite a state and another friendly face is just what she needs.'

'I was worried about her,' she said. 'Is it about last night? Did something else happen?'

'Ah, yes... last night.' Zara stepped back and gestured for Anita to step inside. 'I'm afraid she'd been suffering the ill-effects of alcohol withdrawal. Her mother was an alcoholic. Did you know that?' She closed the door. 'A bad case.'

Anita's mouth dropped open. She hadn't known that about Vanessa's mother and she couldn't help wondering why a relative stranger had hold of such personal information when she – who had known Vanessa for well over a decade – hadn't been confided in.

'It's in the genes, you know?'

Anita's head snapped up. 'What is?'

'Alcoholism.'

'I hardly think...'

'Oh, not to worry. I have it all in hand.' Zara marched off towards the kitchen, glanced back, and said, 'Are you coming? I've got coffee on.'

Anita followed, bemused and now a little on edge.

Vanessa was seated at the table. She didn't look up when Zara and Anita entered.

Zara winked across at Anita and shook her head. 'She's feeling quite the worse for wear, I'm afraid. Best to let her sit quiet a moment... allow her to come too in her own good time. Coffee?' She walked over and picked up the French Press. 'It's hot and fresh.'

Vanessa took that moment to lift her head. Anita had never witnessed such an expression in her eyes. They seemed haunted.

Zara was too busy pouring the coffee to notice the look exchanged between them. She handed both of them a mug and assisted Vanessa to lift it to her lips.

'She's got the shakes, poor love. Drink up, Vanessa, a shot of caffeine is all you need to steady your nerves.' She noticed Anita eyeing some broken glass on the floor, and said, 'That's the remains of a bottle of vodka. I thought I'd cleared it all up.'

Something had obviously happened in the kitchen – Anita was sure of it – and her instincts warned her that it wasn't over. For all her bright, almost giddy demeanour, Zara seemed tense.

Keeping her tone level, Anita said, 'Celebrating the end of the novel?' Well, I guess a drink or two is well deserved, but...'

'The novel?' Zara put in. 'Ah, yes... the book. It's brilliant, isn't it?'

'You've read it?' Anita asked, surprised.

'I was given the honour of helping to pull it all together.'

'Oh?' Anita looked back down at Vanessa, raised a brow in question, and was disappointed when she merely stared up at her with that same haunted look in her eyes.

'I just did some editing,' Zara said. 'And boy did it need it.'

Anita thought she now understood why the text and the formatting was so perfect. Vanessa had help. That was okay. No one expected the author to do their own corrections... not all of them, anyway. Then a tremulous thought batted off her brain. Zara surely didn't have the time to edit nearly one-hundred-thousand words. Had she known Vanessa much longer than a day?

It was suddenly nightmarishly hot. Anita could feel sweat pooling in the folds of her skin and running down the bridge of her nose.

'Would you mind if I opened a window?' she asked.

'Don't bother. I'll do it,' Zara returned.

In the few seconds it took for Zara to walk to the window over the sink, lean over, and push it open, Vanessa had grabbed Anita's arm, dragged her close, and frantically whispered something in her ear.

ANITA SANDERSON (AS)
Sample taken from PART One (CONTINUED) of recorded interview
Date: 22 January 2022
Duration: 80 minutes (TOTAL)
Location: Wood Street Police Station, City of London
No of pages: 16 (total number of sample pages: 2)
Conducted by officers from the London Metropolitan Police
All police officer identifiers have been redacted (Section 38 (1) (A)

AS: I had to pluck up the courage to go back to that house. It was the last thing I wanted to do, but I hadn't slept, was worried sick about Vanessa, and I still had questions about the book. I'd put the events of the night before down to being tired, being wired... to Vanessa's hysteria rubbing off on me. I convinced myself that I'd imagined what I saw coming out of her bedroom wall... imagined everything, including the flies. What else was I to think? It was all nonsense... utter fucking nonsense, and then I met Zara. Just looking at her reassured me. She was so... normal. There was no way that she was what Vanessa made her out to be. At least, that's what I thought when I first met her.

Police: But you soon came to change your mind about her?

AS: Too fucking right, I did... excuse the French.

Police: Why did you come to change your mind?

AS: That's not easy to explain.

Police: Try.

AS: It was nothing tangible. There was just something off about her, and Vanessa seemed scared of her. She'd made herself right at home. Apparently, she'd even edited Vanessa's book. That didn't quite compute. I mean, she was only supposed to have known her a matter of a day. How could she have edited a one hundred-thousand-word book in a day? That would've been impossible. Then there was glass on the floor and Vanessa's weird behaviour. She let that little woman dictate everything… the conversation… everything. then

Police: She seemed frightened of Zara?

AS: Too scared to even talk to me. She didn't say a word until that woman's attention was diverted. I think she went to open the window, or something and that was when Vanessa grabbed my arm and whispered to me to find her journal. She told me, if anything happened to her, I had to find it.

Police: That was the only time she mentioned the journal to you?

AS: Yes because I never got to speak to her again. Zara turfed me out on my ear and that was that. Vanessa didn't do or say anything to stop her from kicking me out. It was then that I knew for sure.

Police: Knew what?

AS: That she was bad news. That Vanessa really was frightened of her.

Police: Then what?

AS: Then, nothing. I left and that was the last time I saw either of them. Vanessa stopped taking my calls. When the worry got the better of me, I went to the house and the rest is history.

Police: You left it for two weeks. You couldn't have been that worried.

AS: I was, but put it this way… I knew, if I went round there, I wouldn't be welcome. I kept thinking that any day, she'd get in touch… ask what was happening with the book… moan about Richard… but I finally had to concede that it was up to me to be the one to act. Welcome or not, I finally decided that I should go to the house. Yes, it was a couple of weeks and, yes, I probably should've gone sooner, but we are where we are. There's no point in me beating myself up about it.

Twenty-Seven

'What do you want, Anita? I'm busy.' Richard threw himself down onto the sofa and took a long swallow of coffee as he listened to Vanessa's literary agent sound off on the other end of the phone. 'No,' he interrupted. 'I haven't heard from her and, if I had, what business would that be of yours?'

He rolled his eyes and listened some more. The silly bitch seemed worked up about something.

'You do that,' he said, 'and she'll probably rip you a new one for using that key – the one that I didn't know you had to my house. By the way... just why do you have a key to *my* house?'

He wasn't satisfied with her response, rolled his eyes again, and said, 'Well, good luck with invading her privacy. Don't come crying to me when her tongue takes the skin off your face.'

He ended the call, looked at his phone for a moment, then brought Vanessa's number up on the screen.

He could try calling her again. If Anita was that worried about her, then perhaps he should be too. He thought that he knew why she'd been avoiding him. She didn't want to hear any more talk of divorce or of putting the house on the market. Like always, she was simply burying her head in the sand.

He was past being mad at her. Anger wasn't going to get him what he wanted. Sugar always worked better than vinegar and, as Simon's birthday was approaching, he'd planned on surprising her with an album he'd made of photographs he'd taken of their son before his illness. He hoped that, when he finally got to see her, to talk to her, that there would be no more mention of Hell. All that talk had really freaked him out, especially since his recent experiences had knocked him completely out of kilter. He'd tried to convince himself that it was merely one coincidence piled on top of another. His rational brain couldn't accept a grain of any strangeness in anything Vanessa said or what he'd witnessed for himself. Thankfully, since that last telephone call with her – apart from suffering his own fair share of nightmares – life had returned to normal. Nothing out of the ordinary had occurred... except that he couldn't get a hold of his wife. That was enough *out of the ordinary* to finally concern him.

Part of the reason he hadn't pursued things with her was Fiona's mood. Only that morning she'd threatened to chuck him out. He was skating on very thin ice with her and jeopardising their relationship further wasn't in his best interests. But he no longer believed he had a choice and would use the album as an excuse to be permitted to visit her. Even Fiona couldn't be so hard-hearted as to refuse him permission to mark his dead son's birthday alongside the still grieving Vanessa.

He remembered his boy as a chubby toddler and then as a thin, wan, very sick little boy. In the end, he didn't have many memories that he could look back on that would give him solace. Over the years, he'd made a point of not thinking about him, not remembering him, because there was no way he could have coped with the guilt. For years, he hadn't looked at the photographs. If it hadn't been for the need to use them to get to Vanessa, he knew they would've remained locked away forever.

Luckily, Richard was blessed with the sort of brain that could lock unpleasant things away. That's why he could have affairs with impunity, how he could keep taking money from Vanessa without feeling any remorse, and why he had succeeded in surviving the death of his son virtually unscathed. Vanessa should have taken a leaf out of his book. She should've shelved her grief in some dark recess of her mind and moved on. In the long run, it would've saved her a whole heap of misery.

Richard had never flinched from his belief that nothing could touch him – not physically and certainly not emotionally – and yet he found the mild concern he'd recently had for Vanessa growing like a lump of concrete in his chest. The phone call from Anita hadn't helped. Although he tried to brush it off, fear poked at him. It was the same fear he'd experienced over the nonsense with his wedding ring. The fear touched him on a deep, almost primitive level, and he didn't quite know how to deal with it.

Although there had been no repeat of the ring issue, or anything weird with the photographs in his study, he'd continued to suffer nightmares. The nightmares also hadn't helped his overall equilibrium. He was tired and jittery from lack of sleep, and he knew that, if it hadn't been for those damned dreams, he probably would've shrugged Anita's phone call off and only given it scant attention.

But he couldn't shake off the phone call, or the memory of the most recent nightmare. It didn't help that Simon had been in that dream and that his wedding ring had been hanging around his son's neck on a chain.

As the details of the nightmare solidified in his mind, he broke out in a cold sweat. It played across the back of his eyes like stills in a horror movie.

His son... oh, God, his son... bloodied, emaciated, screaming in agony.

He shook his head in a desperate attempt to rid himself of the images. They wouldn't shift, and he groaned deep in his chest, a single tear escaping to run down his cheek.

His fear swelled. He tried to tell himself that he was being irrational, that it was only a fucking dream, but he couldn't convince himself that it wasn't more than that.

For the first time in a while, he tried to recall everything that Vanessa had said about Simon during their last phone conversation. Was she having the same dreams? Had she mentioned having nightmares about him? He couldn't remember.

He really ought to go to the house, not leave it up to Anita to discover why Vanessa had gone off the radar, but he knew that he wouldn't go. He didn't want to know what was going on. He wanted to be the old Richard, the one who turned his back, and he was determined to be that Richard again. He much preferred that version of himself.

He would post the album, follow it up with another phone call, leave well alone for the time being. Yes, that would be for the best. He could afford to wait another week or so before broaching the subject of the divorce and before attempting to persuade her to put the house up for sale. In the grand scheme of things, what were another couple of weeks?

He heard Fiona banging about in the kitchen. Lately, she had become much noisier in her activities around the house. It was as if she needed to constantly remind him that it was her house and that she could be as noisy and as annoying as she desired. She knew that he appreciated peace and quiet. She probably believed that the noisier she was, the quicker he would leave but, as far as Richard was concerned, she had another thing coming because he had no intention of making himself homeless – not before the money from his divorce settlement began to roll in. He needed the cushion the money would provide to set himself up somewhere else, and then neither Vanessa, nor Fiona, would see him for dust.

Vanessa. What the fuck was she playing at? Despite his best efforts, he couldn't stop thinking and worrying about her. He decided that he would give Anita a call later... find out what happened when she went to the house. With any luck, she would've discovered his wife in need of a stay in rehab.

In the end, he didn't call Anita. He decided that he didn't want the aggravation of knowing what was going on. He reverted back to the idea of posting the album, of leaving things for a while. He concluded that he was quite content to let Anita sort her out.

RICHARD ARTHUR PARKER (RAP)
  Sample taken from PART THREE of recorded interview
  Date: 23 January 2022
  Duration: 40 minutes
  Location: Wood Street Police Station, City of London
  Total number of pages: 6
  Total number of sample pages: 5
  Conducted by officers from the London Metropolitan Police
  All police identifiers have been redacted Section 38 (1) (A)

Police: I want to remind you that you are still under caution, Mister Parker. For the recording - present are Detective Sergeant (redacted) and Detective Constable (redacted}, Richard Arthur Parker, and Mister Parker's solicitor, Sebastian Cooper (SC)

SC: I've advised my client to remain silent until such times as you inform him of the current position on your investigation into the disappearance of his wife, and until such a time as you explain your interest in him regarding that matter.

Police: You are refusing to answer any questions, Mister Parker?

RAP: I plan to follow the advice of my solicitor.

Police: Even if it means obstructing our investigation?

SC: That's enough, sergeant. Your passive-aggressive tactics won't work here.

Police: Very well, but if it's all the same to you, we'll still ask our questions. Mister Parker, would you like some water? You don't look very well.

RAP: I've not been sleeping, and is it any wonder? My wife is missing and, instead of using your resources to find her, you're wasting your time with me. I told you...

SC: My client is making no further comment.

Police: We'll see about that. Tell me, Mister Parker, did you know about her journal?

RAP: What?

Police: She kept one and it's come into our possession. It makes for interesting reading.

RAP: Vanessa didn't keep a journal.

SC: Mister Parker...

RAP: Yes. Okay. No comment.

Police: She mentions you in it. Would you like to know what she said? I can read a few passages to you... if you want, that is.

RAP: It will all be bullshit so, no... I don't want to know what she wrote about me.

SC: Does this journal shed any light on where she might be? Do its contents incriminate my client?

Police: It's my turn to say... no comment.

RAP: You know she was a drunk, mental in the head. I wouldn't place any store on her ramblings.

Police: It's interesting that you say that Mister Parker.

RAP: Oh, why is that, then?

SC: Please, Mister Parker, don't let them bait you.

Police: t's interesting because her writing, although somewhat... how can I put it? Ah, yes... although somewhat bizarre, certainly doesn't come across as rambling. She is very coherent, very sure of her words.

RAP: Well, she is a best-selling author, after all. If there's one thing Vanessa can do, and do well... drunk, or mental... is write. But you have to remember that she's adept at making up stories. It's what she does for a living, for fuck's sake.

Police: You seem a little worried about what she might have written in that journal.

RAP: I'm not worried. Why should I be?

SC: Yes, sergeant... why should he be? Perhaps it's time for you to put your cards on the table? If you have no intention of being forthcoming, then I will call a halt to this interview.

Police: Not if we arrest your client.

SC: On what grounds?

Police: I'm sure we can find some.

SC: Or make them up? Really, sergeant, there can't possibly be any evidence that my client has done anything wrong. He hasn't seen or spoken to his wife in weeks. You know that. He told you that already.

Police:::He didn't mention the phone call Vanessa made to him shortly before her disappearance.

RAP: How do you know about that?

SC: Mister Parker...

RAP: No. I want to know.

Police: How do you think we know?

RAP: That fucking journal?

Police: Got it in one.

RAP: Then, you'll know that it was an amicable conversation.

Police: What we'd rather know is why you didn't mention it in your last interview.

RAP: What would've been the point?

Police: That's the thing about police interviews, Mister Parker. We get to decide the point of things. It's not up to the person being interviewed to pick and choose what's relevant. We asked you, quite clearly, if you'd seen or spoken to her again. Would you like to change your answer... to both seeing her and speaking to her? You did, after all, go back to the house, did you not? You did, in fact, speak to her.

RAP: Only that one time on the phone. Yes, I went to the house, but I didn't see her. She'd locked and bolted the door. Look, I'd forgotten all about that phone call, okay? Give me a fucking break. My wife is missing. Someone broke into the fucking house... you told me as much. I've been upset and I'm entitled to forget some piddling little phone call.

Police: Have you been in the house since the last time you told us about?

RAP: No comment.

Police: Do you know where your wife is?

RAP: No comment.

Police: Did you have something to do with her disappearance?

RAP: No comment.

Police: Do you know a woman called Zara?

RAP: What? No.

Police: You've never met anyone called Zara?

RAP: No comment.

Police: Did you speak to Anita Sanderson after she let herself into Vanessa's house?

RAP: My house, and no comment.

Police: Has your wife been in contact with you since the day Anita Sanderson went into the house?

RAP: No comment.

Police: Would you care to make any further comment on what you believe has happened to your wife?

RAP: No comment.

Twenty-Eight

Anita left. Zara stayed. Vanessa hoped that Anita understood her message about the journal. She'd had to whisper it hurriedly and she wasn't sure if she'd made her request clear. Worse, she wasn't sure if Zara had overheard her. If she had, then the shit was about to hit the fan.

The journal was the only record of what had been happening to her, and what had happened to Simon. Perhaps no one would believe her scribblings, believing them to be the product of a psychotic brain, but any record was better than none. When Zara was finished with her – when she was either dead or spirited away to take Simon's place – and, as fanciful as it might seem, the world had to be informed about what happened.

Anita was sure to be worried. Zara's behaviour hadn't exactly been what would be considered normal, and neither had hers. She'd permitted herself to be dictated to, had sat mute and unresponsive during Anita's brief visit, and that alone should have raised alarm bells. Anita knew her only too well. She would be curious and the garbled message about the journal would surely have put a fire under that curiosity.

Or, at least, that's what Vanessa hoped.

A shift in Zara's body language brought Vanessa back to the moment. The woman... the demon... now held herself stiff and her expression had lost its amused mask. As she made her way across the kitchen, her footsteps sounded heavy and almost stompy. She appeared angry. Vanessa watched her with heightened trepidation. Her body was so slick with sweat that she feared she would slide off the chair. Her heart was so loud in her own ears that she knew Zara must hear every thump.

Zara seemed to thrive on fear and Vanessa didn't want to give her the satisfaction of feeding off that fear any more than she already had. Despite her mounting terror, Vanessa forced herself to relax back in the chair. She unfroze her jaw and eased her features into a semblance of a smile. She could see that Zara was immediately confused, causing Vanessa to become concerned that she had put two and two together and concluded that her suspicions were correct – that Vanessa had managed to convey some sort of a message to Anita.

'What are you smiling at?' she asked, her brow settling into a frown. 'What's tickled you? You shouldn't be smiling right now.'

Vanessa immediately lowered her eyes, lest Zara see the defiance in them. She let her smile slip and huffed in a breath. She hoped the breath sounded agitated. She wanted Zara believing that she was cowed. Far better that she feed off her terror than suspect her of anything underhand. It wasn't that difficult because Vanessa really was terrified.

Vanessa no longer had such a thing as a survival instinct. Any defiance that survived beneath the heavy blanket of fear was aimed at her son's survival, not her own. She couldn't be saved. She knew and accepted that. She was acutely aware of the torment that awaited her, and being human, feared the consequences of that torment, but it would all be worth it to save her son.

Her fear for her son far outweighed the fear she had for what was to come. She felt an urgency to get it over with, but Zara had made it clear that the time wasn't right.

When would the time be right? How long did her little boy have to suffer before she would be allowed to free him? Zara seemed preoccupied with the publication of the book, but why did that matter? Vanessa didn't care a whit about it. If Zara believed that her decision to sacrifice herself would be thwarted by a need to cling onto a successful future as an author, then she was very much mistaken. If she believed that the sacrifice would be all the greater because of the relinquishing of that future, then she really was quite stupid.

Only another mother would know how little everything else measured against the safety and wellbeing of their child. Nothing – *absolutely nothing* – compared to that.

'What's going on in that head of yours?'

Vanessa lifted her chin. The air pulsed around her. Something told her not to reply, not play Zara at her own game. She didn't believe she had anything to lose. Tight-lipped, she merely stared up at her.

Zara's face became a sullen mass of contradiction. Her mouth tried to smile but her eyes flashed with irritation. Vanessa felt an intense satisfaction. The fear began to evaporate and something of the old Vanessa took root. She decided that she was going to face her fate, and that of her child, on her own terms. She was well past allowing Zara to call the shots.

'What did she say to you?'

'Who?' The word popped out before she could stop it.

'Anita. I heard you two whispering together.'

She didn't know. Zara might be a demon, but it was obvious that she wasn't omnipotent. Vanessa's mood lifted further.

'I don't know what you're talking about. You must've imagined it.' The lie rolled effortlessly off her tongue. 'What could I have possibly said to Anita anyway? The truth? If I told her the truth, she would have sent for the men in the white coats.'

Zara seemed satisfied with that. There was just enough truth in Vanessa's words to reassure her. She said, 'No one can help you. I am your only salvation.'

'My special friend?'

Zara finally succeeded in smiling. She nodded, pleased that Vanessa understood. 'At last, you understand,' she said.

'Understand what... that you're a psycho bitch from Hell, pretending to care about me... about my son? Get real, Zara. You're not my friend, so stop with all the bullshit. Just do what you have to do and let's put an end to this.'

Zara shook her head and made a tutting sound. 'Bravo,' she said. 'At last, you've grown a pair. Where was *this* Vanessa when her son's soul was safely tucked up in heaven? It wasn't *this* Vanessa who hunched over a Ouija board and opened the portal to Hell.'

'Screw you.'

Clearly confident in the total control she had over Vanessa and the situation, Zara continued to smile. No longer irritated, more bemused than upset, she leaned forward and, much to Vanessa's surprise, brushed her lips across her forehead.

'I almost love you,' she said, straightening up and clasping her hands to her breast. 'At least, I think I do.'

Vanessa leaned further back in her chair and swiped a hand across the spot where Zara's frozen lips had seared her skin. 'You're deranged. What do you know about love?'

'Much more than your feckless husband,' she returned quickly. 'How many women did he screw during your marriage? Do you think he told every one of them that he loved them?'

Her words stung. The truth hurt.

'But don't you worry about him. I have plans for him.'

'What do you mean? You leave him alone.' Vanessa was on her feet. 'He's got nothing to do with this.'

'He's got *everything* to do with it. Don't you see, Vanessa? Don't you see just how culpable he is?'

'No.' She shook her head violently. 'I forbid you to harm him. None of this is his fault.'

'Oh poor, pathetic Vanessa... still clinging onto the belief that, deep down, Richard is a good man. I know that his soul is as black as soot. We have a special place set aside for him and you can spend an eternity watching him writhe in agony. Won't that be something to look forward to?'

Vanessa's eyes widened as the shadow cast on the wall at Zara's back began to grow. At first, it was quite clearly the dark silhouette of Zara's small, slim frame, but – as it grew and widened – it took on the form of something else entirely.

Zara let out a tinkle of laughter, pulled her head up, and backed towards the wall. By rights, the closer Zara got to the wall, the more the shadow should have shrunk. But, instead of shrinking it grew larger and more grotesque.

'You're anxious to move things along,' Zara said, her voice booming and now entirely unrecognisable. 'What are friends for, if not to oblige the whims of their pals? So be it.'

The shadow began to creep over the ceiling. Vanessa tracked it with ever widening eyes. Suddenly, it seemed to peel itself free. It was almost something alive. Vanessa reared back in horror. Nothing remained of her defiance, of her wish to get things done and dusted. She backed away but there was nowhere to go. She couldn't escape the encroaching ink black apparition and she found herself gasping for breath, choking, panicking as the inky form heaved its malevolence ever closer.

It was going to swallow her, suck her down into its fetid belly. She was going to die and suddenly she didn't want to die.

A gaping maw opened, and Vanessa had no doubt that the jagged teeth, now bared, were real.

Bile rushed up as the stench of sulphur seared her throat. Then there was no air to breath, no sustenance for her burning lungs. She struggled against the terror of a merciless suffocation. She fought with every fibre of her being to keep herself alive.

Zara's insufferable laughter was the last thing she heard before everything went black.

EXTRACT FROM THE JOURNAL of author Vanessa Parker, discovered by her literary agent, Anita Sanderson.

Now I understand. Now I believe. I thought that I did before – when Zara exposed what lay beneath her golden skin, when she exposed her true self – but the brain doesn't like to accept even what it sees with its own eyes. The doubts set in. When something is so fantastic that it can't really be true, then your brain does its best to convince you that it's not true. You can't help yourself. I guess it's a sort of defence mechanism... something your mind does to protect your sanity.

But the mind can't stand against all the senses being affected. When you are not only seeing, but smelling and tasting and feeling, then the doubts vanish. Then, you believe, and then, you understand... completely. The mind caves, hoists the white flag, and you surrender.

Knowing what I know, believing what I believe, I realise that there is no hope for me, but I have to believe that there is for Simon. I can end this. My free will can end it. That is the promise Zara made to me.

I have no choice but to accept that promise. I can't dwell on the fact that it was given too freely, too glibly, and I can't question its validity. If I did, then all bets would be off.

But perhaps my mind hasn't quite thrown in the towel just yet. It gives rise to many questions. Questions such as – is it wise to trust the word of a devil... a demon? Don't they exist to lie and cheat, and don't they strive to annihilate all hope – hope that they build up and then so cruelly crush? Don't they feed off the tears of the innocent?

How can I reconcile with such questions?

I am not innocent. I won't delude myself into believing that I am. I could never cast the first stone because I am not without sin. I'm vain and proud, selfish and arrogant. I cast off friends as if they were worthless. I respect no one. I can bleat and complain that my loss of innocence isn't my fault. I can blame an alcoholic mother, an unknown father, a cheating husband, the loss of a son. I can give every excuse under the sun, but it would make no difference. You are either innocent, or you aren't, and I'm not.

I cannot hope for redemption, but I pray for it. And I pray for my boy. I pray for him first and foremost, and then add the prayers for myself. If God is listening, then I beseech Him to save Simon, even if it means me burning in the fires of Hell for all eternity.

Yes, I know that I said I would never pray again but I no longer fear Zara's wrath. What more could she possibly do to torment me? Pain and anguish already consume me. If she set me alight, I would barely feel the scorch of the flames, and good luck to her if she tries to mess *further with my mind, because my mind is no longer the sponge it once was. It no longer soaks up any of the crap she throws at it.*

I've been to Hell... literally. Once you've been there... well, nothing else will ever come close to touching you. The experience overwhelmed every bad thing that has ever happened to me, and I count the loss of my mother and the loss of my son amongst the worst of those bad things.

I saw a different Hell to the one portrayed in books and in movies. I think that Dante's Inferno comes close, but even that epic masterpiece barely scratched the surface of how it was ultimately presented to me. I can't bring myself to describe the sounds, the smells, the utter hopelessness of the beings trapped in its fiery pit, but I can describe how I found myself there.

There came a shadow to my kitchen. It came, summoned by Zara, to take me and to show me the place where my son was trapped. I think that Zara wanted me to understand the enormity of my situation. I think she thought I was being a little blasé about the whole thing because who in their right mind would want to embrace such a fate? I think she wanted me to experience the reality, to finally understand the enormity of what was planned for me, and I think she wanted me to change my mind, to do battle with my conscience, and try to save myself. She didn't want me to go easy. She wanted me to choose myself over Simon and hoped that a brief glimpse of Hades would bring me to my senses.

    Zara is one big contradiction. She told me that she was my special friend. She told me that she thought she loved me. How preposterous is that? Her one purpose was to persuade me to sacrifice myself for my son. My sacrifice had to be a costly one. She tried to make my living world as precious as possible so that the pain of leaving it would be all the greater. And yet, part of *her wanted to save me. I'm sure of that. I think she wanted me to remain in the world with her at my side. After all, it made no difference to her who it was who took her place in hell. She would be quite content to allow Simon to remain as her replacement.*

The sick bitch actually thought that she had a chance with me so she summoned the shadow, and she used it to teach me what the consequences would be of a wrong decision.

To be embraced by something so cold, so lifeless, and so malevolent, was excruciating. Its embrace... no, it's grasp... completely enveloped me and I found myself unable to breathe. Weightless, by body sagging in the suffocating prison of its arms, I couldn't move. Because I couldn't move, it meant that I couldn't fight.

I wanted to fight. I didn't want to go quietly. I wanted to fight in ways that I'd never done to save myself from the influence of my mother, to save my son from death, or to save myself from a loveless marriage. I was sick of not fighting. I wanted to kick and scratch and claw, but I couldn't move. I couldn't breathe, I couldn't think.

How can that be imagined? How can that be overcome?

It couldn't.

I'm not sure how much time passed before my ordeal came to an end. I was gone for what seemed like forever. I woke up on the kitchen floor, gagging, choking, spitting out the vile taste in my mouth, and now, I wonder... am I a ghost?

I walk the rooms of my home, write in my journal, watch the birds from the kitchen window as they stomp on the grass to summon the worms to their beaks, but I am not seen, and I am not heard. I am a wraith, wretched in my agony. I bore witness to the evil that is yet to come. I made a bargain with one of the Dev-

il's minions, and now I wait. I wait to pay the piper.

I'm hoping that Anita will come. I won't blame her if she doesn't. I doubted her friendship, treated her like shit, denied her right to be respected, but I'm hoping that she will follow up on the calls she made that went unanswered, follow up on her failed messages. I pray that she will pop around to check up on me. If she does, I'm sure that she will see that I am gone.

Because I AM gone from this place. I may watch the birds, run my hand along the banister as I climb the stairs to my bedroom, but I am truly not here. If you looked, you would not see me. You wouldn't even sense my ghostly presence.

Richard won't come. He won't be worried enough. I'm not even sure if Anita will ultimately be worried enough. I fervently hope that she does, because I don't want that last novel... the novel I'm not sure that I even had a hand in creating, to be the lasting mark I leave. I want this journal to be my legacy, and I want Anita to be the one to find it.

Twenty-Nine

Richard woke up screaming. He fought to free himself from the sofa, terrified that it was swallowing him whole, and finally succeeded in throwing himself to the floor.

On his knees, the scream still hot in his throat, he blinked furiously in an attempt to rid himself of the images sparking in his brain. Those images wouldn't shift. If it had merely been the pictures in his mind, if it hadn't been for the terrible smell and the reminiscence of a fierce heat scorching his skin, he could have coped. He'd had nightmares before. Nightmares were no big deal. He forgot the majority of them as soon as his eyes popped open in the morning. No grown man was afraid of a bad dream. No grown man would wake up believing that the dream was real.

The rush of blood to his head made his ears whoosh. The smell, still caught in his nostrils, made him gag. The scream had died to a whimper and to Fiona, alerted to his distress and standing in the open doorway, he looked a sorry sight.

In the dim grey light of dawn, she saw the flesh on his naked body sag from his bones and droop towards the floor as if pulled there by some unseen force. She knew that the unseen force was the gravity that came with age, and she suddenly realised that she had tied herself to an old man. She had given him a week. She began to think that a week was six days too long.

He looked as if he was about to be sick and the only concern it brought was for the mess it would make of her carpet.

Richard wasn't aware of her presence. He was too far gone... still in the throes of the nightmare.

His son was aflame. He burned – his flesh blistering and blackening, peeling away in huge strips before hanging, like tatters, from his body. Then, he was dust, even his bones, but that wasn't the end of it. Like countless times before, Simon rose like a phoenix from the ashes, to scream again, to writhe in agony once more, and to suffer unfathomable moments of agony before he was, once again, dust.

Fiona stepped into the room. She had made love to the man on the floor too many times to count. She'd told him that she loved him, that she wanted to spend the whole of her life with him. Looking down at him, she wondered at the level of her insanity. He disgusted her and the sight of him made her hate herself. She felt nothing but shame and revulsion – shame that she'd welcomed his kisses, his touch, his flaccid cock, and revulsion at the memories.

'Get up,' she said. 'Put some fucking clothes on, and don't you dare be sick on my floor.'

He heard her, as if through a wall of fog. Relieved not to be alone, he tried to raise his head, tried to understand what was being said to him, tried to shake off the last of the dream, but – though shifting to wakefulness – the dream remained vivid behind his eyes.

He'd had nightmares before, but nothing like the one he'd just lived through. Previous nightmares hadn't included experiencing the whole scene through every sense and every fibre of his body. In that particular dream, he'd felt the heat, tasted the air, felt real agony and not just the usual fear that everyone suffers when living through a bad dream. It was as if he'd been plucked from the real world and actually placed inside the very bowels of Hell.

Fiona's voice kept at him, her angry tone prodding him further awake. Finally, excruciatingly slowly, the vision of his burning son receded. Regardless, he knew that the image of the boy's ordeal would forever be stamped on his brain.

On his knees, his forehead pressed to the floor, his stomach roiled, and his shoulders heaved. Bile surged up from his belly and burned his throat before erupting from his mouth in a vicious yellow stream.

He heard a scream, but it wasn't Simon's scream. It was a woman's scream, and it was one of fury as opposed to one of pain.

He bucked to the side as a foot landed on his ribs. It took him a few seconds to realise he'd been kicked. She'd fucking kicked him.

Fiona couldn't help herself. The vomit had been the final straw, but shocked at her action, she stepped back and gasped. She didn't quite know how to excuse herself.

'I'm sorry,' she said, watching as he rolled onto his back, groaning, and clutching at his belly. 'I know I shouldn't have done that.'

'No,' he moaned. 'You shouldn't have. What the fuck's wrong with you?'

'What's wrong with me? You're the one who's just spewed up over my brand-new carpet. Jesus, Richard, look at the fucking state of you.'

He blinked himself fully awake, took in his surroundings, and swallowed back on the remaining bile. For long moments, he simply lay on the floor, composing himself. He thanked God that the images of Simon were receding but was only too aware that the stench of burning flesh was still in his nose and the evidence of sulphur still in his lungs. None of it was real. He wasn't stupid enough to believe that any of it actually existed, but the sense of it, the taste, and the smell of it, most certainly was.

'What was all the screaming about?'

He was stunned. had she heard Simon's screams all the way from his nightmare? He realised not, and said, 'Was I screaming?'

'Were you screaming?' She shook her head. 'Too fucking right, you were. You nearly brought the ceiling down.'

'I had a bad dream.'

'You don't say? It must've been a doozey.'

'It was.'

'Well, you're awake now. It's time for you to shift yourself and get packed.'

He pulled himself onto his elbows. He still felt woozy, affected, but not enough to miss what Fiona said. He gazed up at her, half focussed and bleary-eyed. 'Packed? What are you talking about?'

'I want you to leave.'

'I *am* leaving. I never said that I wouldn't, but you gave me a week, remember?' He shivered and dragged the quilt off the sofa and draped it over himself, immediately appreciating its warmth. 'I still have six days left.'

'Fuck six days. I've changed my mind. I want you gone today.'

His eyes and his head cleared. Was she having a fucking laugh? 'No chance,' he said. 'I've got nowhere to go.'

'That's not my problem.'

'Don't you even care?'

'Not a bit.'

'Bitch.'

'Sticks and stones, Richard. Is *bitch* the best you can do?'

He saw that he'd gone too far. 'Look... I'm sorry. I didn't mean to say that. Can't we work this out? You don't really want me to go, do you?'

'There's nothing I want more.'

'I thought you loved me?' He hated the wheedling tone of his voice. He was beginning to disgust himself, but he had no choice. He had to win her around, at least until he could get his head screwed on straight and a plan worked out. 'You can't, baby,' he said. 'You can't just turf me out onto the street... not if you love me.'

'Who says I can't? This is my house, my home. You've got a home of your own... go crawling back there. Go back to your wife. I'm sure she'll greet you with open arms and open legs. And, as for loving you...' She snorted out a short laugh. 'In your dreams, Richard.'

He refused to beg. He wouldn't give her the satisfaction.

'Can I at least have a shower before I go?'

'Suit yourself. As long as you're gone by noon, I don't give a shit what you do.' On those final words, she about faced and stomped from the room.

Richard dropped back off his elbows, sighed, and listened to the gentle rumble of his belly. Thankfully, the remnants of his nightmare had all but disappeared and the last of his fear had morphed into a slow burning anger. He was angry at Fiona, but equally angry at Vanessa. Both of them had abandoned him. He couldn't, or wouldn't, admit that he'd been the one doing all the abandoning. He'd been onto a good thing with Fiona. It wasn't meant to last, but he'd been sure that he would be the one to end it and end it on his own terms, but it seemed that he'd underestimated just how much shit she'd been prepared to accept from him. The wedding ring debacle had been the final nail in the coffin of their relationship and the irony was that it wasn't even his fault.

As for Vanessa? He would never have imagined that she would blank him, that she would completely ghost him. He'd really believed that she would walk through hot coals for him, forever pine for him, and never, never cut him loose.

He was obviously losing his charm.

He was reminded of Anita's telephone call of the day before. She was obviously worried about Vanessa and maybe he should take a minute to wonder if he should be too. Moreover, maybe he ought to be worried about himself? The wedding ring and the nightmares notwithstanding, there were times when he thought he was losing his marbles. Maybe Vanessa's craziness was rubbing off on him?

The thought, though bizarre, made him shudder.

For a while, all he felt was the steady rise and fall of his chest. Fiona was being extraordinarily quiet, so there was just the sound of his breathing to break the silence in the house. He imagined what it must have been like for Fiona to be woken by his screams. She probably thought he was being murdered. He wondered if, for a moment, on waking, she'd even cared. Most likely not.

It was a sobering thought.

In his mind, in the quiet of the room, he began to run through all the possibilities of where he might stay. He needed someplace where it wouldn't cost him anything and because – since hooking up with Fiona he'd burned his bridges with all of his other women – the pickings were slim to none.

That left only one option – he had to go home.

Thirty

Anita was reluctant to use the key. If Vanessa was inside, as right as rain, and simply refusing to answer the door, she would have her guts for garters. She'd considered calling Richard again and asking him...no, begging him... to stand with her, but he was as much use as a chocolate teapot, and it wasn't worth the bother trying to persuade him. She thought that it would take her finding Vanessa's corpse to have him shift himself.

Her reticence at upsetting Vanessa was grounded in the fact that she was going to share in a ton of money from the sales of her latest book. She didn't want to do anything to jeopardise either Vanessa's mood or her willingness to go along with the plans the publishing house had for marketing what the CEO had described as a masterpiece. In the couple of weeks since Anita had shared the manuscript with the publisher, attitudes had dramatically altered. Vanessa was right back up there as a valuable commodity and, as her literary agent, Anita shared in the kudos. She wasn't about to fuck that up.

She tried knocking on the door once more, then moved to the side of the house and rapped on the window. The possibility of her not being at home never entered Anita's head. Vanessa was always at home. The fact that she hadn't screamed at her to fuck off, seriously worried her and she had visions of finding her corpse after all.

'Right,' she said, throwing her shoulders back and marching back around to the front of the house.

'I'm coming in, Vanessa,' she called out at the top of her lungs, then turning the key in the lock and pushing on the door. It stuck on something on the floor, and it took some effort to force it all the way open.

'Jesus,' she sighed, staring down at the pile of letters, bills and junk mail littering the space just behind the door. 'What the fuck are you up to, Vanessa?'

She closed the door and then stood still for a moment, taking in the silence and the musty smell.

Dead bodies smell something awful, she thought, reassuring herself that, at least, it wasn't likely that her search would find the lifeless form of a deceased Vanessa. At least that was something, she supposed.

The problem was that it was much too quiet. The house felt unlived in. She automatically thought of Zara and then recalled Vanessa's hurried words before she'd left those weeks earlier.

Had the other woman taken her somewhere? It seemed the only possible explanation, but had she gone willingly?

She hoped so.

She didn't expect a reply, but nevertheless called out Vanessa's name. Her voice bounced back off the walls and then the silence dropped once more.

Twenty minutes later and she'd searched every room, looked in every nook and cranny, and found no sign of her anywhere. She'd left Vanessa's bedroom until the last. She'd been afraid to go in, to look at the wall where... She refused to think about that. It hadn't been real. That face had been nothing more than a figment of her exhausted imagination.

There had been nothing out of place in the bedroom. The bed was made up, there were no clothes scattered around, and the whole room was as neat as a pin with no sign of a struggle or a hurried departure.

Satisfied that Vanessa wasn't in the house, she began to search for the journal. She knew to look in the garage. She couldn't recall if

Vanessa had told her it would be there, but she knew that's where she would find it.

And she did.

It was just an ordinary lined notebook, nothing special. Vanessa's hand had obviously been steady when she made the entries and Anita could quite clearly see – despite her obvious angst – that she penned the words carefully. She only got as far as the first couple of passages before closing it, hitching in a breath, and calling the police.

She hadn't expected to be taken seriously. Vanessa was a grown woman, there had been no sign of a struggle, no blood anywhere, and no reason to believe that anything untoward had happened to her. She was surprised, therefore, when an hour later, two police constables turned up at the door. Before they arrived, she'd read another entry in the journal but was so spooked and so upset that she couldn't bring herself to read any further.

The police officers conducted their own search of the house, looking in all the places that Anita had already visited, and then questioned her for a few minutes before telling her exactly what she'd expected to hear.

'We'll give it twenty-four hours,' one of them said, 'and, if she fails to make contact, or doesn't come back home, we'll escalate the matter.'

Anita wasn't having any of that. As far as anyone knew, Vanessa had already been missing for weeks. Waiting a further twenty-four hours seemed folly. Then, there was the journal. It clearly suggested that Vanessa either suffered a full-blown mental breakdown – in which case she was extremely vulnerable – or someone had been playing a rather nasty game with her and that person could've ended up hurting her, or worse.

She demanded that more be done. She insisted that Vanessa was immediately classed as a missing person, and she even went so far as to suggest that maybe she'd taken herself off to commit suicide. She waved the journal under their noses, recited some of the passages, and threatened to go to the newspapers with the story that a famous author – missing, vulnerable, and probably in great danger – was being ignored.

The police constables did the only thing they could – they passed the buck.

DETECTIVE SERGEANT, John London, had a wife who was a big fan of Vanessa Parker. She always seemed to have her nose stuck in one of her books, so when he heard the name, he immediately knew who and what Vanessa Parker was.

When he read the journal, his immediate thought was that she had some imagination but, of course, she was a writer, and a bestselling author, so, that ought not to have come as a surprise. It was the last entry that gave him pause for thought, and it was those words that initiated an investigation into her disappearance.

EXTRACT FROM THE JOURNAL of author Vanessa Parker, discovered by her literary agent, Anita Sanderson.

I don't know if I will be able to write any more. Every day, I'm finding the act of wielding the pen to be more onerous and more nerve-wracking. I can't be sure if Zara knows that I'm making a record of what's been happening to me, and I can't risk her finding this journal and destroying it. Quite apart from that, I'm also finding that holding the pen, ordering my thoughts, and placing the words on the paper to be more and more exhausting. I get confused. I seem to drift off into a sort of fugue state quite often. I can be holding the pen, words fluttering like discarded paper across my mind, and an hour will have past without me noticing. It can be daylight outside, and then, when I snap out of whatever it was that gripped me, it's suddenly dark and the pen is on the floor and the paper smudged as if from drops of forgotten tears.

I have watched the sun come up thirteen times since my return from Hades. I've been here, alone, and frightened, for nearly two weeks. Two weeks without seeing or speaking to a single soul. Even Zara doesn't visit.

My phone rings intermittently. I've attempted to answer it many times, but some invisible force prevents me from doing so. I can't touch it, have it near me, or even look at it without feeling sick. It's not a nausea that is bearable. It is an experience that leaves me reeling, leaves me believing that I'm being turned inside out. So, I quickly learned to ignore the phone calls, and deny myself any attempt to listen to the many messages that I'm sure were left for me.

This morning, I found myself no longer alone. SHE came back... Zara. I blinked and, suddenly, there she was.

She looked different. She no longer smiled or sounded out that annoying trill of a laugh. She was taller, fuller at the hips and breasts, less waif-like. Her hair, usually bouncing with curls, hung down her back in long greasy coils and she smelled to the high heavens. She moved as if she had a stick up her arse, all stilted and stiff. Her limbs seemed to belong to someone else and her control over their movements was limited to jerks and jolts.

I didn't know what to make of the change in her. She saw the fear and confusion in my eyes and all she said was, 'You'll see.'

I'll see? What would I see? I didn't ask her for an explanation. I didn't believe that I would get one and, in asking, I thought I would lessen myself even further in her now scant estimation of me.

But I did have to ask her one thing. I had to ask her when the whole ordeal of waiting would be over.

She was disappointed in me. She thought that I would be desperate to cling to life, that sacrificing myself was no longer what I wanted. For all her insight, for all her powers, for all she'd learned about me, she really didn't know me at all.

'Soon,' she said. 'Be patient.'

Patient? I think I screamed then. I could hear it, high-pitched, yet mournful, and I was sure that it came from deep inside me. Zara had merely looked at me. Her eyes were quite dead. Her face expressionless.

'You're already dying,' she said. 'Do you feel it?'

I nodded. I knew that she was right. I asked her if that was what the waiting was all about. Did I have to experience a mortal death before an end would be put to the whole thing?

Again, those dead eyes, that expressionless countenance.

She wanted me to work it out for myself.

'I'll kill myself,' I said, determined to do it if it meant it would all be over. I was afraid... terrified... but that terror paled in comparison to the agony over my son. I went so far as to reach for a knife, but just like the times when I'd gone to answer my phone, I was stopped by an all-consuming wave of nausea that bent me double and drove me to my knees. Apparently, suicide wasn't permitted. I was to slowly starve to death.

Funny thing is... I don't want to eat. Starvation isn't being forced upon me. And the best of it is, I don't want to drink either... not vodka anyway. For the first time in years, there isn't a drop of alcohol in my body.

I've been living on coffee and water. I'm getting close to being nothing but skin and bones. If I stop drinking altogether, I think I can bring this to an end in a matter of days. I remember some research I did a few years ago. I can't recall what book I'd been writing at the time... I'm sure you'll remember, Anita. Anyway, I discovered that a person could go quite some time without food, but dehydration would finish them off in a matter of around three days.

Three days and my son could be free. The devil would have me, and Simon's innocent little soul would be released. Three days would seem like an eternity to him, and I only hope that God's arms will heal him and make him forget.

It's dark now and I'm beginning to panic. What if someone comes? What if you come, Anita? I wished for it, I know, but not now. If you come, or if Richard comes, and if either of you saw me...

Will you see me? I don't think so. I believe that there is a cloak around me, concealing me, but I can't take the risk. You would have me in the hospital before I had a chance to explain. You would take one look at me and be right on the phone to summon an ambulance.

You wouldn't understand. You wouldn't understand that I don't want to be saved.

Three days is all I ask. Just stay away for three days, then bury me with my son.

Thirty-One

She was dead. He knew it in his heart, but he didn't know how to feel about it. He felt something... he couldn't deny that much... but it wasn't tangible, wasn't something he could take out and look at, and it wasn't something he could bring himself to talk about.

He dreaded waking up and feeling a sense of relief. He didn't want to feel that... not that. She didn't deserve so little of him.

The police hadn't found the body. They didn't say as much, but he knew that it was a body they were searching for. He was no longer under suspicion and the consensus was that she'd done away with herself whilst the ... how had they put it... whilst the balance of her mind was disturbed.

He hadn't read the journal. It was out of bounds but, as her next of kin, he'd been promised – once it was no longer required as evidence – to have it given into his possession. Apparently, it was because of what was in that journal that the police didn't believe she'd been abducted or murdered.

Although he hadn't read it, Anita had shared what she knew, and he'd been left in no doubt that, over the past few weeks, his wife had slowly gone off her rocker. Not that Anita believed that was the case. She wouldn't say why, but she seemed to accept everything that Vanessa had written.

He conveniently forgot his own nightmares, as well as the parallels between what happened to Vanessa and what happened – and was still – happening to him. His mind simply refused to go there. That was one rabbit hole he had no intention going down.

If he'd known, if he'd learned of the later entries in the journal describing their son's torturous experiences in hell, then – like it or not – he would've gone down that rabbit hole all the way to the bottom, because those entries perfectly described his dreams.

The nightmares had ceased. He hadn't experienced one since he'd been told that Vanessa was missing. That didn't mean he slept any better. He was still on Fiona's sofa. She'd relented and allowed him to stay but refused him entry back into her bed. He wasn't that bothered because sex was the last thing on his mind. All he could think about was Vanessa's body slowly decomposing as he sat and waited on the news that she'd been found. He expected to be told at any moment and lay awake most nights expecting his phone to ring or to hear a knock at the door.

The part of him that remained avaricious, the part of him that made him a selfish bastard, worried that her body might never be found. If that proved to be the case, then he was fucked because she wouldn't be declared dead, so he wouldn't be able to get his greedy mitts on her money, not for years.

Anita told him that there was going to be tons of money... eventually. Vanessa's latest book was on hold, awaiting the outcome of the search, and publication would then roll out once probate was settled. She expected, once news of her death spread, that the royalties from her other books would hit an all-time high. Just like dead artists, and dead pop stars, a dead author sold more books than a live one. Again, he wouldn't see a penny until after probate... not unless they found a will which – up until that point – they hadn't. Not that Richard had a chance to look for one. He wasn't allowed anywhere near the house and Vanessa's safety deposit box at the bank was strictly out of bounds.

He dreaded what a will would show and hoped never to clap eyes on one. He wouldn't be surprised if she'd left him nothing... just his half of the house which she couldn't deny him. The good part of him

– the part that still existed beneath the tight layers of self-interest – wouldn't blame her if she'd stuck two fingers up at him at the end. That part of him knew that he didn't deserve a penny from the sales of her books. Truth be told, he didn't even deserve any of the proceeds from the sale of the house. She'd bought it, furnished it, looked after its upkeep. He hadn't contributed one red cent. Nevertheless, she'd included his name on the deeds, so it was a certainty that he would get his half. There was nothing she could do about that from the grave.

'You've got no one now, have you?' Fiona said from the doorway. 'I feel a little bit sorry about that.'

It was dark in the lounge, but she stood, backlit from the glow in the hallway, and he could see that there was a tiny smile playing at the corners of her mouth. The bitch wasn't sorry, not even a tiny bit. At that moment, she seemed like a complete stranger.

Fiona had never been vindictive or heartless. Okay, she'd wanted to chuck him out on his ear, but that was more because she felt hurt and abandoned, and not out of any sense of revenge or because she'd truly stopped caring about him. Now – although she'd graced him with a few days' respite – he knew that she'd grown to hate him and all because – strangely enough – she felt a sort of solidarity with his missing wife.

You couldn't make it up, he thought, watching her through half-closed lids. His mistress hated him because she blamed him for causing a sister to suffer unimaginable pain and anguish.

She'd actually called Vanessa her sister earlier... her fucking sister, for Christ's sake. It was obvious that she'd taken feminine solidarity a little too far and it was on the tip of his tongue to remind her that she'd been the one – far more than him – to cause Vanessa pain. She'd ensured that Vanessa had ended up losing him.

Unlike his other mistresses, Fiona had insisted that he leave his wife. If he'd decided to stay home, stayed with Vanessa, then it would've been business as usual. Vanessa would've accepted the affair in much the same way as she'd come to accept all the others so, if anyone had caused her mind to skydive off the deep end, it certainly hadn't been him. It was the sanctimonious bitch standing with the smirk on her face who was to blame, but he kept his tongue still. He didn't lash out with words of accusation and blame. He knew what side his bread was buttered and, until the police allowed him access to his own house, he had to bite down on his ire and suffer the insults. It was either that or find himself homeless.

He shivered. The air had suddenly grown cold. Fiona turned her head, as if something had moved behind her. Her eyes widened and she wrapped her arms across her chest and almost hugged herself.

'What is it?' he asked, alert to the expression on her face. She looked scared.

'Nothing. I'm cold,' she replied. 'Do you feel it? Are you cold?'

Before he could reply, Fiona's head suddenly snapped back. He saw it but couldn't quite believe it. It snapped back so quickly and so violently and at such an angle that its very movement seemed an impossibility. Then, before he had a chance to blink or to react in the slightest, her whole body jerked to the side and her head was violently flung forward and the sickening thud as it hit the doorframe made Richard's stomach lurch.

'Fiona?' He made a small movement, making to stand. 'What...?' He hovered half on and half off the couch. 'Fiona?'

She didn't lift her head to look at him. She couldn't. She was out like a light. She didn't crumple to the floor and that fact added to his confusion. He looked behind her, saw nothing, and turned his eyes once more to the bloody mess that was her face.

She should be on the floor... she should be... He shook his head, as if to clear it. For a brief moment, he thought he was living through another nightmare. Any moment, he would wake up.

The seconds ticked past. Everything felt still and ominous. Fiona continued to hang there, her knees bent and her body flopping forward. It was as if she was being held up by some unseen hand. She sagged, unconscious, and the blood pouring from the gash in her forehead mesmerised him.

Richard felt himself grow frozen with shock and disbelief. He'd dropped the few inches back onto the couch and he now sat there unsure what to do, what to think.

Even if he'd wanted to – which he didn't – he could no longer make the effort to move from his place on the couch. He sensed an evil presence. It was so strong that it seemed to make the air hum and some primal instinct warned him that, if he moved, if he went to Fiona's aid, he would be struck down before he'd even got to his feet.

He suddenly realised that it wasn't a nightmare. It was really happening. All he could do was to sit and wait in dumb horror to see what came next, because something was definitely coming next.

He didn't have long to wait. Before his eyes, he saw Fiona yanked backwards then dragged back on her heels to the bottom of the stairs. From his vantage point in the middle of the lounge, his view of the stairs was uninterrupted, and he followed her progress with wide, stupefied eyes as she was dragged by her hair, bump by loud bump, up every step.

When she disappeared from view, his ears were assaulted by loud banging and crashing. At one point, he thought that the ceiling was going to crack and crash down on his head.

His body jolted with every sound. Tears welled in his eyes. He had no doubt that Fiona was being smashed to a pulp.

At last, he was on his feet and stumbling from the room. It had grown quiet. The silence was almost deafening. He made for the bottom of the stairs, halted, and peered all the way to the top, alert for any sound or movement.

'Fiona?' he called out, knowing he wouldn't hear a reply.

He placed his hand on the banister, intent on going up, but failed to haul himself onto the first step. He didn't want to bear witness to whatever had been done to her and, coward that he was, he turned, grabbed his car keys, and hurried through the front door.

He was certain that his car wouldn't start and almost sobbed with relief when the engine turned over on the first attempt. Burning rubber, he screeched onto the main road, turned left, and blinded by tears, navigated towards the nearest police station.

Behind the wheel, he made low guttural sounds from deep in his throat. He was trying not to scream. If he screamed, he would lose control of the car. He had to calm himself, but it was impossible. His hands were so slick with sweat that they slipped on the steering wheel and the car veered all over the road as if being driven by someone pissed out of their skull. He barely missed colliding with an oncoming vehicle and its blaring horn sounded the alarm just in time.

He began to come to his senses. Realisation dawned that it would be a mistake of incredible magnitude to go to the police. What would they say? What would they think when they saw Fiona's broken body? They would blame him.

He turned off the road and brought the car to a shuddering halt. Before doing anything, before speaking to a single soul about what he'd just witnessed, he had to try and make sense of it.

In his mind, he replayed the scene of Fiona being dragged up the stairs. He pictured himself doing the dragging and, for a brief horrifying moment, he wondered if he'd actually been the one to kill her. He'd been angry enough. He remembered that much, but he knew he couldn't have done such a dreadful thing.

But the police would believe it. They wouldn't be able to get their heads around any other scenario. How could he explain what he'd witnessed? How could he ever hope to convince them that there had been something evil, something supernatural in the house? He couldn't, so there was no point in him trying.

There was only one person who might believe him. Anita.

Thirty-Two

Until that night, Anita had never thought she would have to sit and listen to such a horrifying yet fanciful tale. Richard had turned up out of the blue, looking as if the hounds of hell were after him, and she'd let him into her home because she didn't have the heart to turn him away.

She'd never liked him. She had no respect for him. He was someone she'd hoped never to see again, but he looked so pitiful, so frightened standing on her doorstep that she waved him in without giving the action much thought.

He asked for a stiff brandy and, once she'd handed him the glass, she had to wait an inordinate length of time before he was calm enough to explain his presence.

He began haltingly. His words were barely above a whisper, and she had to ask him to repeat himself several times before she grasped their meaning. When he got to the part where Fiona was being dragged up the stairs, she held up a hand and shook her head – more to gather her thoughts and to try and understand the significance of what he'd been telling her, rather than to stop him talking – and he obliged by closing his mouth and simply staring silently at her through watery eyes.

'Let me get this straight,' she said, after a long moment. 'You're telling me that Fiona is dead?'

He nodded.

'By some... *thing*... some invisible thing?'

He nodded once more.

'Do you know how fucked up that sounds?'

'Yeah.'

'Did you see her? Did you see the body?'

Anita couldn't believe how calm she sounded to her own ears. Deep down, she realised that she didn't believe him. She didn't believe that Fiona had been attacked, and she didn't believe that she was dead. She wasn't sure if he'd imagined it, dreamt it, or if he was playing some cruel joke on her and it was those doubts that kept her voice level and allowed her mind to remain unaffected.

But when she looked at him – really looked at him – those doubts faded. He presented as a man driven to the very edge of sanity and she began to wonder if he'd killed his girlfriend and that his horror-stricken mind had conjured up an elaborate story to excuse his deed.

'No,' he said. 'I couldn't bring myself to go up to her. I was scared, Anita. I didn't know what was up there with her.'

'That's ridiculous,' she snorted. 'You had a nightmare, that's all, or...'

'Or I killed her? Is that what you're thinking?' He rose slowly from his chair, placed his empty glass on the small coffee table in front of him, and ran an agitated hand through his hair.

She watched him. She remained poised to flee the room should he make a move towards her. She made no effort to make a reply to his question about whether she believed he'd been the one to kill Fiona. She still didn't quite believe that the woman was dead.

'I... I don't know what happened, okay?' he said. 'All I know is that I didn't kill her, and I didn't do anything to help her either. Things have been happening... I've been dreaming about Simon. My wedding ring...' He couldn't go on and flopped back down into the chair. 'None of it can be real, can it?'

'Why have you come here with this story, Richard? Why here? Why to me?'

'Because... because you believe what Vanessa wrote in that bloody journal.' His voice had risen, had grown harder, less controlled. 'You know something's been going on... something fucked up.'

She remembered the flies, recalled the image coming through Vanessa's bedroom wall, blinked away the memories, and huffed in a breath. She was losing the battle with her common sense and was wavering towards at least considering that what he'd told her was true.

'You should go to the police,' she said, trembling with suppressed emotion. 'They'll get to the bottom of it.'

'Are you mad?' He was up on his feet once more, leaning towards her aggressively. 'They'd lock me up and throw away the key.'

Pressing herself against the back of the sofa, Anita raised her hands. She feared that he would strike out at her, hurt her.

Richard saw the fear in her eyes and immediately drew back.

'I'm sorry,' he said. 'I'm just so fucking scared.'

'Yeah, me too,' she returned. 'I wish you'd sit down.'

He stood still for a moment, then nodded and retook his seat.

Anita visibly relaxed. 'Vanessa mentioned something about nightmares... in her journal,' she said. 'They were about Simon being in hell... being tortured.'

Richard's jaw dropped. 'That's... that's what I dreamt.'

'I didn't get to read everything. I asked, but the police wouldn't let me, but I read enough... well, I've already told you this... but I read enough to think that something had forced her to have those nightmares.'

'Yes.' He nodded quickly. 'That's it... exactly.'

'It doesn't mean...'

'No, I know but...' He dragged in a mouthful of air. 'Do you really think...?'

'I don't know what to think.'

'Fiona... oh, God... Fiona, and what's happened to Vanessa? I can't deal with this, Anita. It's sending me off my fucking head.'

'I still think that going to the police is for the best. If... if Fiona really is dead...'

'I should've gone upstairs. I should've checked. Perhaps she was still alive, although...' He closed his eyes, as if in pain. 'I can't imagine how she could've survived.'

'Do you want to go back?'

'God, no.' He was aghast at the thought. 'I'm never going back there.'

'But, if she's still alive? She might need an ambulance.'

'I told you... I'm not going back there.' His words put a finality on the subject.

Anita remembered why she didn't like him. he was all about self, self, self.

'Then call an ambulance from here. At least send someone to check on her.'

'Absolutely not. She's dead. I know she is.'

'So, what are you going to do? You can't stay here. I don't want anything to do with this.... Whatever the fuck *this* is.'

'You believe me, don't you?'

She sighed. 'I don't know.'

'Then how can I expect the police to believe me? They'll think I killed her. Part of you believes that doesn't it, Anita?'

It was a challenge. Anita's sense of danger heightened. She should never have allowed him in the door.

'Well?' he prompted. 'Admit it... you think I killed her.'

'I don't even know if any of it happened. You could've gone off your trolley. For all I know, you could have imagined the whole thing.'

'Do I look as if I'm deranged?'

'Do you want an honest answer to that?' Despite her growing fear, she couldn't stop the snippy remark. 'You might not like what I have to say.'

'Say it anyway. Let's hear what you really think.'

'Just forget it. Do what you want but do it somewhere else.'

'No... go on... spit it out. You never liked me. I know that, but I thought you'd at least be honest with me.'

'I'm always honest.'

'Oh, I forgot... Saint fucking Anita.' He glowered across at her. 'You do know that Vanessa hated you, don't you?' His words were meant to sting, and, by the way, her mouth opened in a perfect O, they did sting.

He felt suddenly ashamed. *Why was he such a fucking dick?*

'Sorry,' he said. 'I shouldn't have said that. 'You know what she was like. She hated everybody, but never really meant it.'

Anita took several deep breaths. She knew exactly what Vanessa thought of her and she didn't need that prick to enlighten her.

'You don't have any blood on you,' she said, her voice flat.

'What?' He looked down at his hands, at his clothes. 'So?'

'So, you couldn't have killed Fiona. If you had, you would be covered, saturated in her blood.'

He nodded, understanding. 'But you still think I could've imagined the whole thing?'

'It makes more sense than the alternative.'

'I didn't imagine it.'

'Okay.'

'Okay?'

'I believe you. Now what?'

'I need to know how... I need to know why, and I need to know what happened to Vanessa.'

'I think she's dead.'

His head jerked up. 'So do I. God forgive me... so do I.'

'We might never know what happened to her... what happened to Fiona.'

'I know what happened to Fiona. I saw it with my own fucking eyes.'

'Not all of it.'

'No, but my ears didn't deceive me.'

'Whatever's going on, it's beyond us.'

'You may be right, but we're in the thick of it.'

'You are, Richard. Not me.' The image of the flies returned to her mind. She knew that he was right. She was as involved as he was, but she refused to acknowledge it as fact. 'I told you... I want nothing to do with any of it.'

'Do you imagine that you have a choice?'

She thought about that a moment, then said, 'It's not up to you to take that choice away from me. I think it's time you left.'

'And go where?'

'I don't care.'

'You sound just like Fiona.' His eyes sparked. 'She said as much when she told me to fuck off out of her life.'

'She saw sense, then?' She regretted the words as soon as they left her mouth, knowing it wasn't wise to antagonise him.

Instead of flaring with anger, he merely nodded. 'You're right about that. No woman is safe around me.'

Her heart leapt in her chest. 'What do you mean by that?'

'Not what you think. I just mean that I piss all over them and their feelings. I'm a first-class shit, but you already know that don't you?'

She gave him a thin smile but, otherwise, kept her thoughts to herself.

They lapsed into an uneasy silence. Richard made no move to leave. Anita was just about to tell him again – to insist that he go

– when they were both jarred out of their reverie by the sound of a phone ringing.

Anita looked across to where her phone sat on a small occasional table at the side of the sofa. It wasn't hers.

Richard reached into his back pocket and pulled out his. The ringtone immediately grew louder.

He looked at the screen, screwed up his eyes, and then turned it so that Anita could see the name.

Vanessa.

Thirty-Three

Anita stared at the screen then looked into Richard's shocked face. 'I thought... I thought the police had her phone?' she said. 'How can she...?'

'I don't fucking know.'

'Well, answer it, for fuck's sake.'

He shook his head. He didn't want to.

His phone eventually kicked into voicemail and the ringing ceased. The silence was even more ominous than the jarring sound of the call and both of them shifted uneasily in their seats and continued to stare at one another, not knowing what to say.

'That was weird,' Richard finally said, breaking the silence and the eye contact simultaneously. 'It could mean...'

'What? What could it mean?'

'That she's okay. That the police found her and gave her the phone back.'

'I think we'd know if that was true.'

'She could've told them not to say anything... said she wanted to tell me herself.'

'Could be.'

'Yes, that's it... she wanted to tell me herself.' He looked back down at the phone in his hand. 'There's no message. She didn't leave a voicemail.'

'She'll ring back.'

He nodded absently.

'She will.'

'I'm sure you're right.'

'You could call her.'

The thought of doing just that sent a shiver the length of his spine. 'No. I'll wait... see if she rings back.'

It was Anita's turn to nod. She was glad that he'd decided to wait. She wasn't sure what would happen if he tried to return the call. 'I can't believe that she's all right,' she said.

'Me neither. I wonder where she's been.'

'If it was even her on the phone.'

'Who else could it have been?'

'The police... using her phone?'

'To call me? Don't be stupid. Why would they do that?'

'To trick you, I suppose.'

'I don't think the police play games like that, do you?'

'Probably not.'

'So, it must've been her.'

'Maybe, but you're conveniently forgetting everything that happened to you tonight. Something might be playing games... messing with you.'

'Shit, Anita, don't put that thought into my head.'

'I'm just saying...'

'Yeah, right... I get it.'

'I said that I believed you... about what went on with Fiona. I just think that you shouldn't jump to conclusions about who was on the phone.'

'I won't. I'm not. Let's drop the subject, please.'

'Are you sure you don't want to call back?'

'Fuck, no.'

'Okay.'

When the phone rang again, both of them rose an inch off their seats in fright.

'Jesus,' Richard said.

'Fuck me,' Anita intoned, grabbing her throat, and going rigid. 'Is it her?'

'Yeah. What should I do? Should I answer it?'

'How should I know?'

The phone continued to ring. It didn't drop into voicemail.

'I'd better answer it,' Richard said.

'Are you sure?'

'Yeah.' He pressed the button to accept the call, held the phone to his ear, said, 'Vanessa?'

Anita held her breath.

'What, the fuck, Vanessa? Where have you been? We've all been... Okay. Okay. Calm down.' He looked across at Anita, hiked a brow, shook his head. 'I'm at Anita's,' he said into the phone. 'Never mind about that. Where are you?'

He listened for a few moments, nodding now and again, then said, 'Right. Of course. But...'

'What is it? What's she saying?' Anita hissed.

Richard held his free hand up, silencing her, then listened some more before holding the phone against his chest and saying, 'She's at the house. She wants us to go over.'

'Both of us?' she whispered.

He nodded and looked questioningly at her.

'I'm not sure,' she said, suddenly more frightened than she'd ever been in her life. She wasn't sure what scared her. She should feel relieved, ecstatic, but a niggling doubt grabbed at her and shook her very insides. 'Did she say where she'd been? I mean... Jesus, Richard.'

'She wouldn't say. All she said was that she's okay and needs to see us.'

'That's all she said?' She didn't believe him. It sure sounded as if she'd said a lot more than that.

'She's been rambling. I didn't catch most of it.'

'And you're sure it's her?'

'Of course, I'm fucking sure. I happen to know the sound of my own wife's voice.'

'You've not been very sure of much tonight, have you?' she snapped back at him, but keeping her voice low so she wouldn't be heard on the other end of the phone. 'So don't bite my head off for asking.'

'Sorry. Look... it really is her and you've got to come with me to the house. She insists.'

'After all that's happened? Are you nuts?'

'Forget what's happened. We can't do anything about that. It's Vanessa. Come on, Anita... it's Vanessa.'

Sweating, very aware of her pounding heart, Anita couldn't rid herself of the dread blossoming across her chest and up into her throat. Something wasn't right. She was sure of it.

'You go. Call me when you get there... when you see her,' she said. 'I can follow on later.'

Richard made to say something, to argue with her, but thought better of it. Back on the phone, he said, 'I'll be right over. Stay put.'

He smiled, put his phone back in his pocket, and leaned back in his chair. 'Do you believe this shit? I can't quite believe it.'

Anita steadied herself. She wasn't sure if she could squeeze out another word. Finally, she said, 'What did she have to say for herself? Why didn't she tell you where she'd been?'

'She was upset... crying. I didn't want to badger her. I'm sure that it'll all come out in the wash.'

'Haven't you forgotten something?'

He frowned. 'What?'

'Oh, just a dead body.'

'You mean Fiona?'

'Of course, I mean Fiona. Don't you find all of this a bit strange? Don't you think it's a coincidence that Vanessa suddenly turns up, phones you, just after everything you've gone through? Aren't you scared?'

'Fucking terrified, but it was her, Anita. That's all I know for sure. Everything else is just... well, God knows what everything else is. I can't think about that now. I have to get over there.'

He stood and Anita joined him in the middle of the floor. She placed a hand on his arm. 'Don't go. Call the police. Find out from them what's happened.'

'You're being ridiculous. I'm going, and that's all there is to it.'

She dropped her hand. 'Then, you're a fucking idiot.'

He rolled his eyes. 'I'll call you as soon as I get an explanation from her. And Anita...?'

She looked him square in the face. 'What?'

'Don't you dare call the police.'

He left without another word. Anita didn't follow him to the door or watch from the window as he headed off into God knew what sort of trouble.

Before she could talk herself out of it, she immediately picked up her mobile phone. There was no way on God's green earth that she wasn't getting a hold of Detective Sergeant London. Richard might be all sorts of a fool, but she wasn't.

No signal. She walked through to the kitchen. Still, no signal. Frowning, she went to the house phone, picked it up and discovered that the line was dead.

She was being fucked with.

She looked for shadows, her eyes darting in her head. She listened for any sign that she wasn't alone in the house. Everything was still, deathly silent. She didn't see or hear anything out of the ordinary but, regardless, she maintained her vigilance knowing that the lack of signal and a dead phone wasn't a coincidence.

Okay, she thought, *I'll drive there.* It was only three or four miles, and she could be there in a matter of ten minutes.

Half expecting the front door to be locked and barred, preventing her from opening it, she was almost apoplectic with relief when she pulled it towards her and immediately felt the cool night air on her face. Wasting no time, she headed straight for her car.

The car door also opened without incident, and she had no problem starting it and pulling off the driveway. She began to relax. She even felt a little foolish for her haste. It was only as she drew near to the police station that she felt something amiss. Instead of slowing down to take the final corner, the car inexplicably built up speed.

What the…?

Anita eased her foot off the accelerator and pressed down on the brake pedal. The car didn't respond.

'Fuck,' she said, under her breath, before offering up a softly mumbled prayer.

Then, holding onto the madly vibrating steering wheel with one hand, and grabbing the handbrake with the other, she desperately tried to take control of the vehicle.

But the car was having none of it. As if possessed, it veered across the road, narrowly missing a lamppost, and headed off in the opposite direction. Anita could do nothing to stop it. The handbrake was fully engaged, but it was worse than useless. The brake pedal refused to shift. In a final desperate act, she put the car into reverse gear. It was a mad thing to have done. Madder still was the speedometer continuing to rise.

The car took on a voice. It screeched and whined and something under the bonnet banged. By that time, Anita was screaming at the top of her lungs and desperately trying to free herself from her seatbelt. She had every intention of throwing her great bulk out of the door, not caring how many bones she broke when she landed.

Her chest heaved. Her screams were lost in the roar of the engine. The seatbelt wouldn't unclip. She was trapped and knew that she was heading for her death.

A jolt and a sharp swerve flung her to the side, and she banged her head on the window. She saw stars, and then she saw Zara. She was in the seat next to her, smiling and reaching out to pat her leg. Anita's continued screams now left her throat in one long high-pitched agony of terror.

Before the car ploughed, head on into an oncoming vehicle, it was travelling at eighty miles an hour.

Anita died instantly.

Thirty-Four

Richard's journey to the house went quickly and smoothly. He met no obstacles and his car behaved itself perfectly. He admitted to himself that he was a little fearful. Anita's words had planted a few seeds of doubt in his brain, but he drove on stoically, if somewhat anxiously.

When he reached his destination, he remained in the car and studied the house. A single shaft of light told him that Vanessa was in the lounge. All of the other windows were dark, and he couldn't imagine her sitting in the inky blackness all alone.

Vanessa didn't like the dark. She hated it almost as much as the outside world. That thought brought him up short. She'd been out in the big wide world for weeks. *How had she managed that?* he wondered. It was one of the questions he was determined to get an answer to.

He had a sudden inexplicable desire to lock the car doors and stay there, the quiet of his surroundings suddenly spooking him.

It was strange to have only one light on in the house. Vanessa always kept the little lamp on the hallway table switched on, but there was no glow showing through the glass in the front door, meaning it was off.

Stranger still, was the fact that the sensor hadn't gone on when he'd pulled up. The driveway should've been bathed in yellow light, but it had remained dark except for the sweep of his headlights.

He turned sideways in his seat and peered out the window on his left, searching the front of the house for movement. He had a strange feeling that he was being watched.

His phone pinged and he jumped with fright.

Silly bugger. Get a fucking grip.

It was a text message. It said, *Come in. The door isn't locked.*

He felt foolish in hesitating. She was his wife. What was there to be frightened of?

Bloody Anita... putting thoughts into his head. It wasn't Vanessa who'd killed Fiona. Of that, he was sure.

Fiona was in his head. He couldn't shift her. He hadn't needed Anita to warn him. He was well aware that he could be walking into a trap. He wasn't fucking stupid.

Swallowing back on the lump in his throat, he opened the door and climbed out. There was nothing he could do for Fiona, but perhaps there was something he could do for his wife.

About bloody time, he thought. He should've looked out for her more. God only knew where she'd been... what trouble she'd found herself in. If it was even half of what he imagined, then Christ help her... Christ help them both.

He found her in the lounge, sitting as still as stone, her hands folded in her lap. She looked up when he went through the door. She smiled and it was radiant. The only thing was – it wasn't Vanessa.

He did a double take, stepped back in surprise, and said, 'Who the fuck are you?'

The small woman – and she *was* small, hardly noticeable in the large wing-back chair – didn't reply. Instead, her gaze raked over him in an almost insolent silence.

'I said...'

'I heard you.' Her voice, when it came, was high and musical.

'Then how about an answer? And, whilst you're at it... where's my wife?'

After a leaden moment, she said, 'I'm Zara.' She spoke it as if he would automatically recognise her name. 'I'm afraid that Vanessa is otherwise engaged.'

His eyes panned around the room. It was brightly lit, and he could see into every corner.

No Vanessa.

He knew that the rest of the house was in darkness. Was she sitting somewhere in the dark – alone, afraid?

Once more, his eyes rested on the woman. He wasn't taken in by her diminutive form or reassured by her smile. He thought that he had come to know evil, had come to have a clear sense of it, and he was certain that something monstrous lurked beneath her alabaster skin. He wished he'd heeded Anita's advice. It seemed that, after all, he was a great deal more stupid than he'd given himself credit for.

He could feel the powerful thump of his beating heart and was well aware of the tensing of his muscles as his body shifted into fight or flight mode.

His fists balled at his sides. He made a concerted effort to make his voice sound unaffected. 'Is she here? Is she in the house? Can I see her?'

Why, the fuck, was he asking permission to see his own wife?

'What I meant to say was...'

Suddenly, her smile was gone. 'She's not here.' The words were rapped out, fired like bullets from a gun. 'Stop asking about her.'

He screwed up his face, stepped further into the room, consciously flexed his fingers. He wanted to rip her fucking face off.

If she sensed his intent, she didn't show it. She continued to sit perfectly still, her hands still in her lap, and merely followed him with her eyes as he moved towards her.

Her eyes were abnormally large and, as he drew closer, they appeared to be filling her whole face. He suddenly felt weak, as if those eyes had sucked the energy right out of him. He faltered, weaved on his feet, then dropped to his knees.

He had enough strength to lift his head, but he couldn't speak. He tried, but all that he managed to utter was a strangled croak.

'You wanted to hurt me,' she said, quite matter of fact. 'I think that you'll find that no one can hurt me.'

Another croak. He closed his eyes in frustration, tried to get back onto his feet, but ended up on his back on the floor like a stranded turtle.

'You came like a lamb to the slaughter. Why did you do that, Richard? You care for no one but yourself? Why place yourself in danger?' She paused for a moment, then went on, 'You must have known there would be danger. Anita warned you, and the memory of what happened to Fiona is still fresh in your mind.'

He had enough about him to wonder how she knew about Anita's warning and Fiona's death. When something close to an answer popped into his head, he was stunned.

It was her. It was all her. What he didn't know was why. *Had it all been evil for evil's sake?*

'Simon?' he managed to grind out.

Her smile returned. 'The nightmares?' she said, through a giggle.

The bitch had actually giggled. He tried to summon the strength to fly at her, but his body refused to obey his furious command. He was forced to lie there, all but paralysed, and take whatever she threw at him.

'I'll tell you about Simon,' she said. 'You won't like it and you'll blame me, but it's really Vanessa you should blame. Simon's plight is all her fault. Your son's agony can be securely laid at her feet.'

What was she going on about? How could any of it be Vanessa's fault?

'Tell... me...'

'Not yet.'

'Tell... me...' His tongue felt bloated, huge in his mouth. The words came out muffled. 'Fucking bitch... tell me.'

He succeeded in pulling himself onto his elbows. Whatever spell she'd cast to immobilise him was wearing off. He could see her expression much more clearly but then had to blink to clear his vision because... because, holy shit, her face seemed to be melting.

Like molten wax, her skin stretched and dissolved then turned to liquid. She no longer had any recognisable features. Digging in his heels, he scooted back, horrified and in a state of complete confusion.

Soon, her whole body began to melt and dissolve, then the light hanging from the ceiling – the one that brightened the room – flickered. A dark, shapeless, shadow floated up from the chair and seemed to suck what was left of Zara into its midst. It crawled up the wall, along the ceiling, then dropped.

He wanted to scream, desperately needed to scream, but no scream came.

Not until the shadow came for him, did that scream finally explode from his throat.

HE JERKED AWAKE. HE was cold. His hands, clenched around the steering wheel of his car, were like blocks of ice. The car rocked, buffeted by a wind that had grown high. He was confused, disorientated, yet frightened.

Suddenly, he remembered. He let out a gasp, swivelled around in his seat and, swallowing air in ragged gulps, he stared out into the dark night.

He was in the driveway. The house stood tall, almost looming beneath an ink-black sky. There were no lights in any of the windows, no shadows, and no movement.

Had he dreamt it? Was it another nightmare? He couldn't be sure.

His phone pinged. Startled, he reached for it.

It was a text message. It said, *Come in. The door isn't locked.*

Thirty-Five

He didn't want to leave the car, but he did. His feet crunched on the gravel. The wind messed with his hair and rocked him as he fought his way to the house. Terror grabbed him and held him, but his steps didn't falter.

The front door stood open. It looked like a gaping black mouth. Still, his steps didn't falter.

He wasn't being brave. He felt anything but brave. What he felt was a sense of inevitability.

He went inside and closed the door behind him. It took a few moments for his eyes to grow accustomed to the gloom and he stood for a full minute before venturing further.

An incredible force pressed down on him and leaned into him from both sides. When he walked forward towards the lounge, he felt as if he was wading through a river of waist high treacle. It was as if the house had decided that it didn't want him there.

Just inside the door to the lounge, to the left, on the wall, was the light switch. He reached in and turned it on.

The room immediately blazed bright. He blinked, closed his eyes, counted to ten in his head before opening them again.

She wasn't there. The chair was empty. He thought he might feel relief but, instead, felt disappointed.

'Vanessa?' he whispered, not really expecting a reply, speaking more to himself than to the room. 'Where are you?'

'Hello Richard.'

The voice came from behind him. He stiffened, then turned.

'You took your time. I thought your arse was glued to the seat of the car.'

She sounded so normal, so... Vanessa... but she didn't look anything like the wife he'd seen only a few weeks before.

She'd lost a tremendous amount of weight, was mere skin and bones, and she was dirty, filthy.

'It's all right,' she said. 'Everything is going to be okay.'

A figure appeared behind her. He immediately recognised her.

It was Zara.

'You came back,' the demon said.

He thought of her as a demon. She had been a demon in his nightmare... if it had been a nightmare ... and he knew that he would always think of her in that way.

'Yes,' he said. 'I came back for my wife.'

'Too late,' she said. 'She's lost to you.'

It was completely surreal. He couldn't believe that he was standing there, talking normally, as if the whole of his whole insides weren't in turmoil, as if he wasn't scared almost to death.

'It's never too late,' he returned, his voice steady and sure. 'Is it, Vanessa?'

Her expression was sad, resigned. She nodded. 'I'm sorry,' she said. 'The clock can't be turned back.'

'You said that everything would be okay.'

'For Simon.'

He looked to Zara, was almost dragged into her eyes, and asked, 'What does she mean?'

'I'm glad you asked,' she said. 'Go and sit down, make yourself comfortable. It's quite a story.'

And it was.

It was a story about a Ouija board and a demon. It was a story about Simon, about Vanessa's quest to free his soul from Hell. It was a story that explained his nightmares, Fiona's death, and everything else that had happened.

It was a story that didn't quite have an ending and it didn't explain why Vanessa wasn't dead, why she wasn't languishing in Hell instead of their son, and why he was even there in their presence.

It was a story that neither shocked nor surprised him. he believed in its essence, but it was a story that left him with a lot of questions.

'It'll be okay,' Vanessa said for the third time. 'It will all work itself out.'

'You can't believe that?' he said. 'You can't trust the devil.'

'I trust God,' was her only reply.

'Why aren't you dead?'

She shrugged. 'I don't know.' She turned to Zara. 'Why am I not dead?'

For the first time, Richard saw doubt in the demon's eyes.

She doesn't know. She doesn't fucking know.

The pressure in the room grew, intensified. Zara's expression became angry. Richard saw her stiffen, ball her fists.

You're reading my mind. He projected the thought right at her and was gratified to see her eyes widen in shock.

In retribution, she filled his mind and his ears with horrendous images and heart-rending sounds. He saw his son, heard his son, and he let out a long, slow wail of anguish.

'Stop,' he implored. 'Enough.'

Vanessa hunkered down at his feet, rested her head in his lap, and mumbled words of comfort.

There was no comfort to be had. The story needed to be concluded and that meant losing her – losing her to an eternity of torture. The alternative was his darling boy's continued torment.

There had to be another way.

'There is no other way,' Zara said. 'The deal has been struck… sealed in the blood of others.'

'Fiona?' he choked out.

The demon nodded. 'And the other one… Anita.'

Vanessa groaned, buried her face deeper into his lap.

'So, Anita, too?' He felt immensely sorry, hoped she hadn't suffered too much. 'What about me?' he asked. 'Why am I here?'

'I wanted you to know… to understand,' Vanessa said, lifting a tear-stained face to look directly at him. 'I wanted you to know that Simon was okay, for you to know that he's in heaven… *will be* in heaven.'

His heart broke to look at her. He was sad for her, proud of her, fearful for her. His shame grew. He couldn't help recalling all the shitty things he'd done to her over the years whilst all the time she'd been grieving for their son. Now, she was prepared to sacrifice herself just so Simon could live an eternity pain free and in peace. He felt like a turd, knew that he was a turd, despised himself.

'I forgive you,' she said.

Jesus fucking Christ. He couldn't bear it a moment longer. Her forgiveness was the final straw.

'It's okay,' Zara said, showing once more that she knew exactly what he'd been thinking. 'You can leave. No one will stop you.'

'Yes, go,' Vanessa put in. 'It's almost over.'

He wasn't ready to leave. He felt that he still had a million questions. But it ultimately wasn't his choice.

He was pulled to his feet, virtually yanked in the air by some invisible force, and then propelled towards the door. He tried to look back, but his body was no longer his own.

The front door blew open. It slammed against the wall. He banged his head on the way through and, his ears ringing and his body feeling as if it was weightless, he landed on the ground outside. He landed in a heap and rolled, feeling the gravel take chunks out of his face.

He then heard the door bang closed. The wind had blown up into a proper bluster. There was thunder followed by lightning and a sheet of rain soon drenched him.

He had to get to his feet. He wasn't ready for it to be over.

The door remained closed to him. He battered on it with his fists, screaming out Vanessa's name, Zara's name, at the top of his lungs. The wind carried his voice away and his words flew to the heavens.

It was all going to unfold without him. There was nothing he could do to stop it, nothing he could do to save Vanessa and his son.

He dropped to his knees, pressed his forehead on the cold, wet step, and sobbed.

Although he felt less than worthy, he prayed. He told God that he was sorry. He said sorry a dozen times. He didn't beg for forgiveness, knowing he didn't deserve it. Instead, he begged for the souls of his son and his wife.

'Make them take me,' he pleaded. 'You can do it. You can do anything. She doesn't deserve it. Vanessa doesn't deserve it.'

The thunder crashed and boomed. The sky became a churning mass of swirling storm clouds, blue-black against the forks of fiery lightning.

'Please... please... please...'

A scream rent the air. It was so loud that it surpassed the resounding wildness of the storm. Beneath the scream was a fury so resolute that it shook him to his core.

She was coming. He sensed her and he dragged himself to his feet. It was difficult to maintain his balance and more than once he felt himself being pushed almost back to his knees by the wind.

The door exploded off its hinges. Heavy as it was, it was picked up by the storm and carried away.

He saw her, then realised that it wasn't truly her. It was something else... something ugly and grotesque. Its chest heaved and it threw his head back and screeched its venom to the sky.

He saw Vanessa, so small and vulnerable, clinging to the doorframe. She was mouthing something at him and shaking her head.

Then, the shadows arrived – swirling, surrounding, and engulfing him.

He didn't fight. He went quietly. He knew that he was finally getting what he deserved.

Epilogue

Vanessa put both hands on her stomach and held her breath. The kick, when it came, was strong and almost painful.

They said it was a miracle that the baby had survived through those first weeks of its conception – weeks when she'd starved her body of almost all nutrition.

She knew that it was a boy... Richard's son. She would name him after his father. It was the least she could do.

Everyone believed that Richard was a killer and Vanessa did nothing to disabuse them of that belief. It didn't matter to Richard. He was beyond caring that everyone thought that he'd murdered Fiona.

Poor Fiona. Vanessa actually felt sorry for the other woman and often wondered where *her* soul had ended up.

Vanessa was the only one who knew the truth and, apart from sharing it with their son when he was old enough to understand and to believe, she would take that truth to her grave. Not that anyone would believe the truth. Sometimes, even she doubted its validity.

For the first few months after being found, there had been questions, lots of questions, but she was too traumatised to answer a single one of them. Eventually, they stopped asking.

She never believed that she would heal, and it had taken the knowledge of her pregnancy to make the shift from silent resignation to hope.

The pregnancy changed everything. Suddenly, she had something to live for, something to make her carry on. She had no doubt that the baby was a gift from God. God had been the One who had allowed Richard's seed to find purpose and to flourish. For some reason, God wanted her to be all right, and she was learning to be.

Turning her face to the sun, she dragged in a contented breath. She was at Anita's graveside. She was comfortable there. She enjoyed talking to her and believed wholeheartedly that her friend could hear every one of her words.

'I hope you'll forgive me for taking credit for the book,' she said. 'My son needs the security it'll bring and, anyway, it's as much my book as Zara's. I'm sure you understand. You were the only one who truly knew me, Anita and I wish I'd been a better friend.'

There was no answer, of course. It was only demons who threw their voices over the great void.

She said goodbye for the final time. The next day, she was moving to Scotland, to the wild beauty of the Highlands, knowing that it was the only place where she would find total peace.

She left the cemetery, unaware of the eyes on her and oblivious to the presence following her.

There was no tell-tale shiver running down her spine, no goose bumps exploding on her skin. There ought to have been. After all her experiences, Vanessa should have sensed the presence, known of its existence.

The baby kicked, as if panicked. Vanessa rubbed her stomach, made soothing noises, and made her way slowly to her car.

Behind the wheel, she adjusted the rear-view mirror, her eyes blind to the image reflected in the glass.

She drove away, totally ignorant of the small woman sitting in the back of the car and oblivious to the tinkling laughter that filled the air.

Printed in Great Britain
by Amazon